The History of Light Book I:

THE HISTORY OF LIGHT

VOLUMES 1 THROUGH 5

THE GHOST WITH A KNIFE AT HER THROAT

THE BOOK OF SIGHT

THE HISTORY OF LIGHT BOOK 1

KEVIN HINCKER

CONTENTS

A WORD ABOUT THE CITY

Skysill Beach Master Plan

Skysill Beach is an art colony on the Southern California coast. It is stylish and quaint, wholly dedicated to taking money from tourists, and hosts a multitude of art galleries that *compel* shoppers to buy, using special ultraviolet paint. This is a town where ghosts and psychics and magic *light* are the pressing mysteries. Ringed by high coastal hills, resting in a bowl tilted toward the Pacific, it feels at once wild—filled with parks, pressed against the sea, separate from the outside world—and oppressively controlled. An unseen power oversees the painters of Skysill, who have lived for generations, trapped without knowing it, in a city they can never leave.

THE HIGHER COLORS

~

1. **choke** - *accumulation/dissipation*
2. **compulsion** - *attraction/repulsion*
3. **reason** - *transparency/obscurity*
4. **crush** - *large/small*
5. **farewell** - *beginnings/endings*
6. **wander** - *near/far*
7. **bleed** - *destruction*

CHAPTER ONE

I can't paint anymore. It's too dangerous. Instead, I drink. I've tried them both, and by now it's clear the vodka's less likely to kill me. So I was meeting my less-likely demise from my stool at The Charles, where it tastes best, when Waylon Goodman called to leave his fifth message that day. Like the first four, I deleted it without listening.

Five messages meant he was honestly w orried he'd picked up a forged painting. Sometimes he calls just to get me up to visit, because being rich is that boring, so I screen him. He doesn't know the pair of deadly risks I confront visiting his high hacienda. One, his majestic, ocean-view gates, and two his gallery of priceless paintings. Those are terrible risks, for eyes broken like mine anyway, and I won't go up there on some millionaire whim.

But for forgery? I'll go every time.

So I closed out at The Charles. I exited to morning light, which some people think is a bad light to be seen coming out of a bar, but not me. And I went hair-pinning inland and up, along Seacliff Drive, watching Skysill Beach platter out below me. From up there Skysill looks like a sleepy, seaside arts colony—a little paint drop lost between Los Angeles north of us, and San Diego south—but it's really an elaborate cash register. Tourists pour through and we take their money. They think they're coming because our art's amazing. It's sad. I'd almost feel sorry for them, except I'm pretty consumed by my own problems already.

Seacliff Drive switch-backed up to a vista, and there, where the horizon bent ocean water along the rim of the sky, I started to feel my *sight* yanking its leash. My eyes, begging to be allowed to suck ultraviolet color off the waves. I snapped my eyes down though, and I held them on the road, because prudence. Prudence is a lot more work than people tell you, but I've made certain promises. Now I try to keep my eyes under control. Or whatever this is I'm doing.

I took my time getting up Waylon's hill, just to remind him in advance that it was mine. But eventually, Seacliff Drive peaked over a high saddle and cul-de-saced, right in front of risk number one: Waylon's ocean-view entrance gates. I probably wasn't drunk enough to be there, I thought, trying not to stare. This view in particular is a trigger, how his endless aqua skyline backdrops his latte stucco bougainvillea gates. It's something in the sub-shades. Too perfect. I get color seizures and pass out.

But his potential forgery kept me in the car idling and indecisive, which some people say is one of my character flaws. And as the seconds passed, my eyes—my lunatic color magnets—craved harder, though we all knew this craving mostly ends in blackouts. My eyes don't care about blackouts. And after the blackouts Amelia calls fifty times, *I thought we were passed all your blah blah*, but my eyes don't have to deal with my sister. My eyes have their own agenda. Sometimes I wonder if it's healthy, how I think about my eyes in third person so much.

And I idled just long enough for an ocean-blue universe to bloom up off the water. My eyes opened wide. It came at me like a magic tent of color, swirling, surrounding me. It was too much. I'm only human, or whatever, and I'm an addict. And honestly, sometimes the colors slam so hard there's just no looking away.

So we were doing this now.

I reared in my seat and moaned, while prism light rang me like church bells. Nothing but visible-spectrum of course, just the standard rainbow, the red-blue-greens. I kept the seven Higher colors, the ultraviolet spectrum, zeroed out. Because yes my prudence has been halfhearted for years. But it's not like I'm insane anymore.

My mouth fell open, and chromatic seascape washed into me. It came in tide-wrinkle, shale-razor, whale-eye blue, and brought all the sub-shade blues and reds and greens that only Fenestram artists ever see. I heard myself gasp *oh fuck yes* and felt control failing. On the steering wheel my hands closed toward fists. That's how I know the seizure's coming. Fists. I probably had five seconds.

I spent my five-second margin for error drinking color, as addicts will, while the blackout train barreled in, and only at the very last second did I scream and plow myself cross-eyed and apply the brakes. The color brakes—crossing my eyes. Most of the time it works. A *lot* of times. This time, sweat sheeted, limb stiffened, squeezing my pupils together like the world ending, my *chroma storm* faded. Which, if I'm being honest, was surprising. This one had felt like it could have gone another way.

Once the giddy washed out, the ocean past Waylon's gate was nothing but cold water, and when I uncrossed my eyes I felt fine. My hands trembled in my lap for ten minutes but I felt fine. Very dizzy. The brakes had been getting harder to apply recently and I didn't know what that meant for me. And there was no one to ask, not even Amelia who'd figured out I had brakes to begin with. You can't talk to her. She's too solutions-oriented, it's super irritating.

When my hands got steady enough I turned the car off. I still had Waylon's gallery to get through, and my colors were now spiky and threatening, but the idea was nailing Waylon's forgery was going make this whole exercise worthwhile.

I left the car in the cul-de-sac and walked onto his estate. Waylon prefers people drive in but I like to remind him his preferences are meaningless to me. On foot, light and unbalanced but upright, I let his lane curve me onto his palmy compound all the way to the five-car garage where usually I'll see his convertibles sunning. But not today. Nothing stirred today. I heard a distant jay call and the soft echo of shovel work which quickly stopped. The path eased me around the garage toward the main house where I found the walk cut by trenches ringed with stakes and string, a shovel abandoned in the mud. The shovel probably belonged to Waylon's handyman, who trims his bougainvillea and digs his useless, millionaire holes.

I got around the string and up on the porch and rang Waylon's bell, but nobody came. Behind me I heard the jay again, underscoring his silence. More bell work, same result, my unsteady head wanted out of the sun, so I turned Waylon's handle for him. And his door swung open, to a quiet hallway. Very still. Not even a blue jay.

This entrance is where I gird my eyes for problem number two: the masterpiece gallery. I started down the hall toward the corner and I checked for fists as I went and shook my hands—a *chroma storm* here would be inconvenient and horrible. Then I was taking the corner, and slowing to face the atrium galley where Waylon Goodman hangs his money.

My personal problem with it is so much of the work is by *sighted* masters. Waylon can't see sub-shades like we do, and for sure can't see ultraviolet. He's visible-spectrum only, he doesn't know Higher color exists. But his mini Louvre is full of all-time masters—the great ones. And all through history the greats have tended to share our Fenestram way of seeing *light*. Waylon's gallery hides secrets he'll never see, himself. But for me, it's a minefield.

I held my breath, which does absolutely nothing, and headed in, past the first Monet. Monet hadn't had ultraviolet paint like we do, but like any *sighted* artist he'd seen a hundred million sub-shades, where visible-spectrum eyes were only sensitive enough to see a single, solid red or blue. And Monet loved the sub-shades—*all* the sub-shades—so he comes off a canvas like a fucking color blizzard. Still, I got past him. I got past van Gogh, the Renoir triptych,

Waylon's Vermeer with the composition so unbalanced I sometimes get trapped studying it. I put my head down. I almost made it.

But the final painting stopped me. Sometimes it still can. It's just confusing, seeing my name here.

The card reads, *Paul Cézanne, Bouilloire et fruits II,* ***Forgery*** *(certified, Asher Gale).* I don't know if *certified* is the right word. All I know is the first time I saw this painting it raked me like broken glass. Cézanne was *sighted.* An authentic Cézanne is a masterclass in sub-shade layering, but whoever this forger had been, they'd had nothing but visible-spectrum color. So the fake was an empty travesty. A corpsy hack any *sighted* painter would scan. I know a lot of ways to spot a forgery, but visible-spectrum forgers stealing from *sighted* artists? That's the easiest.

I'm told that once, at a party here, before Waylon and I were so fond of each other, after he wouldn't stop bragging about his priceless new Cézanne for hours, I supposedly started screaming his fucking Cézanne was a fucking fake fucking piece of ass fucking bullshit. And it's true I do remember some screaming at a party, but it doesn't mean much because forgeries are everywhere and so were parties, back then.

In those days I couldn't help screaming. It was before I became to well balanced. If you steal another painters work you're a worthless piece of shit—that's the one pure truth I know. A forgery is soul theft. If you're a forger I despise you—which is *exhausting*. But as a side effect of exhausting myself, I'd saved Waylon's ass on the Cézanne, and he'd labeled it and hung it, then started expressing the opinion that we'd become partners. He's the kind of millionaire, it's hard to talk him out of an opinion. He got cards made for us.

I finally stumbled from his gallery into his oceany living room, still in one piece, and I drew a deep breath because I'd pulled it off. I started peering for my draped easel. He always drapes them, I have no idea why. On my right was Waylon's bar, gleaming in wealth mist. In the center of his expansive great room were a lot of light linen cushions on driftwood couches. And along the far side, a wall of sliding glass doors stood open to inhale the vast, standard-blue, Pacific Ocean air. Cool air. A Hockney swimming pool lay back, above the fireplace.

Waylon faced away from me looking out his doors, watching his ocean put its time to productive use. His greying hair was loose and wild, not Albert Einstein wild but more like an abandoned terrier. Everything else about him snapped tight as a rubber glove. He wore a plaid shirt belted over a small paunch and linen slacks that complimented all his driftwood.

"I don't know why anything happens," he said, sort of straining. "Do you?"

I kept looking for my forgery but started sensing a new kind of ominous in the room. It's always something. Because was it odd, the way Waylon was slouching? He's not naturally a sloucher. I checked my hands for fists. The colors were jumping.

Then Waylon turned and his heavy features fell on me. He had thick brows and a broad chin without much room between them, but he managed to work expressions there. Today he wore it beaten and gut-wrenched.

His grief stretched face was instantly triggery. And this time when I checked my hands, I was worried I'd find not fists but fingers straining into stiff salutes. Which is my other color issue: the dangerously inquisitive *Gray*.

I felt the *Gray* lurking in Waylon's great room. It likes taking me over. It likes swooping down when there's excess drama. And I was *definitely* sensing excess drama from Waylon. In many ways, the *Gray* is worse than a *chroma storm*. I get a lot less predictable. Was it too late to leave? The thing I needed least was going *Gray* in Waylon Goodman's living room, spinning out in some curiosity-fueled amoral crime spree.

The right move, I knew, was leave immediately, which I didn't do.

"I need you for something," he urged, coming forward.

"If there's forgery," I said, "let's see it fast, I'm running out of time."

"You're the only person I trust," he told me, and I saw him weeping, which, *definitely* extra dramatic.

He didn't have a forgery I realized. This was something else. I'd been lured up on a bait and switch, or maybe not a bait and switch, maybe I should've listened to one of those messages. I turned to run but I'd started too late. That'll happen with me. Waylon had the exit covered like he knew what I wanted, and now came my way wringing a photo in a driftwood frame where a girl scowled in a graduation gown. I tried not looking, but he wanted it seen.

"Do you know who this is?" he asked. She had electric hair, Waylon's lips, eyes either flirting or warning you get the hell out of her way. His daughter. She was my age and I'd seen her rage-drive off the compound in a pearlescent sport something a few times, but didn't know her. I don't know anybody. I work hard at that. I told him so.

"Samantha, my baby," he moaned, "my baby's *dead.*"

And... drama threshold exceeded.

My fingers spasmed straight, stiff as fork tines. Dead or missing family? Yeah, that'll do it. Every time. Then the *Gray* rolled in and took me.

All color drained from the room. The furniture, the bar, the distant ocean, everything faded to charcoal and talcum. A greyscale world. And slightly sociopathic tranquility rose inside me and around me and it felt *fantastic.* It always feels so good.

Amelia's the only one tracking all my color problems, or I hope she's doing it since I don't even try. I have the basics memorized: sometimes I *storm* and have seizures, other times I'm *Gray* and unpredictable and violent. Amelia calls the *Gray* a self-protective maladjustment, but that's only random words she read online. I know the truth; the *Gray's* just one more symptom of my broken eyes.

"I'm sorry for your loss," I heard *Gray* me tell Waylon, which wasn't true at all, but *Gray* me often says what I *don't* mean just to find out what it feels like, because *Gray* me loves trying things out. Any things.

I'm sorry for your loss, I discovered, felt fantastic and I stood appreciating Waylon's cougar-grey living room. I took luxurious breaths. My cheeks eased and I grinned and my stress dropped away. Such a relief! I felt like a different, much *much* better person.

Waylon's shoulders shook his wet face. It was so easy to push down and sit him on his couch because of how strong I am when I'm *Gray*. It was fun. I did it to see what it felt like, and his plaid shirt felt like, which was *excellent*.

Then I left him crying to pour myself an awesome tumbler at his sea-grey bar and rocked a moment there, feeling better and better, like a greyscale Superman. I carried my drink back to stand behind Waylon and wiggled my toes and wondered what the back of his skull would feel like if you squeezed, like, how much pressure to pop a human skull?

"They say she killed herself," Waylon told me.

"I'm sorry for your loss," I heard me say, and this time it was boring, which was hilarious.

"They say she cut her wrists and bled to death... my baby bled to death?"

While Waylon cried about his dead daughter *Gray* me smiled and spotted the Hockney over the fireplace. Would it feel pretty amazing, shattering my vodka glass against that priceless canvas ripping it? Or would that be boring too? I drained, reared, and fired—the glass sailed over Waylon, over the chairs, flashing, dropping to break and scatter on the hearth. Out of range but fun! Now I needed more tumblers. Waylon looked back at me, frowning.

"My baby, Asher. How can she be gone?"

The longer I'm *Gray* the harder it gets remembering to even want to come back. Over the years that's gotten worse. Now if I wait too long it's nearly impossible in the short term, and it can take days to get normal, or whatever I am. Sometimes weeks. And even when I do remember to want to come back, escaping the *Gray* isn't straightforward like the eye-crossing brakes to stop a *storm*. The *Gray* has to be debated. But the *Gray*'s flitty and has a short attention span, so it's like having an argument with a moth, where you and the moth are both drunk. Sometimes I win and sometimes I don't.

This time I won. I gasped back up into a room of bright color, disoriented, leaning, and by instinct pulled the whole visible spectrum shallow, desaturated it pastel, the safety range. I stood, blinking, weak—it never happens this way. *Chroma storms* then the *Gray* —one right after the other? What was going on?

The gut wrench had cleared Waylon's face by then. Maybe I'd done him good being sorry for his loss so many times. I levered a hip against the couch to push for the door, but Waylon twisted and grabbed my arm.

"Help me," he said, "I have to know what happened to her."

"That's in the police report," I said, and pulled, but couldn't get free. Waylon had dead family strength. I recognized it.

"The police are idiots," he said. "I need you. Go look. At her body. Oh god... her dead body. Go use your eyes."

"Send your handyman, he gave up shoveling, his eyes are free."

"I need *you*!" Waylon roared, because he'd decided to try some rage, which was impressive even though I'd seen it before. "I told them *don't move her*! You *will* go! You'll investigate for me—stay there! Don't move!"

It was too much. I was too shaky. I watched him take command at the bar and come back with my drink, face hard, eyes dry. It was his millionaire face, the face behind all the others, making everything happen.

"Finish that," he told me, "then go investigate!"

"I will finish this, you go call a detective."

"But we're partners in a whole agency! *Asher Gale: Investigation and Authentication.*" He grabbed cards from an end table. He loved those cards. He had them everywhere.

"There's no *agency*," I would have shouted if I had energy, "that's just you—whatever tax dodge—I never said use my name, even—look, Waylon, I'm sorry about your daughter, I am, but *our* thing, it's just *forgery* and—"

"*Then go look at Samantha right now or you'll never see a forgery from me again*!" He was all over the place. It was hard to follow. "I gave you an office," he cried, "You're like a son to me! I put you in the news," and then he was weeping again and I'll admit it was getting harder not feeling sorry for him, but I wanted to keep trying.

"I'm not qualified to investigate anything," I complained. "Have you seen me?"

"Just go *look*. My daughter's *dead*," he cried. "My only family's *gone*. Do you know what that feels like? Losing your family?"

That. Why I didn't see that coming I do not know. He probably planned it this way—it's not like my family history's a secret—or maybe it was just his millionaire instinct for personal weakness. Either way yes, I do know what losing family feels like. In my case technically it was family losing me. Me and Amelia. What it feels like is a hole in your life that isn't pretty to look at so I don't. That's my system and I'm great at it. But now here was Waylon pointing at his own hole, like we shared a hole trauma. Were we bonding, or... ? My god I hoped not.

I drained the glass and pointed it at him. "What are you asking me to do *exactly*?" I did not whine, exactly.

"Go. Look around her place. You see things. You have special eyes."

That one about buckled me. He'd really lined them up today. First my family, now we were going to talk about my eyes? What?

You can't get a single Fenestram artist in Skysill to talk about the secret of our *sight*. Not even Amelia. They'll hardly admit Higher *light* exists, except around Gala Lumina, like they have a mental block. So what could visible-spectrum Waylon Goodman possibly know about my ultraviolet eyes? He wasn't a Fenestram artist—he wasn't *any* kind of artist. Waylon's just a *collector*.

"I don't know how you do it," he relieved me after a moment, remembering, "but I watch your eyes, watch you, how you scan a canvas, how you see when whatever's wrong. You spot every forgery. Nothing hides from you. It's a gift! So go to Samantha's! Just go, look around, tell me what you see. My daughter wouldn't ever kill herself. Tell them I sent you. Show your card. Well?"

"If I do this," I said, slowly, "if I go *look around,* then god damnit you will never call me again unless it's a painting. Don't call like this Waylon. I'm serious, I already have problems. Do you understand?"

"Yes. Fine! Go—why are you still standing there?"

I was going to do it I saw. These people have so much energy. They wear you out. And I had color still jumping around. A dead girl. It was going to be exhausting.

"No more calling," I warned, handing him the glass. "Do you have any more daughters?"

"No. Why?"

I sighed. "I don't know. Figuring my odds, I guess."

He texted an address, Bluebell Lane in Catalina Village. I went out the way I'd come, escaping the gallery, leaving the *storms* and the *Gray,* thinking how precarious my control felt these days and how vodka's perfect for that. Trenching back through Waylon's holes I looked for Damien to apologize for all the string I was taking down, but the shovel was the only sign he'd ever been there at all.

CHAPTER TWO

Anybody in Skysill Beach who's rich and isn't busy buying something else picks up a rental in Catalina Village, a beach accessible Airbnb slum. The buildings are beige and thin-skinned, maintenanced just enough to keep them earning. In another city they'd be diced into apartments but we don't do apartments in Skysill.

Waylon owned 1687 Bluebell, the stucco box Samantha had occupied. Bluebell turned out to be a gravel finger of Airbnb alley lined with sagging redwood fences, where Audis and BMWs slummed anyplace they damn well pleased. 1687 Bluebell sat on the ocean side of the alley, one house from the corner, riding the continent up out of the sea. The second story balconies on adjacent houses held daiquiri-handed short-term lodgers who'd stopped whale watching to watch emergency vehicles.

Yellow warning tape roped spectators out. I parked across the street. My head hurt when I slammed the door. I filtered the scene purely pastel, for brain safety. Like vision Pepto Bismol. I approached Samantha's alley where I saw a big cop standing by his car playing a game on his phone. He lost as I watched and sat hard on the hood.

There was a space cleared at the yellow tape. When I reached it I tested it on my legs, then looked to my right.

The spectators had pulled away from the oil-brown man mumbling beside me. He had a spray bottle and watched the open, ground floor door of 1687. I knew him. Peter by the Beach, a slow and methodical pier dweller, with dehydrated eyes and wind-torn beard, and tattered tennis clothes like the second waiter on a cruise ship. We had a longstanding relationship enjoying conversations Peter never remembered afterward. I valued him for his willingness to say whatever the hell he thought up and because, in all the years I'd known him, he'd never pushed me *chromatic* or *Gray*.

Something here, in the crowd or the lights, had drawn him from his 7 Eleven.

"Hey," I stood close and spoke low. "What do you see?"

"I hear pebbles," he rumbled, his voice subsonic. The voice didn't fit the thin body. "Not enough oxygen for this."

He showed his spray bottle. If you gave him a dollar in the parking lot he'd use it to spray dirt from one side of your windshield to the other. If you gave him five dollars he'd make the windshield look like it wasn't there. If you gave him more than five he gave you change.

"The weather," I guessed, "but oxygen always comes back. Don't worry. Keep your head up." We spent a minute watching nothing happen on the other side of the tape. I wondered if, like me, Peter was putting off some task he didn't feel qualified for which he never should have agreed to do in the first place.

"A girl died there," he rumble-whispered.

I told him I knew and asked how he'd found out.

"All these buildings are clouds," he showed me the balconies. "Cloud people live there. Some of them have pets."

The balconies were growing raucous. And I didn't need full spectrum color to see the confusion and pain in Peter as he looked at the cloud vacationers in the sky. Music blared on one balcony. A girl in a pastel pink bikini danced, while other people cheered.

"The dead eye is here," he shrugged. "It won't leave me alone. The whole past is a whale. The buildings are empty, no one's there. A house without a place to stay."

"You know," I told him, letting out an idea, "if you ever *are* looking for someplace to stay, and I'm serious, I know of an office, no one's ever there. It has my name on the door, apparently. Go live in it. Maybe you'd like it."

"My bank gave me poison," Peter shook his head. "It's all they had."

One man on a balcony lost a margarita, which splattered to the gravel. The cop glanced up but kept working his phone.

"Ok," I sighed to Peter. "Great talking, I've got a thing." I found five dollars and let him make it disappear.

"Which car?" he rumbled.

"I don't care, something convenient."

I fed more color into the scene, took a breath, hooked the tape and slipped under.

Right away I got the cop's attention. Still working his phone he made his legs straighten and made one arm stick out with the palm showing. He held me stationary while he lost another game. He was smaller than a horse trailer as long as he wasn't breathing deep, and had rebar eyebrows rising and falling and consuming a lot of energy. He came forward spinning a bored finger to show that my job was turning around.

"Can't come back here," he ruled, stepping in fallen margarita and liking it not at all. I pointed at 1687.

"I'm supposed to look in there." His attention lifted from his boot.

"Says who?"

"Waylon Goodman. He owns the property. He's the father of, you know. The girl."

"Oh—the girl?" That focused him. "And you know what about the girl?"

"Nothing."

"And yet here you are, on the know something side of my tape."

"I'm surprised too."

He sucked his teeth. "You have a name?"

"Yes."

"It is?"

"Asher Gale."

"Let's have the card." I held out my license. He didn't look at it. "Did I say license?"

"No you didn't," I admitted. He asked straightforward cop questions, it was good. I scraped around my wallet and found a card, surprising both of us, that read *Asher Gale: Investigation and Authentication.* The top was worn. It was bowed from six years of ass curl. I handed it to him.

"So that's it," the cop said, snapping it on his palm. "Investigator, huh?"

"No," I said. "Probably not, not the way you're thinking. It's complicated."

"Complicated to *you* is what you mean."

"I do forgeries."

"Nice. I do suicides. And the man said wait, I waited. Are you from him or not?"

"I'm not from him. I *know* him."

"He calls, you take a veeery long nap now you're here, you're his investigator."

"I don't like putting it that way, I'm not his."

"Yeah, okay I recognize you now. We've had you down at the station. A few times."

"Maybe. Sometimes I go in for directions."

"Here's your directions," he snapped, literally snapped, then turned so I could follow him toward the door of 1687, "do not waste any more of my time, leave the investigation to professionals, you call me Officer Hennessy," and we went in.

Whoever'd been living in Waylon's rental had been weaving all over the road, it didn't take forensic expertise to understand that. I moved down a dim interior hall following Hennessy and passed an open kitchen. I looked for cats. It was that kind of smell. Cat food and cat piss and cats being in charge of everything. Plates half-full, tilting on red Formica. Discarded towers of dishes in the area of a sink. An open trash, contents crushed and piled and rolling. Everywhere bottles. It was several weeks of eating, a year's worth of drinking, even for me. It was ammonia and rot and early morning puke.

I stepped down the hall around mounded clothes, boxes, what could have been smashed picture frames, bowling more months of empties against the walls. If the kitchen was an advanced case of *Maybe I'll Get to This Later,* the hall was a terminal case of *Fuck It I'm Done.*

"The girl was found here," Hennessy called from the end of the hallway, "and nobody moved her."

I passed a bathroom. A pile of towels, hardened on the floor from soap or booze, stoppered the door — the walls a Blitzkrieg of filth and hard use—and I started trying to not pass judgements because those are not my thing. And because this could be me ten years ago.

Ahead was Hennessy laughing and someone else talking. Shuffling took me past another door, I assumed bedroom, shut. And final shuffling took me into the living room, where Waylon's cop had his arms crossed, chortling to an EMT. The EMT was worried.

"I can't wait," the pinched thirty-year fireman said. "It's my balls in a vice, the Chief'll bust me."

"Calm," Hennessy told him. "The guy's here. We get this cleared up and you take care of your balls. Am I right, Gale?"

They looked at me. I took in the room. On the back wall were sliding windows aspiring to a view of the ocean but settling for a view of the back of another house. Faded drapes hung open. The space had a couch and a chair and a TV with a side table and bookcases, all given the same treatment as the bath and the hallway. Bed sheets and books and clothes and food, in piles, and again on top of that. You could tell it came this way in layers, over time. Decision by decision. Not one boozy episode. A thousand hours of confusion and despair.

The very glaring exceptions were the framed paintings on the walls. They'd been dusted. Not a single one hung a quarter inch crooked. I'd see that.

"Jesus Christ, what *happened* in here?" I breathed.

Hennessy raised his steel beams, a powerful face lifter.

"You tell me," he said, then shrugged, "or you don't."

Something about her paintings ... I stepped nearer. The frames were antiques, easily two hundred years each. French Neoclassic and older, flaked ornate. But the images they held were prints you'd find at a thrift store. Pets in ruffled collars, gingerbread cabins, children with windmills. Some were hardly more than magazine pages. The images were nothing. The frames approached priceless.

Then I saw the body.

Samantha lay on the floor behind the couch in sun through windows. She wore dark slacks, no shirt, a bra. An X-Acto knife rested in blood in her palm, upturned near her neck. Her arms had several lengthwise cuts from a fading hand, I thought. Despite the copious blood—on neck and arms and elbows and face, on the floor and dry on drape bottoms and under her couch and pants—I had no urge to *storm*, and none to go *Gray*. I checked to make sure I hadn't already gone *Gray*, but no, things were chugging along. It felt no different than a life drawing class where we'd hired a dead and partly mutilated corpse instead of a live model. And while that didn't seem like the right thing to feel, it was my first dead body, so I decided I just needed practice.

"Upstairs neighbor saw the girl through these windows," Hennessy said. "One of her cats scratching for food. That was this morning, ten-ish. We got the call. I'm asked, I wait. You came in via skydiving after getting your calves waxed, so what are we even doing? This case is shut before it even opens."

Waylon didn't believe his daughter had killed herself. What father would? But Hennessy was right. There was nothing new I'd find here for Waylon. Samantha had cut her wrists, sitting on the floor between her couch and her windows, maybe looking at her art collection. But she'd done it, without question. What more was there? Something, I thought. Something more.

Was it her collection? It kept turning me around. Commodity art in priceless frames. Frames creating value. I knew the idea. I wondered if anyone else had ever seen this, and what she'd been like alive. There was impressive scope to the disaster here. She'd worked this project of annihilation hard. Her accomplishment ought to be acknowledged.

And I felt, maybe a hit of color. Just a toke.

Because prudence gets exhausting.

So I slacked the leash and let my eyes loose, and blew past the edges of Lucky Charm colors in a micro second. My eyes gorged. The sub-shades came on. Samantha's blood loomed off the floor, the purple ventral spread where it congealed wet, the sulfur dusted edges where it oxidized hard, the guttural spew of tone stretched between. Her skin the grey of prison sheets. The colors of her life spun up off the wreckage she'd left.

I took deep breaths and drank the entire room. Hennessy stared. My face shifts when I do this, I'm told, my pupils dilate into addict saucers. Hennessy watched as I gave Samantha the only thing I had to give—I opened my eyes and looked around.

I thought for a moment I'd discovered that she was a secret smoker because her living room wasn't an even, apartment beige, but sub-shades of syphilitic orange-brown, fading from the ceiling down the walls. But the stain wasn't Samantha's; I saw where one of her paintings was missing from the wall, and the stain had been here before the paintings ever hung. The work of some earlier tenant.

I felt my grip loosening, the giddy slipping in, but I thought I still had time. Maybe I'd give Samantha everything. Like you'd do, in memoriam. And honestly, I admit, I just really wanted the ice and fire. Like, sometimes you just want to go banging around.

So I brought in the Higher colors.

Color doesn't work this way for most of us. Dialing saturation, filtering spectrum. Even my sister — maybe the most fully *sighted* artist anywhere in Skysill Beach — just moves through her days *seeing* combined spectrums of visible and Higher color, no management required. She can't control it, and has no need. She can paint. I'm the only one who feels paradise in the Highers. Up there it's like god's own garden of color.

Samantha's room lifted somehow, or I crouched. We came together. And feeling tone rode out, ultraviolet streamers of feeling as I turned the Highers on one at a time, savoring them from bottom to top: first *choke,* then *compulsion, reason* and *crush, farewell, wander,* and at the very top, *bleed.* The Higher rainbow. So unbelievable, when you *see* them without *storming.*

When I looked at Samantha's body I was afraid I *had* started tripping *chromatic* because I saw Higher pigment spread on her forearms, down her wrists, caked on her palms. She had Higher paint jammed up under her fingernails, thick as graveyard mud. I blinked. It was no *chromatic* hallucination. Samantha Goodman had Higher paint on her, paint only a Fenestram artist uses. The cops hadn't seen it, or this would be a different kind of investigation. Had Samantha been *sighted?*

It was becoming hard to think, and past time to dial everything down. But I caught a flicker to my right and turned to *see* a Higher color ball, a swirling aurora of insta dust—no, gone. No, *there.* A shimmer near the bathroom in the hall. It undulated and faded, made of seven Higher colors and something more. Something that held the form together, molded it. The form fled down the hall.

I stumbled forward with the world shifting. I was too high, I felt the mania, I had to dump this or I'd go *storming* — but what was down the hall? — something *else*: a glint. Something Higher glinting by the front door. I staggered through trash, fell on a picture frame, got to the entrance.

"Gale!" I heard behind me. "What gives?"

On a half round console table was a harpy-blue ceramic bowl

and the Higher *glint* within it was a key ring. One key radiated. I lift the ring. One key had been coated in every hue of Higher paint in existence. Just one key, with a sushi-green plastic top.

I was feeling dumb. Thick. I tried dropping the ring in the bowl but it wouldn't drop. It was trapped in my fist. I had a fist. Both my hands locked, and then it came. I dropped to my knees and crossed my eyes. The *storm* began to fountain, this time with Highers, and it's hard to stop the Highers. I pushed, crossed eyes as far as they'd go, crossed them like the world was ending. Then it did.

CHAPTER
THREE

Rolling back from unconsciousness is like a memory game. I'm an expert. What you do is, you work the pairs. First match your fingers to your corresponding toes. Then wrists to ankles, knees and elbows, and so on, until you remember all the pairs back together and wake up and you're a winner. There was a time I'd been world champion. I'd averaged five *storms* a day and also blackout drunks prior to my recent reforms.

My eyes blew open. I jingled my hands —keys, no fists. I pushed Hennessy and his EMT off my chest and struggled sitting up.

"Hey, hey," said the fireman, "take it easy fella, hold it fella, hey —"

My emergency had jammed all three of us into the narrow hall in the Bluebell Lane doorway. I didn't think we'd come to that intimate stage in our relationship, though I admit there was something hot about it. I crawl-rolled out, while they watched, and slipped over the bottom step down onto alley gravel, and groaned and tried crouching to my feet.

"Okay I'm fine," I said out loud.

They considered being convinced against their better judgment.

"I get migraines," I slurred.

Amelia helped come up with that too. Migraines are impossible to disprove. I watched the two of them mull me over. Only a thin thread of professional impulse had drawn them to my unconscious body to begin with. I was already more trouble than I was worth and we all knew it. They put on their wishful thinking faces.

"Well you need to get hydrated, man," said the EMT, like if people only drank more water his job tending to suicide bodies would be so much simpler. He turned back into the house. Hennessy watched me a few seconds more, not out of concern, I thought, but from law enforcement considerations, then dismissed me from his mind. I got myself uphill to my car.

The sun was setting. It seemed early for that. The breeze was cool and getting damp. My eyes hurt, starting at the back of my brain and coming out the corneas. My hand had clamped around Samantha's keyring, and now I found it hanging off my index finger. Several distinct and possibly unrelated things had just occurred, and I didn't understand any of them, which happens often enough so it's hardly worth mentioning. I knew which bar was the best solution for it, though booze wasn't going to make my eyes any clearer. Which, neither would anything else.

The Charles is north, upbeach, at the edge of town where a modest shoe emporium and a Thai restaurant ply themselves. Tourists never find my bar, and *sighted* Fenestram artists never look for it. I share it with people like me who don't know anything and want to stay that way. It took me thirty minutes of coastal crawl to get there, where a black pole held aloft a top hat and a cane on a royal red background. It'd been called something else before I'd been born. I heard the crowd through the door. A welcome sound like an empty stool.

Different people like different things at The Charles. I like that there's no ultraviolet pigment, not anywhere. It's the one bar in town where I can't pay the tab off my Fenestram stipend, but the upside is, no ironic Higher tchotchkes and no *crush* stencils over the bar. No *wander* lipstick smiles glowing in the shadows and not a single flirty *farewell* biceps tattoo. Most of all, no *compulsion.* All of Skysill Beach's success flows from *compulsion.* But there was no hint of success in my little ultraviolet free bar.

A long mural spanned the dim walls in boozy neglect, left from the earlier bar with the other name. The best thing about it was, it was neither clever nor interesting. In the mural, faded English gentry rode horses facing prosperous factories and distant hillsides. It was the least ironic painting in three hundred miles. If you squinted you could just see it behind Michelob neon, which was also true of the patrons, who were mixed young and old, not-drunk and very, jukebox smeared in conversation or mostly numb.

I held the color low, Highers off, got my stool and nodded Serena to the shelf. While Serena worked I reached Samantha's keyring out of my pocket. I gave it a jingle. I pinched the key with the green top and started prying it around, until it dropped into my palm. With the Highers off there was no glow, just a silver key. I put the rest of the ring in my pocket. The problem key I held with my finger on the bar, since I wasn't ready to think about keys. Serena brought my glass and lime, and I worked that.

The facts seemed to be I'd *chroma stormed* and passed out. And before that, there'd been a suicide and this key ... and some swirling light leading me down a hall. For a second I caught myself thinking I'd actually seen swirling light in a hall instead of it being purely imaginary, like swirling light is generally. I kept holding the key with my fingertip. The Higher painted key. If it glowed, it made everything less imaginary, right?

I dialed up the Highers, just a touch, and the key popped off the bar in ultraviolet technicolor. I stared at it. That much, at least, was real.

My phone buzzed. Waylon. I sipped and then answered.

"Asher," he yelled, "what's going on? God dammit, I told you *call* me!"

While he yelled I set the phone on the bar and reached for my tumbler, took a drink, then got my napkin to dry the bottom of the glass, twisting to get all the moisture, then used a second napkin to wipe the bar puddle and put my drink back down, then picked the phone back up. Waylon had stopped yelling.

"Waylon," I said, "I didn't hear anything you just said, so listen. I went to your Bluebell place and *looked around* at Samantha. Do you have questions?"

"Come up to the property!"

"I'm not going to do that, I'm drinking."

"God dammit Asher!" His voice got quiet. "That was my daughter. My family."

"Stop reminding me. I went and looked. What do you want to know?" Silence. The moment of truth. More silence. "Do you want me to describe her body?" That was cruel and I was sorry I'd said it, mostly.

"No! God, no."

"I met your cop."

"Who, now?"

"Your cop Officer Hennessy. Why do you need me if you have him?"

"Hennessy's just a cop. He looks around and jumps to the most likely conclusion."

"Samantha killed herself."

"Yes, exactly! He's a cog in the god damn machine!"

"I mean that's what happened to her. As far as I can tell." A thought came to me. It doesn't happen like that all the time. "Is there a reason to think it's not suicide?"

"I know my daughter, Samantha would never kill herself!"

I fingered her key toward me across the bar.

"You might not know your daughter as well as you think," I told him, watching it glow.

"What does that mean?"

I tapped my phone's camera and framed the key against the bar and talked at the same time, and it felt good to do more than one thing simultaneously. Like I was a genius. "So Samantha was a painter?" I asked. Click.

"She never *painted.* God no. She did little journalism things. She hated art." A note of bitterness. A rock in the porridge. "She hated me, I think. She had a collection—did you see it? That collection was mocking me. Mocking what I do!"

"Sure it was. I just texted you a picture of a key. Do you recognize it?"

"No. Am I supposed to?" He didn't stop for an answer. "I don't know—was I a bad father? No, of course not! Then why? Oh, god. Did she really do it, Asher? Is she really gone forever?"

I was tired of this topic of his, family members and tragedy, he was obsessed. I shot vodka to hold off the *Gray*, which is a strategy I hope will work someday.

"Text me a picture of Samantha," I told him. "Look, whatever you think, *I* think your daughter was a painter." Higher colored paint is very tightly controlled. The only people who get it, or can see it to use it, are Fenestram artists. "I'm going to ask a couple people. If I find anything I'll call you."

I'm pretty sure he was talking when I hung up.

Even considering how long I'd been out of circulation, I knew just about every artist in Skysill who had a Fenestram stipend. We *all* know each other. Someone as prominent as Waylon's daughter, if she'd been *sighted* all of us would have known. Unless she was keeping it secret. But why do that? Being *sighted*'s already a secret. The outside world somehow never notices us.

There was a gash on the finger I was using to hold the key on the bar, cut falling in Samantha's hallway. When I thought about trash, cat piss, blood diseases, I stepped away from the bar to the washroom, and leaned against the sink and flushed as much of it down the drain as I could. I wiped my hands and in the mirror saw my face, white as a sand dollar, dark hair very neglected, obviously I could eat better, shave with more diligence or at all. I do have attractive symmetry—I've done a lot of figure studies, I see my potential—but like all my potentials I fail to live up to it.

Behind me something *choke* glowed in a toilet stall. I guess I was still riding a little Higher.

My first instinct was outrage — my ultraviolet-free sanctum violated — but that was hilarious because The Charles bathrooms are pretty hard to violate. Still, I slammed into the stall to stare at the wall above the toilet where a variety of standard color pens in different hands had made a list disparaging the Dodgers for their sexual and athletic failings. Scrawled recklessly over the top of all that, in greasy *choke* marker pen, was, *these sightless cocksuckers can all SUCK my DICK BAAABY!!!*

Some charming lordling came into my toilet and spread his art pen *color* all over my inane Dodger complaints. The boundaries between the kingdoms in my world were shifting, becoming permeable. I didn't like it.

With toilet paper and palms I swiped the Higher scrawl, though none of the regular drunks would ever know it was there. I wiped until the words were a *choke* smear and my palms gleamed with ultraviolet oil. Like Samantha's.

When I left the bathroom I kept walking to the car. Whatever I couldn't figure out was not likely to show up in a tumbler at this point. Convenience like that never happens to me. I went home, emptied my pockets, and in the moonlight falling through my window I considered my life and all my unfulfilled ambitions, which only took a minute, then I sat on my little bench. Some of Tante Celine's macramé, with Higher beads and textiles, hung in the bay window weaving moon shadows on the floor.

In the center of the empty room stood the last painting I ever started, unfinished. Whenever I'm home I look at it constantly, which is a waste of time and one reason I stay at The Charles when I can. I watched the silver moon lighting those opening strokes, *choke* and *bleed* in yellowtail hues, a rough outline. It might have been great. A lot of it was then.

Resist the impulse to dip a brush and paint, and then tilt crazy, pass out, rise and do it again. Pretend that impulse doesn't exist. That is what I always say to myself instead of doing the thing I most want to do. When the *Gray* took me the first time, ten years ago, at sixteen, I'd been painting this moon glow canvas, about to go lights out. But instead I'd dropped into a pool of calm, grey, soul Novocain. And the *Grey* somehow made it possible to completely stop painting, for the first time in my life. And so now I have my life working perfectly.

In the moonlight I lifted the brush to the canvas, without paint weight, washing it back and forth and stroking out ghost images.

CHAPTER FOUR

Dedrick's Fenestram Color paint store squats, wide and self-contained but a little confused, between a hipster dentist and a hipster barbershop. It wears a goofy six-foot painter's palette on the roof with colors weathered into dust puffs. The neighborhood around Fenestram Color has been gentrifying for decades, but Color keeps its legs tucked in depression era overalls. It knows its clientele. It knows its place.

It's the only art store in Skysill, maybe the world, selling Higher paint. If Samantha bought her supplies anywhere, she did it here.

The *OPEN* sign blinked across the street. I leaned out of my car and put my legs under me and stood. It was a cheery morning. Or other people on the sidewalk seemed to be having that kind of morning. Probably none of them were looking into a dead painter girl.

I chewed my lip while traffic cleared and came back and cleared again and then I still wasn't ready to cross but I did, wondering what Dedrick would say when he saw me. Apologies are second nature to me, they have to be with my history—I serve them two-handed like happy hour jello shots—but this apology to Dedrick wasn't going to be easy like the others, since I would mean every word I served.

Sweet linseed alkaloid tang hit me when I opened the door, and I shivered. Turpentine resin, virgin paper, varnish on oak, perfumed endless afternoons with a brush and a canvas here, trying to manage my problems. It all hit me.

I drifted inwards, tracking the colors, tuned a little too high probably, along a honeycomb stuffed with a thousand bubble gum chalk sticks, too dreamy to be safe so I dialed everything back. I followed the chalk to the end, just before turning right to Dedrick's counter.

I subvocalized a few practice excuses there. It's not that I'd done anything so wrong with Dedrick. I'd just stopped being around for a decade without explanation. The day the *Gray* took me and I stopped painting I'd really started living out of a bottle, and all the other parts of my life took a back seat. He'd understand. I'd tell him about the *Gray*.

I stepped around, started forward, and saw... not Dedrick.

"Welcome to Fenestram Color," said the woman who wasn't Dedrick. She had snowy skin and white hair falling taut off one shoulder, the way starlets played nuns in the 50s. Her eyes were nocturnal shadows. She was dressed in white painter canvas. She wore pale *choke* mascara, though no other makeup, as a little secret handshake. *Sighted* of course. Her mascara focused on me.

"What can I do for you?" When she smiled her mouth went the right directions but the rest of her, I felt, reserved judgment. Or she was bored and bad at hiding it. Who knows? I try not to care what people are thinking because I'm so bad at it.

"Where's Dedrick?" I said. "I'm here for Dedrick." I noticed myself sounding a little unbalanced from the smells and colors and all the guilt. A night of sleep had left me unrested and confused. I hoped it was not going to be another of those days.

"Dedrick," she repeated. She made it sound dubious.

"Right. Dedrick. Is he here?"

"No one is here but me, can I—"

The nun had to be a new employee, I thought.

"The owner isn't here?" I interrupted her, which I know, I wasn't at my best, I was distracted. "The *boss*?"

"Oh the *boss*," she lilted, "you're looking for the *boss*."

She liked saying *boss*. She had a British clip. Close in she seemed older and less like a nun—more like a mother superior regretting the nights of immorality she'd never have, which you knew she'd make her nuns pay for.

The *authorized access* door where the Higher paints lived was closed. But I knew Dedrick wouldn't be back there. He preferred it in front with the customers.

"I'll leave him a note," I told her. I wanted to write, *Dedrick, sorry, haven't been around this decade, need to talk to you about a dead painter girl,* but that seemed wrong. While I thought about my note, the nun lady watched me.

"Dedrick retired," she said. "He's gone. I'm Veronica. I own the store. Which makes me the boss I suppose."

"Retired?"

"That's right."

"You're the boss? Dedrick retired? That's not possible."

"Oh, it *is* possible I'm happy to say. It happened more than four years ago. I've been the boss every day since then. Perhaps you can talk to me. Would you like to try?"

I was disappointed hearing myself not drop the subject. "This is extremely ... fishy," I told her, "Because Dedrick ... I'd have heard about him *retiring,* I mean, leaving the paint store? He's a friend of mine, and no someone would have told me. Why wouldn't ... why wouldn't he tell me or anyone tell me, if this is true? It's *fishy*."

I didn't like how I kept saying the things I kept thinking, or saying *fishy*, or how the Veronica woman looked. She had a speculative twist on her face. She pinched her lips quizzical, wishing she could help me. It was subtle mockery, the kind that confuses me.

"Hm," she wondered, "fishy, yes, how could this have happened? To you! Of all people! Here is one theory—perhaps the people who never mentioned your dear friend Dedrick selling the store to me assumed he'd already told you himself, as he was your friend. I would have done the same thing in their place."

The mockery was pretty twisty. I took it as a compliment she expected I'd follow it. I tried to get back on track. If Dedrick was gone —and there shouldn't be much surprise to that, he might not even be alive anymore, it had been ten years—my questions about Samantha remained. So I turned on the charm, which shows how low I was on other options.

"Look Veronica, I sincerely apologize for calling you not the boss. Dedrick's gone and you are the boss. I should have seen it. You have all the classic signs."

"That's a *tremendous* sincere apology! Extremely sincere. I wonder what Dedrick would think of it?"

I put my phone on the counter with Samantha's picture and turned it toward Veronica. "I'm willing to forget Dedrick if you are. I have this picture, of this girl. I just wonder, she might have come in to buy Higher paint. Do you recognize her? Can you look down at the picture on the phone?"

She couldn't. She didn't need to, apparently.

"Higher paint?" she asked. "I wouldn't think so. That girl does not have a Fenestram Stipend. And of course we know the rules. Dedrick told me. Such a lovely man. Too bad you missed him. If this girl had come in, she could never have purchased, or learned about, Higher color materials. But of course you know that too, don't you, Mr. Gale? May I call you Asher?"

I stated the obvious because sometimes that helps me. "You know my name."

"I *do,*" she subtly astonished herself realizing. She put her hands on the counter with snakey grace. She smiled again, with her whole face this time, but it wasn't any better.

"I thought it was you," she nodded. "I must say, you're ruder than I'd expected. It's Asher Gale the prodigy!" Her dark eyes in her white face were fascinated. "Tell me, after you stopped painting, they say you lost the ability to *see* Higher color. Is it true?"

"I don't think they do say that., Veronica. People who *see* Higher color never seem to say anything about Higher color."

"So true," she said. So tiresome, was what she meant.

"But *you* talk about it," I observed. "Is that right?"

"If I wanted to talk about it I could. So tell me, Mr. Gale, why *did* you stop painting?"

"I ran out of brushes. We're getting sidetracked. I was asking about this girl. You still haven't looked at her, so how can you be sure she never came in?"

"They say your work was unbelievably powerful. But you gave it up. I always wondered if something happened?"

"Can we focus on the girl? Is this a familiar girl at *all*?"

Veronica reached under the counter and lifted a tube of Higher oil paint and pretended my phone didn't exist. She held the tube between us. "I have also heard that you *see* as high as *bleed.*"

"Is there some Asher Gale wiki I don't know about?"

"Is it true? You *see bleed?*"

"Would you be able to tell if I said yes but was lying?"

She bent, her body flexible as her voice, and rifled through something below the counter then put a paper beside the register. It was The Test. The assessment to determine how much, if any, Higher spectrum a person *sees*. It showed the seven ultraviolets, labeled lowest to highest. They get harder to *see* as they rise to *bleed.*

The Test finds your Higher limit. Scattered on the paper were several dozen jumbled circles, each printed one Higher color. Test takers worked their way through the circles with matching Higher markers, stamping the ones they *saw* with a dab of the corresponding color.

Veronica lifted the *bleed* tube the way you showed someone the Russian roulette bullet before putting it in the gun, unscrewed the cap, and put a dab of *bleed* on the tip of her little finger. For anyone who couldn't *see,* that would be nothing but transparent gel. She used her fingertip as a little stamp, applying it to every *bleed* circle on The Test except for one.

So she could *see* to *bleed.* Not many can.

"What's my grade?" she asked, studying me. "Do you think I could catch you if you lied about your *sight*?"

I looked over The Test.

"Veronica," I sighed, "I tried apologizing about the boss comment, you remember?"

"Yes. Your Herculean efforts at apology—how trying that must have been for you. If you grade my test I will tell you what I know of the girl."

I was tired of the subtlety. I twisted the cap off the tube and turned it down on the last *bleed* circle and squeezed, then put the cap back.

"B minus," I said. "Now my girl."

She examined the test for just a moment, then shifted her gaze to Samantha's picture, a grinning image of a girl in a boat on an ocean. Veronica gave it a going over.

"Yes," she said, "I have never seen her before. She has not been into the store. She likely doesn't have a Stipend or I would know her. You painters go through an extraordinary amount of Higher paint. Almost like you're addicted to it. Do you think? And she most certainly has not been into the *members only* area. Everyone knows the rules. The rules, the rules."

"So I took The Test, but you still know nothing about the girl."

"Yes. Apparently."

"I honestly don't get it. Are you bored? What is all this?"

"I'm very bored."

"Can you get a hobby?"

"Trust me, Mr. Gale, I have a hobby." Veronica gave me a long look. "Perhaps, someday, I will share it with you."

Her smile went back to its lair. Her hands came back onto the counter. Her eyes considered the possibilities, until she found one she liked.

"Can I help you with any painting supplies? A coloring book or a small sparkle pen? No? Take this, then. You earned it." She slid the tube of *bleed* across the counter.

I abandoned it, escaping out the door, feeling sifted and labeled, like I'd left blood under Veronica's nails. I knew more than I had when I'd arrived, but only at the edges. I climbed back in my car. The clock on the hipster dentist said 10:30 am. I'd gotten up early, brushed my teeth and had coffee. The day had been set aside for asking a few questions of a few people, but I wondered, if it was all going to be this unsatisfying and subtle, should I go home and spend time with my unfinished canvas, or just go to The Charles? Not being a painter was my real calling, after all. Asking people for information was new to me, and I was starting to think I was bad at it.

Still. If Samantha Goodman had been a secret painter—a Higher painter—there were things I wanted to understand. Why hide her *sight*? Was it something about the way she *saw?* Had she *seen* things like I do, broken? I'm always looking for some secret way to get myself back to a canvas. It feels a little pathetic, honestly, or a little Pavlovian. Over and over. Those poor fucking dogs.

Only one other person in Skysill would know Samantha's Fenestram pedigree. He'd know it without question—he knew us all—and I could tell how semi-desperate I'd grown, since despite what it was going to do to me, I was already headed upcoast to meet him.

CHAPTER
FIVE

The Square on the Sea takes in its audiences at the open end of Skysill's only cobbled alley. The renaissance lane starts between a chocolate shop and a sunglass hut, where stout stanchions allow no cars, only palanquins and horse-drawn carriages. The alley hosts life-sized potted plants in bronze, and a bronze boy sitting whimsically on a bench reading, and a bronze girl filled with innocence chasing a sculpted dog. And as you came into the Square itself you saw the sign: *Roman Sutherland - Master of Light and Shadow.* It's as discreet as fine artisans can make any huge, tightly kerned, gold embossed sign hung in coal-black framing.

Other galleries looked into the Square from all four walls, while the sun came down on the bronzes and the shoppers. All the other show places tried to get a piece of the art action. Some of them did a decent job, but Roman owned the gold and black.

Consumers crowded Roman's gallery. They packed in like it was 7 Eleven on a weekday morning. The light was bordello low and the walls cauldron colored, in three retreating, increasingly shadowed rooms. You went through wide passages all the way to the rear, with

Roman's art pinned to the walls everywhere in spotlights. Some people called it art, I mean.

Along the tops of all the walls in all three sections, a word was painted over and over in awkward, sans serif letters unlike anything else in the gallery. All the words were colored *compulsion.* They stood out to me, but none of the other shoppers saw them, though the words leered down at us, as out of place as missing teeth on a glamor model, shouting in spark-smack *compulsion: BUY BUY BUY BUY BUY BUY BUY BUY BUY,* ringing the ceilings round.

They called the color *compulsion* for a reason. The other six Highers lacked any special powers that I know of. You could paint *choke* or *farewell* instructions on a wall and normal brains wouldn't react in the slightest. But *compulsion* is different—for visible spectrum humans, but not the *sighted, compulsion* tends to bend thinking. Make good ideas seem bad, and vice versa. A lot of money rolls through the galleries of Skysill Beach. An absurd amount. Some substantial part of that comes from the secret of *compulsion.*

Different galleries take different strategies. Some lure shoppers to the cash register with winsome *compulsion* flower trails, some fill display rooms with *compulsion* pornography. Some galleries write out *compulsion* appeals to long forgotten loves, invoke charity, shame, flattery. But they all do something. It'd be hard to sell the Mona Lisa in Skysill Beach without *compulsion.* You'd be competing against a sales steamroller.

But Roman had distilled it to a most brutal efficiency. The same mechanics as all the rest, but worse in some real way. I squinted, and reminded myself I'd given up complaining about *compulsion,* along with authentic art and other trivia, for vodka. The power of *compulsion* was one of the *sighted* subjects no one wanted to discuss.

Next to the cash register were puzzles and placemats featuring Roman's pictures. Two older women with handbags as big as St. Bernards stood discussing their shopping plans.

"Do you think we bought enough?" asked one. "What if this is our last chance to buy?"

"We should buy some puzzles," said her friend. "He's such a master of light and shadow!"

"Any canvas you buy can be shipped anywhere in the world," smiled the cashier. "Maybe you should go take a second look? You want to make sure you buy everything you like!"

The ladies agreed. It seemed like a very good plan to them.

I dialed the Higher color away. I held my breath, which didn't change anything but I couldn't stop myself. Then I pushed through the first room and into the second room and then got to the last room where, in a rounded, raised alcove set into the back wall with rugs and candles, Roman sat, discussing being a master of light and shadow with a young couple who fingered their wallets and listened.

I waited for Roman to notice me and I took that time to reacquaint myself with everything I loved about the Roman Sutherland collection. It felt like being inside Disney's world of cartoonishly horrible wonder and drama. The canvases absolutely radiated wonder and drama. The dramatic parts were always very bright, to make sure you didn't miss them, and the backgrounds were filled with wonder and darkness: shimmering garden gate flowers, alive with drama, bridges arcing into clouds, winter midnight cabins where families of angels poured golden drama through the windows onto the snow.

And the real crime: they were all forgeries. Every single one of them.

Roman noticed me at last. "Excuse me," he told the couple and pointed them toward the art products. "Please enjoy, and please buy something, large or small, because art is precious, and it reminds us to value ourselves."

Then he came toward me, hands out in front of him at belt level like a man approaching a wild animal or a holy sword.

"Asher. Oh my friend. But this... what a wonderful surprise!"

"It is? A surprise? I thought maybe you'd seen me." I pointed to the ceiling. The place was surveilled like a casino.

He smiled his beatific face. He was swarthy like a perfectly groomed alligator, with shocking light blue eyes. Inky beard shadow blackened his cheeks further to set off his shocking bright eyes and leave him stupidly charismatic. I'd always wondered if that was where he came up with his brand, *master of light and shadow*. He'd been admiring his beard and his eyes and it'd just occurred to him.

"Please, come, sit," he put a hand behind my shoulder and it was firm and accomplished. I let him sit me on one side of his alcove and watched him slide into the other side and cross his fingers into a prayer, then put that on the table between us.

"Well," he beamed. "A reunion celebration! Let us share a cup." And like magic a samovar was delivered on a tray with two cups, and the steaming oily scent of Turkish coffee and sugar and cardamom came up.

"I am embarrassed, my friend," he told me as he filled my thimble.

"Finally," I said.

He seemed puzzled. "I've forgotten if you take sugar. Do you?"

"Just give me what she's having."

I pointed at *Sleeping Beauty*, a painting where a woman with red hair lit by drama had collapsed in a shadowed forest after sipping drama from a porcelain saucer, probably hoping it was poison so she could escape Roman's collection. Roman laughed, delighted, immune to aspersions or critique.

"Asher! Oh, my friend. You have not changed!" He handed over the coffee. It was amazingly fantastic coffee.

"How's business, Roman? Still selling art hand over fist as if people can't help themselves after coming in here?"

He smiled wider and deeper—he found me delightful.

"Please, Asher, let us not season our soup with that dry old bone." What the hell do you say to that? "Drink! This is a good day!" I drank. It's hard not to drink coffee like that. "So, you are here. You are ready to begin painting again?"

"What?" Coffee got stuck in one of my heart valves, just for a second. "No. No Roman."

"But you are *so gifted!*"

"This subject comes up fast. How long since we talked and right away I'm so gifted?"

"But why, why would you stop? You could do extraordinary things!"

"Let's not talk about me. Let's just call it a dry bone and keep it the fuck out of our soup."

He caused himself to look unhappy with a pout. It was charming and boyish and made me want to beat him.

"As you wish. But. If you ever again lift a brush, I expect you to come paint for me."

"Your problem, Roman, is you won't come out and say what you mean." I felt the bitterness coming up, colors flaring a little. Not a safe feeling.

"Mean?" He pouted harder, making it worse. "What do I mean?"

"If you want me to come *paint your pictures* for you, just say it. Like *minion one* over there." I flicked at three separate garden gate canvases in dramatic spotlights. "Or minion *two,*" I pointed at *Sleeping Beauty* and at two dramatic waterfalls, "or *three,*" I pointed to six pictures of bridges, "or *four,*" one cottage in the woods, a couple of swoony landscapes, "or *five.*" Five was mostly Christmas scenes and a church. I ground my feelings down with a sick push. If I *stormed* here, or went *Gray,* the insult and the injury together might cripple me for days. I'd known it would be bad. I'd forgotten what it really felt like.

Roman stared at his paintings like he was seeing them for the first time.

"It is quite astonishing," he said, easing back to me, "although I do wish you would be a little more circumspect." He glanced around at the shoppers. His voice was low but smooth and full of curves. "How do you do it? My five apprentices are extraordinary, each trained to a very high standard so they can paint with my hand. And yet, as if it were nothing, you pick them out one from the other."

"Anyone can see it."

"No. Only you."

“Not a single painting here is yours!” It just came out. It was more of me not dropping things, and not getting back to the real questions. But then I seldom amaze myself with any new behaviors. “It’s got to embarrass you a little, right? All this forgery. A little?”

“But, Asher, these are all mine. The system of patronage and apprentices is thousands of years old, my friend. You know that!”

“Your customers don’t so you’re selling forgeries. Throw *compulsion* in the mix, it’s not even selling. It’s like you don’t have a soul.” I had no idea what I meant by that. I thought it came out sounding pretty insincere.

“Forgeries!” He laughed, completely ignoring all talk of *compulsion* or soullessness, so he could enjoy the thought he was having. I guess he just loved every second of his life. “My own paintings as forgeries! Now *that* philosophical position had never before rolled through my mind!”

I told him I didn’t picture anything rolling through there at all. I did picture him rolling through money devouring babies though. He just shook his head and laughed. Impervious to me churlish.

“Ah, Asher—I have missed you. Like I would miss my own shadow. You bring so much delight to my life!”

“Ok, Roman. You’re delighted, I’m a shadow. The whole world’s a fucking cartoon.” I made a real effort to turn the stampede. I drank more coffee, which just got better the more you had. I put the tiny cup on the tiny saucer and took out my phone. “I’m here because I need your help with something.”

“Anything.”

“One thing. You know everyone in Skysill with a Fenestram Stipend, right?”

“Of course, my friend.” He took a deep breath. Roman has a bunch of different set speeches. You have to be careful not to trigger them. I’d been out of the game for a while and wandered smack into one. He beamed, because he loved his speeches.

"I am your shepherd. I interview applicants, I review your Tests, I see to your training, mentorships, I issue your stipends and I guide you all into life and work in Skysill Beach. Some few of you I consider friends. But all of you are my *children.*"

"Okay for god's sake, Roman," I said, jumping in fast because who knew when it would end otherwise, "I ask a simple question and it's a god damns stump speach—just look at this picture. Will you please? Do you know this girl? Her name's Samantha. Is she one of your children?"

"What do you mean?"

"I mean is she a painter? Can this girl *see?* Is she on a stipend?"

I was afraid a question about *sight* might run us into a dead end. A thing as simple as that, a lot of people just change the subject. But Roman picked up my phone and stared, and after a moment, which seemed like a strangely long moment, he shook his head.

"She is not one of us, Asher."

"She's a painter."

"That may be. But she is not *sighted.*"

"You're sure?" He actually arched an eyebrow. "Fine, be sure. How about this?" I put Samantha's Higher stained key on the table. He looked at it without picking it up. After a moment he looked at me. His arresting blue eyes started arresting concern.

"Are you in some kind of trouble?" he asked.

"Yeah I'm double-parked. What do you know about the key?"

"Nothing. It is a key. What is all this, my friend? I am worried."

I stood up. It was all I could take. But Roman saw someone behind me before I could storm out, or even leave in a less satisfying way, and it lit him up more, eleven on the scale of wonder and drama. He gestured over my shoulder to someone.

"Asher, do you know Julian Donner?"

I looked. Thin, coiffed, eyes of smoke. I knew his face. I thought I might have passed a portrait of him, somewhere in the gallery.

"Julian, this is Asher Gale. Julian is an extraordinary talent."

Julian admitted it with his eyes and every other part of him. It was his favorite admission to make. He thought he looked fantastic doing it and I had to agree. His eye fell to my phone, and Samantha's picture. Julian gave off a natural suspicion of anything that didn't particularly relate to him. He was suspicious of my phone.

"Julian is my most talented apprentice." Roman's eyes sparkled at me, veritably *sparkled.* "Can you guess which number *minion* he is?"

Roman watched me. I looked Julian over. I glanced at the walls where the forgeries hung. I shrugged.

"I could guess, Roman. But I have my reputation for not giving a shit to worry about."

"Yes, of course," Roman nodded. "He is... *one.*"

Julian could tell he was being served at a feast where he was only a side dish. He didn't like it. He made a frown.

"Oh Julian," Roman said. "Do not frown. It will sour my painting."

"Ok, Roman," I said. "I can't bring myself to use up any more of your time, you must still have a bunch of art you need to force people to buy against their will, so I'll leave you to that. Just forget you ever saw me."

"Asher, these questions you are asking," Roman said softly. He held out Samantha's key, which I'd been about to leave behind. "Please be very careful."

"About what?"

"Skysill Beach is ... a complex balance. People, forces. There is only so much protection I can offer you."

"Protection—if you really want to do something for me," I said, pointing to *BUY BUY BUY BUY BUY BUY BUY* around the tops of his walls, "scrub that shit off. Fire your apprentices. See if you have an honest painting left in you."

"Oh Asher, so young. And arrogance is still your birthright. But your path is dangerous, I fear."

"Well stop fearing. It might sour your painting."

I turned and left as fast as I could part the crowd, still tasting his unbelievable coffee. Passing the cashier I saw the two older women stuffing their trophy bags with puzzles, plus a few extra snow globes of light and shadow.

CHAPTER SIX

I snapped out of Roman's gallery ember hot and fizzed across the Square as far as the alley with the bronze boy reading on his bench, and stopped. Fury like that can push me *Gray* and has to be tamped. But Roman fingers my hottest buttons with his gallery of forgery, calling it art when it's nothing but profit.

The bronze boy on his bench with a book had a leg up, sitting forward in a reader's lean, and that's how he'd stay until they melted him. I sat down on his bench struggling for calm, which seems like a contradiction but is totally a thing you can do. I thought the bronze boy was also doing it, focused and diligent. He'd been given a wide mouth to indicate an accepting nature, and a drawn brow which showed he had purpose, and he sat with his back to Roman's gallery which showed he had common decency.

Talking to the bronze boy helped. People gave me sidelong glances but I live on sidelong attention. I updated the boy. Eventually, I'd smoothed the outrage to some dregs, when I got a text from Amelia: *Hey baby brother. Don't forget the Nagato tonight!* She had an opening at the gallery where she showed. I sent her a thumbs up, which meant, *I love you Amelia but I'm not going to that and you know it*, which she did know.

Samantha's mystery key still pearled in my palm. It was the kind of thing I lose with ridiculous regularity, so I stood and fished out my own keyring, and walking back down the alley I pried the loops open and did the responsible thing so as not to lose the dead girl's key.

There were only a few other keys on my ring. Samantha's slid in between a bike-lock key I forgot to use until my bike disappeared and the extra house key I'd never bothered to hide. Among those duller keys was one that gleamed. It was a key I'd never used, silver with *I & A* emblazoned on the crown. *Investigation and Authentication.*

Downtown Skysill is four or five long blocks. But right across the street was the building where this *I & A* key had a door. Sometimes when I'd drive through downtown I'd pass the Bradley Building and forget to ignore it, like mouth sores. I saw it now, closer and for longer than usual. *Asher Gale: Investigation and Authentication* was in there. It made me think of Waylon, then more forgeries, and didn't help my state of mind.

The Bradley Building is three stories of earthquake retrofitted brown brick with lily pad awnings at street level shading an Italian grill and the Gallery Manifesto. The broad entrance is midwestern, tinted glass and stenciled, with thick concrete steps like a super friendly bank. I wanted to go home but now, on top of my other afflictions, Roman's coffee began working through me, and I thought, how appropriate would it be if I used the *I & A* toilet? If the only thing I ever did there was use the toilet? I did not want to go back to Roman's, and I wasn't drunk enough to use a gallery storefront. So I hurried across the street and pushed into the lobby, where I piped a little Higher around to see if any of the listed businesses were run by Fenestram friends, but nothing bounced back. Asher Gale's office, I discovered, was on the third floor, reached by a clean, slow elevator. I elevated.

Asher Gale: Investigation and Authentication read the sign on the door to the left after I came out into a hallway. Asher Gale's office. The hallway smelled empty, like buffed dust, with long green runners in case you wanted to get in a fairway shot or two. I stood a moment before Asher Gale's door. After a time, I put in the key and pushed the door open, and while it swung slowly shut again I looked in at a large, fully decorated interior. It overlooked the Coast Highway on a prime corner of Skysill Beach—it was blazingly rich real estate. How much money had I saved Waylon, if this was how he thought about repaying me? A few Swiss fortunes? I let the door swing fully closed. I didn't need a bathroom that badly.

Then a voice called behind me.

"Can I get you something?" It was an uncertain voice. I turned to see what there was to be uncertain about. The elevator doors were open and a man with round spectacles and a high forehead and bright Hawaiian shorts stood with a watermelon under one arm and two six-packs under the other. I could tell what made him uncertain —he was as dexterous as a newborn calf, and watermelons are heavy and six-packs can get tricky.

"I said can I get you something?"

"What'd you have in mind?" I asked.

The elevator closed behind him as he asked, "Just what do you think you're doing there?"

"Thinking about bathrooms. What are you doing with that watermelon?"

"There's a *public* restroom two blocks *that* direction." He showed me the direction with his chin. It could have been any direction. His glasses slid down his nose and put him in a tough spot with his juggling, but his tone made it perfectly clear he didn't want any of my type going to the bathroom around here.

I watched him losing his game of balancing things and said, "I bet you wish you had a bag."

"Leave a bag out of it."

"Your watermelon—"

"If you don't get out of here—" he kneeled to catch the melon and forgot to finish his thought. The melon rolled around a second and then he trapped it.

"Look, don't worry," I told him. "I'm Asher Gale. From the sign on the door. I manage the bathroom in there."

He pushed his glasses up and stabilized his breath and kept his watermelon down. Yes, he saw, there it was, the name on the door. That was all he needed. He was done with me. He had Hawaiians in his office. He picked up his fruit.

"Yeah, go ahead, use that," he said. "I'm Phil. That place never has anyone. Homeless guys come in the buildoing looking for bathrooms. Some homeless lady in a sweater's been back and forth all day, hovering around, crying. They're a plague. We watch each other's backs here in the Bradley Building. We're a family."

"Got it. We're the Bradley family. I bet we're something." I stopped him when he wanted to walk away. "But listen, are you saying you believe I'm Asher Gale just because I pointed to a name on the door? Is that Bradley family security? Couldn't I be *anybody*?"

"Okay *are* you him or *aren't* you?"

"Let's leave that to the authorities. In the meantime maybe you know more Bradley family members with an opinion on me going to the bathroom in this office, we'll have a focus group."

I watched for the second time as Phil had to swoop to catch his melon, this time trapping it between his knees and his chest, and then he duck-walked away without issuing any more ideas at me, so I stepped through the door with my name on it and let it close, behind me this time.

Inside was a cavernous modern reception area painted with natural light. At a comfortable distance from the door a glass table waited, where a receptionist could sit and enter wireless data or talk on his office phone or interrogate people who came through his door. Three deep club chairs waited by the windows for people who made it past him. The chairs had marbled orange cushions with coral piping, and gathered at an abalone coffee table to take in broad views out the windows, up at the inland hills, and down at cars and people going by under elm trees. Throw rugs spread over a floor of cream limestone. The rugs did a nice job keeping all of it feeling warm. On the walls hung a collection of the forgeries I'd found for Waylon over the years, a nice touch, if a little sickening.

And there was a bathroom. Bravo, Waylon's property manager.

But as the bathroom door closed I heard Asher Gale's office door open again. Hadn't it locked behind me? Uncertain watermelon feet padded in. This bathroom might not be a bathroom I used or wanted, but enough was enough. I slammed the door back open.

The woman who stood in front of me was startled. She had cat-eye glasses and motionless black hair and a face so heart-shaped it belonged on a card. She'd been crying. Her thin blue cardigan fell off one shoulder and she pulled it up, her jeans hung off both hips like she'd lost weight recently, and one hand clutched a leather bag like she wanted it dead.

"Your office keeps the strangest hours," she told me. "I've been waiting for you all day."

"If you're looking for public restrooms they're *that* way," I pointed.

"I'm looking for Asher Gale."

"Really? Why?"

"What do you mean? Are you the receptionist?"

"I don't think there's a receptionist."

"Who are you?"

This kind of interrogation seemed to come up a lot in the Bradley Building. The woman was distraught. I registered that belatedly because belated is how I roll, when I can get away with it. She seemed to be growing more agitated the more she talked to me. I felt colors flare. I jammed them down.

"Look, come sit here," I told her. "Take a deep breath. I'm Asher Gale. I guess I'm man enough to admit it." I led her to the reception desk and sat her in the chair with the phone and the wireless plastic, and showed her some of my cards in the stack as proof of my identity. It appeared to confuse her, almost to the point of crying again.

"Why am I sitting *here*?"

"Where'd you rather sit?"

"Not at reception! What about the office?" She pointed at a glass-paneled door I hadn't noticed yet, cracked open to expose an inner office where the wood was dark and the rugs less dreamy and more pipe smokey. I saw a standing lamp, a shelf of heavy books, an oak desk. She seemed calmer when she looked in there, it was that kind of office. An admiral's office. I told her *absolutely,* go sit in the Admiral's office. She stopped at the door and looked back.

"Aren't you coming?" she asked.

"I wasn't planning on it," I said, but then she looked like she might cry, so I did.

We got in and she shut the door and sat in the chair in front of the desk. The lights had come on by themselves. Very clever. The only seat left was the leather chair on the serious side of the desk. She held her bag down on her lap. I lingered at the door. As soon as she looked away, I planned to leave. But she stared at me, like she expected me to say something.

"I want you to find my missing girlfriend," she cried after a while. She yanked her bag open, very suddenly, to tear out a manila envelope and throw it on the desk. Then she sat breathing, like all the hard work had been done.

"Ok," I said. "I see what's happening. We don't do that kind of investigation."

"What kind *do* you do?" she demanded, straining at tears again because she hadn't come to the right kind of investigation office.

"Not any. Nobody investigates anything here. It's a mistake."

"Well why do you have it on your *door*? And *Yelp*? I had to come here, this is the only investigation agency in Skysill Beach! I've been out there all morning, knocking and waiting. Please help me. My girlfriend's missing!" She un-pursed money in a handful as she continued, "I need your help. Help me find Samantha."

I felt the world twist. There's just one thing after another all the time.

"Samantha," I repeated.

She nodded, dabbing at her eyes with her cardigan sleeve which I thought had been used that way a lot already. As the mascot of, apparently, the only investigation agency in the city, I stepped away from the door, moved around the desk, and sat in the leather and looked at the envelope she'd put on the Admiral's nautical blotter.

"Is there a picture in there?" I asked. She nodded. I pinched the brads apart. I turned it like a bag of sugar and tapped it empty. It was a big envelope but there wasn't much information. One of the items was a photograph of Samantha Goodman. I lifted it to look. At Samantha's back was a green glass door, riveted with copper bolts. I recognized the door to the Nagato Gallery, the gallery where my sister had her contract. Samantha seemed to be enjoying herself at a party.

"Samantha Goodman was your girlfriend," I said.

"Yes. We live together. She disappeared two weeks ago!"

"And did you tell the police?"

"They won't do anything."

"Why not?"

"Well since Samantha was texting me," she explained, "they say she isn't missing!"

"So she wasn't actually missing? Not if she was texting. Right?"

"Well I don't know where she *is*. What do you call that? Missing! Then yesterday she stopped. Something's happened, I know it, she's in some kind of trouble!" I poked through the few pieces of paper on the desk. I stirred them. She watched me. "Don't you even want to know my name?" she asked.

"Go on. Tell me your name." She was actually pretty good at the investigation stuff.

"It's Felicia!"

"I'm pretty sure Samantha lived by herself," I said. "That mess in her place wasn't by committee. Where do you fit in?"

"What are you talking about? What mess? We live in Skysill Canyon together!"

"So," I had a stroke of insight, a clear-headed feeling I didn't particularly prize but which sometimes I can't avoid, "did you *not* know she had a place in Catalina Village?" Felicia stared. Now I felt I was the one excelling at investigation.

"What are you saying," she asked. But I thought, deep down, she wasn't surprised. I had another funny thought. An investigator thought. I flashed Higher to see if Felicia had paint on her, or if anything else stood out. But nothing changed in the ultraviolet except she looked more upset. I put Samantha back in the envelope and sealed it.

"I'm not the one you need to talk to," I said. "I'm sorry."

"There's no one else! She's acting so—something's wrong! She's erratic, drinking more. She won't tell me what story she's working on, but that's when it started."

"What story was she's working on?" I asked, and Felicia gave me a look confirming to me I was still bad at investigation after all.

"Will you take my case?" she asked. I must really be the only game in town.

My day had done a 180 in the time it takes to lick a stamp. I looked at the office. God damn it Waylon, if you didn't — then I saw it. A nice minibar. I stood and sighed and looked at Felicia pleading. I was going to have to tell her that her girlfriend was dead. It was going to be my job. How do you watch someone hear news like that and keep all your pieces from going haywire? Pretty dramatic stuff. Dangerous territory for a person like me.

I poured a drink, and held it to Felicia. Felicia wasn't looking. And then the drink dropped through my hand, and I couldn't catch it, and it hit the floor — my hand was spasmed open. The ice and the glass bounced but Felicia didn't notice it because the rug was a masterpiece of soft insulation. Oh shit, I thought. Going *Gray*.

The office eased down to become a charcoal still life of smoke and milk and calm. I felt muscles soften, my face relax, my grimace fade. I'd had a grimace. How long had *that* been going on? I floated back to the little bar and poured Felicia another drink and took that and floated it down to her. I balanced it on one finger. In the *Gray* I'm very precise. It's the best thing about me. I smiled.

I remembered doing almost exactly the same thing for Waylon with his drink pretty recently, and remembered saying almost the same thing I was about to say here. That was funny.

"I'm sorry for your loss," I heard myself say. The sun was warm on my right leg. So perfect.

"I don't want this." She pushed the glass away. "What loss?"

"Samantha Goodman killed herself yesterday in her duplex in Catalina Village. You didn't know she had a secret place over there but she did. The inside was amazing!" I floated over her drink again. "I poured this just now."

She took the drink but only held it.

"Why ... are you saying that about Samantha?"

"I saw her, I was investigating for her father." Felicia put her drink on the table. "I'm sorry for your loss," I heard myself remind her with a smile, breathing and enjoying the feel of the leather arm rests. Perfect.

"But you said ... you don't do investigations ... " She was trying to go backward. But I could see she believed me. These words were just leftovers, from earlier in her life, before she learned what she just learned. Her mind was completely filled with believing me.

"Usually I *don't* do investigation," I heard myself agree. "I'm glad I did this time, it was fantastic, you should've seen it. She used an X-Acto knife like this on the veins on her arm, so she really bled, bled to death *everywhere*. It's going to take them a year to clean that place, I mean, there was a lot of blood and she was crazy."

I sat on the business side of the desk and leaned back. The chair was exquisite. It didn't squeak once. The sun streamed in the window medium grey and fell across the ash paper desk. I put up my feet and enjoyed the millionaire vodka.

"What should I do?" she asked after a while. I'd forgotten she was there.

"Do whatever people do. Vacation?" I got an idea. I stretched a leg and reached into my pants and pulled my keyring out, and sorted up Samantha's key. Not a Higher color on it, not here in the *Gray*. "I found this at her duplex. The secret house. Do you know what the key's for?"

"That's for her office," she said. She was surprised I had the key. That can be fun, surprising people.

"Ahh," I heard myself say, enjoying the sound as much as the feeling of putting things together in my mind, "an office. So that's where she painted."

"She doesn't paint."

"That picture of her in your bag was the Nagato Gallery. Did she want the Nagato to hang a show of hers?"

"Samantha's a *writer*."

"You mean was."

"What?"

"Remember she's dead? But I think she's a dead painter, not a dead writer. I have proof."

I love being right.

"No," Felicia insisted, "Samantha doesn't paint. She's going to win a Pulitzer for journalism someday."

"Posthumously you mean? So you're claiming there aren't paint supplies all over her office?"

"I've never been to her office. Samantha can be very private."

"Well that's an understatement!" It felt good, laughing. Then I tickled my arm. The hairs stood up in the sun and made goosebumps. "Do you know where her office is?"

"The Klimt Suites," she whispered. "You're very ... "

I knew I needed to get out of the *Gray*. Experience teaches. The shocking things I do and say while *Gray* are sometimes so shocking people misunderstand. Sometimes I end up accidentally seducing people that way. It's hilarious. And other times the cruelty just lands cruel. I thought maybe that was happening with Felicia. I pushed to get out of the *Gray*, but this time the moonbeam didn't want to let me go. I urged it. We debated. Finally, maybe bored or distracted, like a psychotic puppy, the *Gray* cleared the field.

Color surged back, rocking me in my chair. I racked everything pastel and held the arms of the Admiral's desk. Felicia wept quietly, the envelope open again, the picture of Samantha in her lap. The office was silent except for her. Her cardigan slipped below her hand at the side of her chair, her face hidden by hair.

I gritted my teeth, hurrying.

"I'm so sorry," I grimaced, "I'm so sorry. I ... I'm a little ... "

"Don't be sorry. It isn't your fault," she said and turned her heart-shaped face up and it still didn't understand. "Please tell me what I should do now."

"Honestly... I have to go. Stay in the office long as you want."

I backpedaled out. I did stop and use the restroom on the way. It's amazing how long you can hold things in if you put in a little effort, but even I have limits.

CHAPTER SEVEN

I knew the Klimt Suites, and what I knew made me even more certain Samantha had been a painter. I myself had once had a cozy studio at the Klimt, though I'd done all my real painting either in Brook Hills with with Tante Celine, or at home with Tito's vodka. But free studio space came with the whole Fenestram package. The Klimt was a Stipend House. The first three floors, anyway. The fourth floor was rented to businesses run by the sightless. The Klimt was one of only a few mixed population Stipend Houses in Skysill, for people who wanted to blend in and pretend to be normal. Or pretend not to be.

If Samantha had a Stipend studio, Roman had lied.

The building faces south for soaking in sunlight. Three floors out of four wear balconies and have wide windows to slide light onto paintings. The fourth floor is just rows of little office windows. All the studio window shades were drawn, I saw, as I drove around to the back. It was a confident building, sitting above the beach with its eyes closed. If it could have hummed while it went about its day it would have.

The lot had trellised jasmine to dapple sunlight over parking spaces. I pulled into a space, shaking *Gray* from my brain. The lot had a few cars, almost certainly belonging to people on the business floor. When Skysill Beach geared up for Gala Lumina, our winter solstice extravaganza, all these spaces would fill, and stay full until the very last minute, as every painter in Skysill Beach came to live at their studio and paint the Gala pieces they'd put off until too late. Procrastination is the water that ebbs and flows through every artist's veins, as predictable as seagulls and sand.

Samantha's key had no number or identifying marks, but it had to be one of the studios on the first three floors. I ambled for the rear entrance and spun the Highers up, just enough to notice, in case there was anything to notice, like more keys, or more dead bodies with Higher paint, because I'd had a weird couple of days.

There was Higher pigment everywhere of course. Over the years it had spilled and been tracked, doodled with, smeared around. But since all of it was invisible to the sightless who visited the fourth floor, and those humans who *could see* didn't give a shit, it tended to build up. I pushed the lobby elevator button. The Klimt tried to hold a higher standard than other Stipend Houses. The graffiti marked around was tame. Not *compulsion,* just everyday *choke* and *reason*.

The elevator reached the lobby and the doors opened and someone was inside, and there was no place for me to hide, and it was too late to run.

"Ash?"

"Yeah," I admitted, disappointed it was true.

"It's Harrison."

"I see you."

He held the door button like he'd decided to wait until I got inside, so he could let it close and ride around with me. Like he didn't have anything important that'd taken him to the lobby in the first place, which was almost sure to be true unless Harrison had changed a lot in the past ten years.

"Oh my god, Ash!" If it was going to be a battle of wills at the elevator door it would be no contest. He smiled. "Are you getting in?"

"No."

"You look great. Where have you been?"

"I have a house." We both waited to see if I'd give out any other details, but I didn't.

Harrison was languid with a knowing look he used to keep you from figuring out how little attention he was paying. He was thin, wore *farewell* eyeliner, had silk-smooth dark black skin and was just one example of what used to happen back when I still thought staying *Gray* was the answer to all my problems. Harrison and I had been intensely involved, on beaches and in bedrooms and alleys throughout the drug-fueled summer when I turned sixteen. He was my first *Gray* conquest. The *Gray's* pretty indiscriminate though, and at the end of the summer I discovered his sister who was *sighted* like him, though not as talented or beguiling, and had licked just as nice and brought different drugs with her.

They shared an attraction to cruelty, a family trait apparently. When I go *Gray* and lose all color—when I lose basically everything but curiosity and physical intensity—I gain something in its place. In some people's eyes, anyway. It's just a fact. For certain people, callous disregard is magnetic. Cult leaders know it. When you truly and relentlessly don't give a fuck, you get a certain glow.

"Are you coming back to Klimt to claim a space, Ash? Should we get together?"

He tilted a bit, took his hand off the button to hold himself on the side of the elevator. I'd left recreational drug use long ago, booze excepted, after Amelia convinced me it was killing her to watch, but I could see Harrison still set time aside for it. Once, he'd been one of the best painters in Skysill. That was the reason I'd preferred him, out of my many options. We'd matched. My work had been better than his, back when I still did it, but his landscapes had burned clear and deep, open. They'd appeared in my dreams. The difference between us had been I was dosing to stay sane, while Harrison had been perfecting the skills that would last him a lifetime.

Then the doors slid shut. I didn't wait for him to work back over to the button. I went for the stairs. With any luck he'd forget he ever saw me by the time he got the doors apart. I climbed up to the landing for Floor One, the first Stipend floor, and pushed the heavy fire door open.

Before me was a single hallway running the long length of the building with a window at the end. Loft doors marched away on the south facing wall, hiding studios full of sun. The lofts were all thin, long, sucking in light across the width of the building. The industrial white walls dripped Higher everywhere, door handles and ceiling and long tiled floor. I heel-toed along the doors, listening for human habitation, all the way down to the window that showed the parking lot, and my one lonely car. Twenty-four doors. Very likely no one here. How long could it take? I pulled out Samantha's key.

It could take more than a minute per door, that much I learned, but nothing else, until I was finished and stood back at the stairwell. I'd known I wouldn't find it on the first try. That's not the kind of luck I ever step into. So one of the two remaining floors held Samantha's "office." I surprised myself by feeling anxious. Why did I care Samantha had been a secret painter? What did any of it really matter to me? When I realized I was trying to talk myself out of any more key testing, I hurried back into the stairwell and up.

I pushed out into the second floor hall, which if anything was more chaotically distressed in Higher everything. I wondered had there been a paintball battle? So far I'd seen no one but Harrison, but I was starting to feel jumpy. Like someone was watching. I hurried down to the end of the hall, checked my car through the window again, then started the key to lock process, growing more nervous as I went, because one of these doors was actually going to open. But again I keyed my way back to the stairwell and came up empty.

The third floor was cleaner. Only the door handles glowed Higher, like they'd hired a separate cleaning service. Higher paint dissolves in standard thinning agents, and anyone can be hired to run an acetate rag down the wainscoting, even if they don't know what they're cleaning. But we mostly have to address our own messes, if they're bad enough, because we're the only ones who can *see* them. But cleaning is not a skill the average Fenestram artist is known for. You can adapt to just about any kind of mess, as long as you're lost in your work. That was why my house was clean the way it was.

I was flagging, surprised two flights of stairs and two hallways and forty-eight doors with a very light key had taken this kind of toll, like maybe I was out of training or sober. After a deep breath, I hurried to the far window, looked down at my car because OCD, and worked back the other way. Every door I tried I expected to open.

And then, at door twelve, right in the middle of the row, I heard a click. But the click came from door thirteen, a dozen feet to my right. Thirteen swung open. A figure stepped out, with his back to me, and started toward the elevator, and left thirteen to close behind him while he walked away, one sleeve rolled up. I held very still. Maybe the elevator would open and my problem would vanish into it without turning around. Maybe he'd keep going to the stairwell door.

Instead he forgot his wallet. He slapped his ass and turned back. I saw then that it was Julian, apprentice of Light and Shadow, and he saw that it was Asher, cat burglar. We took time to process our discoveries. Julian had tight black slacks and a belt and a dress shirt and black shoes shined like conquistador jewelry. All he lacked was fringe and a rose and he'd be fighting bulls.

"What are *you* doing here?" His voice was all feline snap.

"What are *you* doing here?" I asked right back and hated myself. Imitation is the highest form of flattery, and I thought he probably already got enough flattery.

He soaked up the admiration. It made his smile sharper.

"So. Asher Gale. *Asher Gale,*" he crooned, "I'd heard Asher Gale was sent to a care facility?"

"That's a rumor. I don't know how it started."

"You *seem* lucid. Thorazine?"

"Vodka and Tylenol." I pointed at his rolled-up sleeve, where his thin veins were black and blue. "You seem lucid too. Smack?"

He drew his sleeve down, smile lazy, layers of self-satisfaction from his shoes to his ears, and stalked toward me, wrist buttoning, a matador before the kill.

"So Asher Gale. I've heard you can pick my paintings from a lineup."

"Just call me Asher. I hate hearing you work so hard."

"Can you? Pick my painting out of a lineup?"

"I wouldn't pick your painting out of a toilet. Your real problem is you don't do paintings. You're a color copier. A little Xerox drone boy. Anything your master tells you, you paint. Good boy."

I was swinging pretty wild because it seemed like it was working. The satisfaction of slapping his pretty smile was a little intoxicating, but it would be even better to see him swallow it.

"That hack?" he hissed, but he did it smiling, so I wouldn't get my satisfaction. "He's not my master." Then he rearranged his voice for curling pleasure and batted his eyes at me. "Well," he said. "We shall just see."

He decided he'd observed everything of interest, and he'd got his sleeve fastened, so he went into his loft and came out pocketing a wallet. I hadn't thought of any place else to stand by the time he reappeared. He watched me while door thirteen swung closed.

"What are you even doing here, Gale?"

"Looking for a bathroom."

"No public restrooms. Maybe one of the residents will let you use theirs." He pulled his door closed, then walked to the elevators, where the doors did pop open as if by magic and he did step in without looking back. I held the key and waited. Then the elevator was gone. I had become very curious about door thirteen while Julian had been going in and out. Hadn't he seen Samantha's picture on my phone, at Roman's? Had there been a flare of discomfort? I slid to Julian's door. Positioned it, pushed in the key—where, for the sixty-first time, it failed to be the right key.

And then, after finishing the final eleven doors, I had to admit that Samantha did not have a Stipend studio at the Klimt. All the way up to the last door, I was hoping. After that I ran through explanations, like maybe Felicia had the wrong building. Maybe Samantha lied to her about the building. Samantha obviously hadn't been helplessly addicted to the truth, so maybe. But the key *had* fit the locks. It was from the right series. It just hadn't spun any of them open.

My energy was really bottoming as I went back into the stairwell. There were still the fourth floor stairs. The sightless floor. The rooms up there had terrible light, you could tell from the street. Who would put painting space up there? But the key. It was from the Klimt.

Up on the fourth floor stairwell someone had markered *land of the sightless and sad* in pop art *choke*. I pushed the door open.

The walls were calming vomit green. The carpet was a triangle pattern from the eighties. This hall was organized to maximize profit, not sunlight. It didn't dead end where it overlooked my car, but turned to the right. The long lofts had been cut in half, and the hall wrapped all the way around the floor for access. These were cubicle spaces, where property managers and medical supply offices had addresses. This floor was a song to human industry. I watched from the stairwell while the elevator disgorged two women in business skirts with bandanas in their hair. They walked into an office and laughed, and another door opened farther down the hall and an elderly man came out, heading around the far corner.

It would be a harder hallway to inconspicuously try a key in a succession of locks. I started a slow amble forward, since it seemed lurky to just hang at the stairwell, moving the way I thought a very slow, distracted property manager might walk, to try to fit in. I had no ideas left. These were the fumes of my plan. Had Samantha been a painter? I would never find out.

Down the hall, near the corner, I saw a flash of Higher paint.

On a doorknob.

Instantly I changed my walk to property manager who can barely believe his luck but doesn't want to attract attention walking too fast, and who has a key that's already disappointed him seventy-two times that day so he doesn't want to get his hopes up. But this time, after the key disappeared up to its fat little neck, and I gave it a twist, it turned. I stepped forward into a dark room, and pushed the door shut fast.

Right away I could tell something extra was going on, even in the dark—there was Higher color all over the walls. The very highest of the Higher Colors, *reason* and *bleed,* come in wavelengths of energy that ignore less dense accumulations of matter entirely, matter like the outer walls of office buildings. Those wavelengths get into the dark inside houses and glow if there's anything for it to hit and reflect off. And anyone there to *see* it.

Bleed and *reason* paint appeared in the dark, randomly applied on the four walls of what seemed like a small room, but it was hard to tell for sure. Depth can be difficult to judge in ultraviolet. The colors seemed to describe nothing figurative, and not to be arranged as a composition. But I understood. These patches of Higher color were just parts of a whole, the rest hidden by the darkness. It was like seeing only the light brown sections of the Mona Lisa. It'd make no sense. You'd want to turn on the light.

I did. But right away I wished I hadn't.

It wasn't a large office, so I'd got that right, but it looked bigger because there wasn't much in it. And what there was... wasn't a studio. There were two low filing cabinets, one with a spider plant, one with a snow globe, both with dozens of taped up notes overlapping like scales. A desk with drawers sat in the center, with a monitor, a cable to plug in a laptop, a desk chair.

All the Higher color I'd seen in the dark on the walls turned out to have been parts of a mural, now seen in full, stretching 360 degrees around the room. The mural depicted, in brutally graphic scenes, a sexual assault. An assault perpetrated, from many different perspectives, on Samantha Goodman.

Most of the color was *compulsion.* The mural was laid on in a Soviet constructionist style, with block-colored backgrounds and human figures treated like cut-outs. There were only two human figures, but they appeared over and over in different tableaus. One figure was Samantha. She wore a dress—in those vignettes where she had any clothing on at all—and pumps, and had her hair pulled back in a ponytail. Some of the vignettes were closeups, some from above, some featured body parts. But whenever it could be seen, Samantha's face stretched tight with horror.

The other figure was a man, who held a serrated knife to Samantha's throat, over and over, and forced himself against her, and on her, and held her down, and, as depicted, seemed to mainline malevolent violence in its purest form. You seldom saw anything painted exclusively in Higher color like this. There were plenty of closeups of the man. Deftly depicted, efficient and hard. In each closeup he had a jackal brow, snarling teeth, and one bruised, dark black eye.

It was staggering. Stomach turning. Why would anyone paint their own office this way?

And then the mural wasn't the main attraction in the room anymore. Because slowly spinning into view in the center of the space came a woman, a form in silvery delicate ultraviolet light that swirled over her head and down her translucent hair and arms and the rest of her. Samantha Goodman. I saw the filing cabinets right through her torso. This, I understood, was the Higher swirl I'd seen at the Catalina Village suicide. It hadn't been formed into this girl yet. This see-through girl.

I slid one step to the right. She did not blink. Did not follow me with her eyes. Did not gesture, or bend, in fact her body seemed frozen in a pose. But her whole figure turned a few frozen inches as I moved, so she continued to face me. And her face... lived. Her unmoving eyes gleamed with some essential impulse. She was urging something on me. Which I hate. I slid one step back to the left. She pivoted, following me.

My nerves tingled. My breath did the cornered animal pump pump pump as I watched a river of crystalline, ultraviolet color move inside her. And I *saw*, mixed in everywhere, I *saw* another color, a color I'd never seen before. A *higher* Higher color, higher than any I knew to exist, a color that gave coherence to the vaporous mad form of the girl of light that floated above the floor in front of my eyes. A controlling color, pinning her with a tendril from above, and a tendril from below.

Samantha wore a pants suit. She wore stylish—if disturbingly transparent—wedged heels. One of her arms hung at her side. The other she held in front of her, toward me, and in her hand she gripped a cup, or a goblet. It was full of perfectly formed round holes.

Very slowly, without switching off the lights, without turning, I backed to the door, reached around and opened it, and slipped out of the office. My heart and stomach were racing and churning, respectively, and I closed the door and I locked it with Samantha's key. To keep the see-through girl inside. The hallway was the same normal hallway I'd left a moment earlier. I started back down it, flat out running now, like a property manager who's seen a ghost and thinks he might be going crazy and needs a drink. Needs one in the worst way.

CHAPTER EIGHT

The Charles went forward into the future around me and my vodka. The first thing you do after becoming a person who just saw a ghost is doubt yourself. I had plenty of good starting places—my eyes, for one. Something wrong with my eyes. It was an easy case to make. I could also easily doubt my brain. Had it finally been pushed too far? By the spectrum jumping, all my regrets? There were plenty of parts of me to doubt. The human-animal, the humans I've known, have fixed ideas about reality, and when reality proves, as it does over and over, that it really isn't that fixed, the animal doubts its senses instead of its preconceptions about reality. We're a perverse species.

By this time I'd mostly stopped trembling. I kept coming back to one thing, something that wouldn't have amazed anyone else—I hadn't, not before, during, or after *seeing* whatever I'd just *seen*, felt a *storm* coming or felt the *Gray* rise up to pull me. It was puzzling. My unwelcome investigation client's sorrow had shocked me greyscale, so shouldn't pictures of violent sexual assault and then a glowing, female specter hit harder than this?

I did feel certain about one thing. However broken I was,

however much I might break in the future, I'd never decorate my own office with images of a violent crime against myself. You had to be even more fucked up than I was for that. No one had known Samantha could even *see*, let alone paint like a little Stalinist protégé. And apparently Samantha had yet another secret studio somewhere in Skysill, because the office I'd just seen hadn't held so much as a watercolor brush.

My vodka and I also speculated about the new Higher color I'd *seen*, which my mind was calling *dominion* because of what it'd felt like: dominion over the other colors. I remembered the way it ran in tiny cat paws over Samantha's arms and legs and back, patting, sculpting, and the way tendrils had stretched above her and below. The other Colors had all done *dominion's* bidding. It seemed to manage the interactions. Keep things together. Made motile the spirits of the dead.

Which brought me back to one spirit of the dead. The ghost with her cup full of holes.

I waved for Selena, my favorite barkeep. Also the only one.

"I have a question," I said to her. "As a bartender. Have you ever come across a cup with holes all through it? What kind of cup is that?"

She barely paused. "Bartenders call those *defective* cups."

I nodded. I heard it now. A cup with holes.

Plus Felicia had shown me a picture of Samantha at the Nagato, which put her in the same gallery as Amelia. The consensus was, Samantha hadn't painted, but I still thought my angle had a chance. So far it was me against the world on that. It's a place I'm used to finding myself.

Amelia had an opening at the Nagato tonight. If Samantha had wanted a show, or been pushing to apprentice there, Amelia would know about it. The problem with that was the opening. Selena gave me another vodka. At that point I started hitting the point of diminishing returns, and I headed out. I nodded to Damien, Waylon's handyman, as I passed him in his corner booth. He glowered, one eye drooping and white. He'd evidently done enough digging for the week and retreated to The Charles to share his own problems with some beer and soccer.

Gallery Nagato fronted the coast highway from a neighborhood arranged behind sentinel elms. It looked, in sunlight, like rising talons spun from green glass, purring and streamlined for social media coverage. At night it glowed like emerald tissue paper, straining to float to the stars. That's what it was doing when I drove up, straining. I began looking for someplace to put my car but anyone who was anyone was already inside drinking champagne at Amelia's opening and they'd overflowed parking for blocks. I had to prowl darkened streets until I found a spot, right on PCH.

I walked back. Soon I was hearing the party—sound bites from a movie, alcohol and cheer edited into atmosphere. I came up to the garden entrance where the cheer escaped through a gate. The gate noticed me and put its other business aside to welcome, *welcome* me to the path that leads to the Gallery Nagato! A raked meditation river of glass beads ran beside the path to keep it company. Buried lights glowed beneath the meditation beads, to act out impressionistic fish and ripples and sunken mysteries. Gallery Nagato was up and coming. It liked to look that way. Amelia was its star attraction. The town could barely contain her, and it didn't deserve her.

I heard a voice as I meditated fast down the river. I recognized the subtlety in it. Of course Veronica from Fenestram Color was one of the anyones who was anyone enough to be here celebrating themselves with Amelia's canapés and booze. She perched on a bench to the side of the path talking on her phone. I wondered if I'd be allowed to walk past without talking to her, but she got off her seat still talking on her phone, and fell in beside me. She didn't like being ignored. Some people don't. It makes them afraid they're doing a bad job taking up space.

"Mr. Gale," she told me, hanging up. "To what do we owe the pleasure?" She seemed a little tired and less subtle. Maybe she was hungry. In her creamy hair and clothes and shoes and skin she slid down the path holding a champagne flute in the air like it might explode and she wanted to see it happen. She drank it off, then pretended to remember.

"Oh! Of course, Amelia *Gale,*" she said. "Your sister. The fabulous Gales. You have the most fascinating family, don't you think? Attractive, talented, mysterious... " Veronica snapped a flute from a passing tray without even looking, by pure instinct. It was impressive. She'd already had a few. She offered the flute to me and when I shook my head she fired her old flute down her throat and promoted the new one, and I escaped through the copper studded front doors while she handled too many glasses to keep good track of me. I left her gazing through green glass. I attract a certain kind. I don't know why. I'm sure I deserve it.

It wasn't a promising start. I'd hit turbulence before leaving the runway, and now here I was, inside and airborne, and it was storm clouds everywhere I looked. From the outside the Nagato might be a feline fishbowl, but inside it was a spiraling cave, throbbing with ultraviolet color, lit and warm and promising treasure at every bend. Amelia's paintings held the strategic high points, most of them her series of portraits. They all had that quality of looking like someone you knew, without actually being anyone you knew, because the painter had painted them from the inside and grown to be them, if only transiently. They were delicate and broken and deeply, terribly real, her people. I loved these paintings. I loved everything she ever painted.

But I forced myself to move past, not look, since I had my mission. Higher color flared around me. The walls of the Nagato were a long scroll of *compulsion* in kanji, which I was glad I couldn't read: on the floor, baked into the glass, striped over all the people, Higher color flowed a river. This event was invite-only. The Fenestram crowd was here in force.

Music shivered the walls. A triptych of dancing girls wove into me and against me, nothing but rhythm in their eyes, faces laid with Higher paint that followed their cheekbones and ringed their eyes, *wander* in blue and pink and purple, like psychedelic Cherokee warriors. One pulled me, crooked her finger, but I'd just got to the party and etiquette dictated I debauch myself at the bar first before trying it anywhere else. I waded into the press. I saw Harrison and a crew from the Klimt, and other faces I recognized. Faces everywhere. It was a yearbook. Finally I came into the main gallery, where Amelia's work was crushed to the walls by the press of bodies. Normally you'd see patrons leaning on the paintings, but these were all artists tonight.

I have no idea how she saw me. That's just Amelia. Tonight her hair was black in cornrows and metallic circlets, bound in a ponytail. She'd gilded a bustle with strips of glitter and copper to make a chrome and fabric gown, and the whole room orbited her in steampunk anti-fashion gravity. Her face lit when she caught me, and her hands went to her mouth. I saw her call out but couldn't hear it, and she began to dodge my way.

"Ash, I can't believe you came!" She hugged me, held me out, eyes narrowed. "Is it *all right,* baby brother?"

It was *the code,* the code that meant, *are you in the Gray? are you storming? are you okay?* I nodded, though the music was too loud. I wanted someplace to talk. I had unsettling things to make into other people's problems. I scanned the room.

The front doors opened then and Julian tracked sullen splendor into the gallery. He had Higher paint on his hands, cleaned and thinned away to a film just barely glowing with *bleed,* maybe out of the range of most of the others in the room—apparently Roman had forced him to complete a dramatic cabin in the woods before giving him permission to go outside and play. He had on the same matador black I'd seen him in earlier that day. He wasted no time cutting a mulish path toward a circle of Skysill veterans—the long established artists, the ones having conversations about how fabulous openings had been in their day, and within seconds he was poised to pounce on Lady Damely. What did Julian want with Skysill's elder hands? That wasn't his sandbox. Patronage? Was he thinking of leaving

Roman? I imagined how much I'd like to see Lady Damely lay him out. She could do it with a glance.

He reached her but before he spoke she'd raised a palm before his face. The palm wore a white glove with lace. Lady Damely had seen me. As soon as our eyes met she untied from her mooring beside her contemporaries and to part the crowd toward me and Amelia, a venerable warship having an outing to the other side of the harbor. Lady Damely carried a cane with a duck bill handle, and was famous for the way she brandished it. People got out of the way.

"Asher Gale," she snapped when she arrived, as if that settled the matter.

"Hello, Lady Damely," I replied. It didn't pay to risk much with her, conversationally. For one thing you had to worry about the cane.

"I have been deeply disappointed in you, Asher. Deeply. For many years. I knew your *father,* you know."

"I didn't know."

"Of course you did. Don't be an idiot. I was his patron."

"I was pretty young," I offered. "I'm sorry you're disappointed. If it makes you feel better, I'm a disappointment to a lot of people."

She squinted at me through bifocals and tight lips and made the sound horses do, thinking about hay. Somehow she managed to keep her disappointment in me confined to a fifteen-meter area. It was finely calibrated.

"I let your sister slip through my fingers, Asher. I will *not* see the same thing happen to you." She cracked her cane on the floor for emphasis. She turned to Amelia. "Not that I think you've made an error, dear. You will be the one to lead your generation out of their wasteland of irony. We are all convinced of it. You are a marvel." She tucked a wisp of lace down on one of her gloves and turned back to me. "If you ever leave your existing patron I expect you will seek me out, yes?"

"If I had an existing patron I might consider it. I'm not patron material."

"Oh? Asher," she instructed, after more disappointed examination, "the world is not a forgiving place. But redemption is possible. Under the proper circumstances. I'm sure you understand what I am saying? Your story is compelling. All your trials, oh dear. Your parents. Your early brilliance and the messiness. And so a return to the pinnacle would be très bien, just *that much sweeter.* I can picture in my mind the title of our triumphant return show. Marketing is one of my gifts. I will leave you with it." She drew her gloves into fists and held them on her diaphragm, preparing a modest aria.

"*From Lunacy to Legacy, The Asher Gale Story.*"

Her hands settled, she awaited applause, but I wasn't moved that way, and it tripled her disappointment. She lifted her duck bill and gave it a thoughtful brandish, waited for me to rethink applause, and then, true to her word, she left me with it, sailing back to her peers. Julian watched everything. Julian had a gifted mouth that turned regular smiling into assassinations. I tried a smile back, but it was nothing in comparison.

Amelia laughed and talked from the corner of her mouth, watching Damely go.

"These people. They'd cut their thumbs off if Damely ever offered *them*..." My face finally got her. "Ok, Ash, out with it. Are you *sure* you're not... you know?"

"No, I'm not, *you know*. This was just a very strange day. I have a lot... there's a girl, Samantha Goodman, who committed suicide. I wonder if you know..."

"Oh my god. *Samantha*? I know her!" Amelia stared. "How horrible. What happened?"

"That's why I'm here," I said. She waited. "It's like this," I tried. She could tell I was circling in. She didn't try to hurry me. And her with all these sycophants that needed petting. Good old Amelia. "I need to ask you a weird question, Amy."

"I'm all ears."

"It's a little funny."

She pointed to her ears.

"Well, first—have you ever heard of any cup, or goblet, with holes in it everywhere?"

"No. Did you go *Gray* and break someone's goblet?"

It was a reasonable guess. I do like breaking things when *Gray*.

"No," I insisted, "I told you, I hardly go... never mind the goblet. So look. You know how we all," I gestured to our crowd, our city, our world, "can *see?*"

"Ashy." She didn't like to talk about it. Of course.

"What if we're not *seeing* everything?" I asked, going in tentative, testing her boundaries.

"Just how weird a day did you have?"

"Listen. Have you...ever *seen* any, ah, what's the word...*specters*?"

"That's the word?"

"Right. You know." I raised my arms and made a ghost face. She thought about it.

"Like in The Shining?"

"No, I mean... real... " I'd have to say it. The word felt like a towel in my mouth, too thick for saying, too crazy in front of the only person whose opinion mattered to me. But I couldn't see any way around it. "Oh fine. I'll call it a ghost. Something like a ghost. Have you ever *seen* something like a ghost?"

She shook her head slowly. She was starting to look worried. There was nothing I could do to help her.

"I'm pretty sure I saw one," I told her, knowing it was not what she wanted to hear. Not at all. "I was ... I *saw* some glowing thing in Higher color, floating, and there was some new kind of color—did you know there's a color higher than *bleed*?—and the ghost was shaped like Samantha. Maybe it wasn't a ghost. I can't be sure. Who could be? Maybe it was..." I gave it a few honest seconds but got nothing.

Amelia stepped close and whispered, fierce, "Ash, *truth*—are you in the *Gray*? Right now? Or *chromatic*?"

"No, nothing—"

Very abruptly she had my hand and we were moving—someday

she'd inherit Lady Damely's position as Skysill's unstoppable force, or maybe its immovable object. She pulled me toward a service door, sloughing well-wishers on the prow of her gown, and dragged us down a short hall and finally outside.

She pulled me to an undiscovered corner of the Nagato meditation themescape where the party could be seen through the tinted glass, and we were alone, and she spun and faced me.

"Cross your eyes Asher."

"Amelia - "

"Do it. Right now. Kneel and cross your eyes. You cross your eyes this minute, Asher Gale!"

"This isn't a *chroma storm*!"

We faced each other. We were panting. She had a sheen on her face. This was about as far as I'd ever pushed her, and ironically this time I hadn't even wanted to. My sister was born with the patience and mental energy that sometimes turns the tides of world wars, but helping people who refuse to help themselves has got to take a toll, eventually.

"Amy, I swear to you, this is something else."

"You've been drinking."

"I had a couple drinks, not the same thing. Please. Can I just... ask you a few things?"

That's what she had on the agenda, it appeared. Listening to me ask questions. She towed us to a bench, sat us, and started. Listening. It was a little intimidating. The surf could be heard back here, over the muted party swell. The waft of cold salt and seaweed mixed with perfume and incense made me dizzy. It wasn't warm out. I felt like I might have a fever.

"Mom and Dad," I said. Her eyes got wide, but she stuck to listening. I started again, not so far back in history. "This thing I saw was real. But I know it wasn't normal. Which, I know, that's a moving target. You remember them better than me. So did they, Mom or Dad, ever mention anything like this? Ghosts?"

It took her a moment.

"I never heard you talk about Mom and Dad before."

"It's a question. I'm not talking."

"It's okay to miss them. I do."

"Amy... "

I saw it wasn't going to be possible to exhume the family corpse without tearing a lot of bitter roots up with it, and I wasn't so far gone in selfishness that I wanted Amelia darkened with my poison, tonight of all nights. I'd end up darkening her, too, if I said any more. She was an open book, open for my thoughts, but my thoughts were just black water.

I'd have to get at the problem a different way.

"You knew Samantha?" I asked. Amelia nodded. "Was she a painter? Did you know she could *see?*"

I was pushing the limits of what Amy would talk about. I knew that. But she was game. She did it for me.

"Samantha couldn't *see,* no way. She was visible spectrum. And I definitely never saw her painting... oh, my god, Ash, is she what this is all about? Were you *together*? I'm so sorry, I—"

"No, I didn't know her."

"Well, she had a lot of boyfriends, that's why I ask."

"Girlfriends, you mean."

"Those too. I met her a few times because she was going out with Tobias. She'd meet him here sometimes. He took her to a party or two. They broke up a few weeks ago. I heard it was bad."

"Who's Tobias?" I was getting a feeling.

"A painter. He's signed to Gallery Nagato. He was here before me."

My body tensed. Another one of my investigator brainstorms bubbled up. They seemed a little untrustworthy, so I kept my enthusiasm banked. I laid it out casual. "Does Tobias, by any chance, have *a black eye*? About this big?"

She thought about it. "Like, permanently?" She snickered.

"No Amy. Recently."

"No. Why? Is he moonlighting as a kickboxer?"

"No, damn it, I don't know Tobias, just, the man with the black eye was in the room with the specter girl! The *ghost,* ok I'm trying to make something fit somewhere, oh my god. Here we go." She'd reached her point. Pealing laughter. The gates opened. When the world got most strained and scattered, Amelia cracked up. Right before she fixed everything.

"I don't *want* to be the guy who saw a ghost, Ames. Plus let's not call it that."

"I'm not calling it that!"

"I saw Samantha's dead body, and later I saw her transparent, and floating, and made of Higher light. Together with even *Higher* light. Did Mom or Dad ever talk about *anything* like this? Before they *left*?"

I had my reasons to suspect there were secrets I'd never been told. It was a well-framed question. And I was proud, I'd asked it without cursing their names or lighting anything on fire. Maybe there was a citizenship badge I could get if I kept this up. It brought Amelia back from her joy ride. When she answered, her voice was soft, like it was just a normal question I'd asked about normal people.

"Never, Ash. Nothing I can remember."

"How about Tante Celine?"

"Celine? No. Nobody ever talked about seeing... specters. But you should go ask her yourself. She'd love to see you."

So that was that. Amy'd never lie to me. I probably was crazy, it'd been the prevailing opinion for years. We sat in the dark, and Amelia drew a gloved arm over my shoulder and leaned in, put the side of her head on my arm and hummed soft nonsense while she looked up at the trees. Through the windows you could see her party gather steam, oblivious to its absent guest of honor.

"You're missing your extravaganza," I said.

"Good. Let them eat each other. I'm glad you came."

"You're the only decent one, Ames. All the rest of them... *compulsion?*"

"Ash."

"Nothing's sacred." I don't mind depressing most people. It's actually one of my few satisfactions in life. But I hate doing it to Amelia. I tacked, to lighten back up. "You should get Lady Damely to buy you a gallery."

"You think?" Her question was lazy, just floating on top of the other things she was thinking. She spilled a few of those then, mild, curious thoughts. "I just had no idea Samantha loved him that much. Tobias I mean. Kill herself over a breakup? I'm assuming that's why she did it."

"Who knows? She didn't leave a note."

"Tobias is talented, sexy, but honestly his mind's on other things. I always wondered if he was using her. I'm surprised he's not here right now, this is his element—dowagers. Look, he's getting scooped!" She laughed and pointed inside, where Julian had managed to engage Lady Damely in conversation at last. It was a sweet trick he was managing, being a fawning supplicant and a knowing peer at the same time. Subservient and lascivious. She wasn't fighting him off with her cane. "Damely gave Tobias her patronage a few weeks ago, and now Tobias isn't here, and Julian's trying to supplant him."

I suddenly had a swell of sympathy for Tobias.

"Speaking of patronage," I told her, "you really should go back in."

"I know, I know. After all, these paintings won't sell themselves. *Oh wait,"* she said, and we snarked, and for a minute the night felt peaceful and almost normal, and I had the sense that maybe it was all going to be okay. Amelia was making it work. She was five feet four inches of talent and bulldozer, and everyone loved her. And even though she'd never had a *storm* or gone *Gray*, she carried the rest of our loss just the way I did, but better. It made me hopeful ordinariness might lurk, somewhere in my future.

Following her back inside down the access hall toward the main gallery, I passed several doorways on the left, opening into darkened, secondary galleries, and I couldn't help looking in. I flipped the wall switch in the first, and saw a derivative collection of Edward Hopper style windows, here a bay window, there a view outside a plump living room, over there a pensive bedroom window being pensive about a pensive cityscape in the distance. Places the artist had never been, it seemed to me, or hadn't been paying enough attention to.

I hurried after Amy, but had compulsive curiosity to see how my fellow Fenestrams were wasting their talent, or their lack of it, so I looked in the next gallery. This space contained expressionist seascapes, expressing mostly boredom as far as I could tell, although there was sensitivity in the composition and some value in the green-silver waves reflecting the cherry sun. Over and over, reflecting it. Because reflections were selling well this week, I guessed.

My appetite for my fellow artists went comatose after that. I passed the third door, just barely glancing as I went by. I stopped. Amy, now far ahead, finally turned to see what I was doing. We stared for a motionless second, then my feet carried me back to the third gallery door, which was good work from my feet because my brain was working a completely different problem. I reached in, flipped the light, and stared.

The show was titled *SUBSCRIPTIONS*. I stumbled out into the middle of the room and turned a circle. The paintings were in bold, Soviet constructivist style. It was the same hand that had painted the assault mural in Samantha's office, though I'd only had a few seconds to appreciate that expanse of grotesquery. These were red and black, angular compositions, each one denoting a subscription in the artist's life. Netflix, Hulu, Spotify, magazines, more esoterically the nave of a church, the American flag, a local beach house, and dozens more. Stalinist art at its most Nagato. But not a single one of them could be sold to the public, because the unwritten rule was no canvas with Higher color ever left Skysill.

These canvasses were thick with Higher color, the lower five of the eight. Every artist in Skysill Beach who *sees* Higher, except for me, has a Higher canvas they are working on. They can spend ten years on a single canvas, since finishing isn't the point. Painting Higher is like masturbation, it's the only way to satisfy a very specific itch. But nobody *showed* those paintings. Except, again, for me, but of course I'd been fucking insane.

So this was a room with something to prove to a very select audience.

Amelia came in behind me.

"He does have some talent, right?" she said. "A little brutal with the *wander*. I respect the fact he did it since it's never leaving this room. I am surprised Damely picked him up though. I mean, communist subscriptions? Irony much? You'd think it would give her acidosis."

"What do—whose work is this? Who painted these?"

"Samantha's ex. Tobias."

The paintings jabbed me in the eyes some more. I tried blinking but that didn't help. Then I said, "I'd like to talk to him."

"He's around. Though come to think of it, I haven't seen him for a while."

We stood, side by side, taking in the collection but probably having very different thoughts about it. Tobias had painted this derivative pop train wreck. He'd put his name at the bottom right of every canvas, like they were something to be proud of. And I wanted to jump to the conclusion that he'd painted the mural in Samantha's office too, because that was obvious and easy, like all my favorite conclusions. But I couldn't jump. Something about the whole spectacle just refused to be that easy.

I stared and stared, and the more of it I *saw,* the less of it I liked.

CHAPTER NINE

The painters who can *see* never leave Skysill. But the downtown doesn't have a designated hippy section, so in the 60s Tante Celine had settled in Brook Hills, which was technically within city limits but up in the coastal pines, to tie-dye Higher t-shirts and make fabric art and compose collages. After our parents abandoned us that's where she took Amelia and me to grow up. In yurts, over solar stoves, with down sleeping bags and heirloom foods. I miss it in spirit, every day. In practice it's too full of triggers to be good for me. And these days I like a good shower. But home will always smell like thin smoke and pine shade beside Celine's main dome, among the smaller huts where her people slept and worked and tripped.

The dust cupped the car when I rolled it to a stop. Her road wanted grading. I slid a preemptive cap over my color, laying the ground rules. Chill out. Don't *see*. Don't see. Just be.

The old rhyme came up like it always does. The sing-song drifted through my mind:

Mommy's got three,
Daddy's got four,
But little baby Asher,
Has got one more.

The single clear memory I have of my mother, here in the compound before they left, is her in bed beside me, sing-songing this rhyme, softly and endlessly, until I finally slept, kissing me to end each cycle. I used to have the hardest time sleeping. The colors kept me up twenty-four hours, forty-eight hours. After she abandoned us, and we came to Celine's permanently, there were plenty of other souls to stay awake and groove with me. I remembered a lot of that, after Celine took us. But of my mother I have only the rhyme. Once I'd told Amelia the words, but she'd never heard them. I'd held it for years, like maybe it explained something about me. Little baby Asher —*he's got one more*. That's why I'm the way I am.

I trod pine needles on the circular deck and pushed Celine's door open into the mudroom, spider woven with macramé in Higher yarn, boots in rows on one wall, many of them mine and Amelia's, even a few that would fit me as an adult. It was dark in there. Celine's solar needed upgrading. Amelia and I would have to lay the law down in the next year or so.

Past the boots and jackets and hats on hooks were the recycled bottles, empty now but waiting to be repurposed. I picked up a liter soda bottle and smiled. For washing and watering and art projects, and *nothing else*. I remembered. When I emerged into the living room, the thin plastic container began to crinkle in my hand. By this time you'd think I'd know what that signified. But I'm endlessly surprised.

Canvases were stacked everywhere around the big curving wall of the main room. The entire Gale family collection. I stumbled. The top popped off the liter bottle, and my hand clenched down. Both hands. Colors surged. It was the paintings, the whole family, together again, that was doing it. The visible spectrum macroscoped wide, fish-eyed fifty billion shades out of the visible spectrum. And one Higher color, too: *dominion.*

It crept and flowed among the paintings. It poked. It sifted. It wanted something.

I fell to my knees. I did it hard. No more Highers. Please. Cross eyes, I said to my eyes. They tried. I bashed them together across the bridge of my nose. My world hung in that balance. I'd come to the *storm* so quickly. What was happening?

And *dominion.* What was that doing here? It didn't belong. There were no other Highers. It moved like water, like gas. With an agenda. But I fought it back. My eye-crossing can be relentless and terrible when I put my mind to it, which I seldom do. I'm capable of committing everything to shovel myself backward out of these fugue states, on those occasions I'm sober enough for that. And so slowly, painfully, my eyes went visible spectrum. They clawed back across the threshold.

Dominion seemed to ... make a decision? ... and it skittered off the field.

I fell forward, and the liter bottle rolled behind one of Amelia's astonishing seascapes, and I saw that it glowed. It glowed *dominion.* The Highers were banished to my mind closet, or wherever I kept them, yet *dominion* remained visible. Infused in a plastic bottle? What was going on?

"Ohhhh," I heard Celine, from behind, her low voice a wood rasp dipped in honey. "Duuude," she moaned, and I felt her old bones bend beside me. "Oh Ashy, I didn't know you were coming today. Oh, dude." She stayed there, and because I knew it had to be hard on her knees I stood up sooner than I wanted. I swayed like a drunk—I know how it looks. But Celine knew too and she just waited.

"What's all *this*?" I finally asked. I didn't know where not to look. The room had canvases in four groups. My father's art. My mother's. Amelia's. And the last pile. The Asher Gale pile: a look within the mind of an enraged cetacean? A collection wrought by psychotic cultists? It was almost all Higher, and the colors tore me down the middle. The canvases screamed three ways at one time. Hues never settled, not anywhere. All the explosions were bigger than all the preceding explosions. It was shocking. Disturbing. Painfully brilliant, in a way you just don't ever want to be.

She had it stacked chronologically. The canvases were eight deep, ten, piled and racked. I wandered forward because gravity made me. It was all here, everything but the unfinished one in my living room. The funny thing was how I remembered every single painting, from my first canvas at three — I remembered how big the brushes had felt in my hand and the *chroma storm* I'd painted through — to my last, at sixteen. I remembered that long stretch where I'd thought painting was the way to work through my problems until the *Gray* had taken me, and I'd emerged and figured out that painting *was* the problem. You can't keep the Highers down if you're going to keep bringing the Highers up to paint. So smother them. Just good, American-made logic.

"What's all this?" I said, for the second time. Celine coughed.

"Well, I've got to get the place cleaned," she said.

"Why?"

"Why didn't you call?"

"I did. I left a message."

"I didn't get it. Do you want goat's milk? I have some spaghetti, let me fix it."

Hunger voted for that. I followed her to the kitchen and sat at the table while she put things together with familiar motions. She brought a plate and a glass and set them in front of me then put herself in the chair across the table. She seemed tired. Older hair. She'd always had a tendency to pajama through the day, but I wondered how many days she'd gone in these.

She coughed. "So *how are you?*" The code. "I didn't mean to set off a *storm*."

"You didn't. I've got it under control."

"Dude. Really. I wish you *could* control it." She wiped her palm on the table, trying to clean up a mess that was far past cleaning. "Maybe we could have tried harder to get you help. You should be painting, Ash! When you stopped... it broke my heart. Do you ever think you'll be able to control it? "

"Tante. Celine. It isn't a problem anymore." I was wishing this could have been a phone call, it would have been so much easier. Celine wanted to go around fixing things, but that was not her skill. Incredibly gifted ceramicist, filled with the best intentions, but she couldn't glue a broken pot together if her life depended on it. "I just haven't seen those paintings in a while and it was a surprise. Okay? Everything's fine. I wanted to ask you... a few things."

I had more than a few questions. I thought I'd do the small subjects first. She waited for me to pick one.

"So you're a potter," I told her, chewing spaghetti casually, like I can. "And, have you ever seen any kind of pot, or cup, maybe something old-fashioned, like a goblet with holes through all the sides?"

"Like something to hold plants? To hold another pot? Sounds purely decorative. Why?"

I shrugged. She didn't look satisfied. So much for the small things.

"I saw Amelia's opening," I told her, easing up into a larger weight class. "And something came up, we were talking about, you know, my mom and dad ... and stuff."

Celine wiped her mouth. She wasn't eating. She got up and drew herself a glass of water and brought it back, and then sat in a different chair. I continued. Neither of us seemed to know how this conversation was supposed to go.

"Amelia and I were trying to remember, how old was I, when they left, exactly?" I found that I'd asked it out loud. A perfectly ordinary question. I am astonishing to myself.

"Well," Celine took a breath and lifted her head thoughtfully.

"You were six, Amelia was twelve. I'm pretty sure that's right." She watched me, wondering what we were doing.

"And so, they just left," I confirmed, chewing but fooling neither of us with any casual.

"I came home that night and they were gone."

"And they just... didn't ever come back," I told her. The basics.

"No one ever heard from them," she said, very careful. This was unknown territory.

"And you never knew why? Why they left?"

She looked at me like a bomb to diffuse, a very confusing, sad, and valuable bomb. She was going to try not to touch the wrong wire.

Her lids grew moist.

"No one knew what happened. I never understood. They were ... free spirits. I mean, you don't remember, but I did tell you about that night. I got home from the beach, found their note. They asked me, take care of you. Didn't even say how long they'd be gone... but your mom and dad... they did want me to take care of you. We looked for them. For years I looked. I gave reports of them missing. I've tried to talk to you. When you were little, you'd just *storm,* and then later, you'd go *Gray.*"

"Do you know this rhyme?" I asked, then sang-whispered, because apparently I was going all in at this point:

"Mommy's got three,
Daddy's got four,
But little baby Asher
Has got one more."

She didn't react. Nothing. I asked anyway, "Do you recognize that? My mom sang it to me."

"No, I don't ever remember hearing her sing. Dance, yes. Sing, no."

"But they were your friends. Right? You have to know something." This wasn't what I wanted to say. I had questions about ghosts. Somehow that had turned into this semi-accusation.

"Friends? Oh. My god. Your dad and I, we grew ... up together. You never let me tell you any of this, it just sets you off. Is it okay? Well, when we met we were fifteen or sixteen, only kids. Right away we were thick as thieves and ... then later when he met your mom, the three of us ... were inseparable. He was a king you know, down the hill? Skysill would've given him the keys to the city, but your mom and him lived up here. Your mom hated it in town. Oh, Ashy, if you could have seen us, so much *life*." She wiped her mouth again on a napkin, and shook her head. "The years'll kick you in the ass, dude. Wear thick pants."

"Tante, straight up—is there any reason that I might be seeing ghosts? Did my parents see ghosts? Do ghosts have anything to do with them leaving?"

It all tumbled out in a word blob. The word *ghosts* does get easier to say the more you do it, I realized, which didn't seem like a good thing. Celine was trying to figure out if I was kidding, or crazy. So I said it again, slow and explicit, like serious people talk.

"Did my mother," I asked, "or my father, see ghosts?"

And Celine laughed, like she'd decided I wasn't crazy, just charmingly misinformed. Even though *all* crazy people are misinformed, that's their main problem.

"No," she laughed, though it was a soft laugh. "No, your mom was too grounded. All she did was dance around and paint. The birds came when she called. She was pretty special but she was all in the here and now. No time for ghosts. Your dad worshipped her. She was his muse. He didn't have time for ghosts—all he ever saw was her."

She coughed again. I noticed something thick to the sound.

"Hey. Are you ok?"

"I'm fine. Tired I guess. I could use a nap."

She wanted me to go. It was unusual but convenient. I let her walk me to the door.

"Ash, you and Amelia? You'll always be my kids. You are my kids. You know that."

I nodded, but I was distracted. We passed my paintings again. My final work at the top; brutal, wild, color on top of color in between color, and in between that, finer and finer shades of color—out of balance, inflammatory, anguished. People had loved it and almost seemed to fear it, but I have no clear memories of them viewing it. I'd been on track for a gallery show, the youngest ever, maybe patronage the next year. There'd been talk I'd have a gallery of my own by the time I was twenty-five. And then. Amelia went to the Nagato Gallery, young for that but I *guaranteed* I could handle things on my own. And that year the *Gray* found me. And more than eight years disappeared without Higher *light*, until I finally fought my way back a couple years ago. Now I'm perfect.

I saw the liter bottle. It wasn't *dominion* infused anymore. I grabbed it and shoved it into Celine's recycling, then got back into my car. All the way back down the hill my final picture hung in my mind. What had that sixteen-year-old boy been *thinking*? How could you ever be that raw, go that far, and still leave a sliver of mind to return to? I'd made promises to myself since then, and to other people, to preserve the small sliver I still possessed. The sorrow of those promises was light as trains falling. I drove fast. I drove to get out from under them.

When I got off the hill the car was covered in dust. The evening's dew would turn it to mud so by morning the windows would be opaque. I stopped at the Chevron with a car wash, started the gas, and went to pay for a basic scrub, but in the end I just didn't have the energy. I went back to the car, replaced the nozzle and slid in behind the wheel—to find that all my windows were as clean as telescope glass. It was handiwork I recognized.

When I rolled up to the highway I saw the familiar figure hunched under the Chevron sign: Peter, squatting in succulents alongside his rusted ten-speed, holding a squeegee and a conversation. He looked up when I slowed, but went on talking. I reached him some bills, but he waved me off. And so I went.

Somewhere on the drive back from Celine's, I'd decided to risk another look at the mural in Samantha's office. now my windows were so clean, I decided it might as well be tonight. Had I been inspired by that last painting, by that boy who looked at everything, though it made him crazy? He'd have looked at ghosts, I suspected. So I would.

CHAPTER
TEN

I found not a single car in the halogen-lit Klimt lot when I got there a few hours past midnight. I'd stopped at The Charles before coming over, to clarify my plan, which hadn't really needed that much clarification. Samantha was the one with answers. And even though she was a ghost, I thought I'd ask them. Samantha, who'd had at least one girlfriend, at least one boyfriend, at least one semi-secret house, a minimum of one semi-secret office — who knew what else she'd had? Maybe answers to my questions? *Why am I seeing a ghost? Why a man with a black eye? What's with your goblet?* And, most importantly, *Do you really exist?*

At 2 AM I found the lobby elevator empty, but I'd decided to take the stairs because it would be safer. My safety began weighing on me as soon as I stepped out of the car. The building was dark. The stairwell was silent when I stepped in. I discovered that silent, dim stairwells at two in the morning in buildings that maybe housed apparitions produce a powerful *hairs up on your neck* sensation. That sensation entertained me as I went slowly up. When I thought I heard a door slam overhead I froze but went on when there was silence. Before I even reached the Floor One landing I was sweating, and it wasn't from exertion.

I leaned on the fire door. Through the little window I saw the unlit hallway, and the Higher paint on the walls, and near the end I saw a loft door propped open. A wedge of light fell into the hall. There hadn't been any cars in the lot—so this was someone who'd walked to the Klimt. They'd left their door open behind them—so this was also someone a little lazy about their two-in-the-morning personal security. Or someone who'd already left their studio to go home but whose door hadn't closed behind them. But I'd seen the Klimt doors close on their own.

With cat careful movements I inched the stairwell door open, just because I was in the mindset to leave no stone unturned. I stepped into the dark hall, cat quiet, and that's exactly the moment the motion controlled lights snapped on. Lesson: *I am not a cat.* Also, I am not an investigator, and I should stop acting like one, and I agreed with all these things, and sighed, and moved down the hall toward the cracked open door. It was jammed at the bottom by what was, I saw when I was near enough, the tip of a trifold easel.

Maybe I'd leave it alone... or maybe... an easel had fallen and caught in the door but no one had noticed? Because they were too drunk? That made sense. Caught in an embrace? Easy to see. Something nefarious? Like murder? Probably murder. And that's how it goes. You start out worried about ghosts, and from there you can get just about anywhere in the dread and mystery game, simple as shivering or snapping your fingers. Or knocking.

I tried knocking because it felt the most conventional. After a moment I tried again. Once more, and made the hallway echo and the door swing an inch inward, then stick. I was feeling more and more like something wasn't right. I pushed the easel with my toe. It wouldn't budge. I pushed the door handle, and that's when the condition of the door got more complicated because in addition to being *propped open,* it also suffered from being *kicked in.*

I gave it my shoulder, something delicate snapped behind it, and I was swinging inside.

The cleaning service wouldn't be happy with this tenant, I decided, this tenant who was a chimpanzee with lots of time on its hands and no respect for personal property. Easels and cans, paint and paper, Higher Colors and all the visible were spilled, smeared, pigment and chemicals scattered everywhere, a model skeleton fallen, chairs, books strewn and cast to the polished floor, drawers from the material chests, desks. The chimpanzee had really had a fit in here.

The one thing I didn't see were canvases, finished or in progress. Not even an easel. But this was a painter's loft. Had the paintings been stolen? Maybe the chimpanzee had broken in. Looking to steal paintings, though why tear the rest of the place apart? Maybe that's what the search had been about, the missing paintings. I enjoyed all the theories I was able to create so quickly. It made me feel better about pretending to be an investigator. I also theorized that the chimpanzee was looking in all the wrong places for paintings, because tiny tubes of paint were open and squeezed on the floor. Maybe the painter painted miniatures, and stored them in tubes. So many theories.

I bent, where a receipt from Fenestram Color caught my eye, to read the purchaser: Tobias Singlebee. I pawed through and found his name enough times it would be an impressive coincidence if it wasn't his studio. Which meant someone had tossed Samantha's ex-boyfriend's studio, looking for something, or he'd done it himself, or there had also been a chimpanzee. I wondered, suddenly, crouched there with my back exposed to the door, if whoever had done it was still around.

And my real problem still floated three floors above me or I was crazy.

I backed from of the room, listening even harder. The hallway was empty. I left the door propped, the way I'd found it, for future crime professionals. I was ready to have this ghost meeting over with, and go someplace other than this too quiet building. I got back on the stairs and went up hard. In a minute I stood just below the Floor Three landing, and that's where I stopped, because once again, from the floor above, Samantha's floor, I heard a fire door slam. Then more than a single set of footsteps coming down fast.

The Third Floor fire door was right behind me, but I remembered the motion lights. To wait on the landing felt suspicious. Should I go up? Down? Fleeing quietly seemed unlikely. The steps echoed like a barrel. So I chose going up. I tried for a confident expression. It was probably a little too much. I felt out of my depth.

After some seconds the feet above me got quiet too, like they'd had an idea. Then around a landing I saw a pair of ankles hurrying in patent shoes and cuffs of silk slacks, and two duplicate versions of one grave South American man, both slimmer than rhinos, came into view.

They read, to me, as suspicious and unhappy and violent. One of them had a scar on one cheek, and on the other cheek, a tattoo of a scar just like it. On their suits they wore a catastrophe of paint, Higher and visible spectrum, wiped and spilled. The suits had toured Tobias's room recently, I guessed, in my insightful way. I gave a confident chin nod to them and passed going up. I felt them watch me.

On the landing above I stopped. Whispering rose, not English—Portuguese, I thought, from the various recognizable curse words—and then footsteps descended. I hurried out of the stairwell.

Before me was the hallway. Last office on the right. I kept the color down, though I wondered if that even mattered with ghosts, or whatever Samantha was if it wasn't a ghost. I padded down, having forgotten I was not a cat, to the door. I was not surprised to find it kicked open. Not when I really thought about it.

The mess inside was less dramatic than in Tobias's room because Samantha left less material to work with. The few objects taking up space had been scattered by someone, though. Like a behavior pattern.

And the walls had been scrubbed. No mural, no black-eyed man, no *compulsion* close-ups. All four of the walls glowed a uniform Higher smear of all eight Colors. It had happened at least a day earlier, too. This much acetone would linger in the air. So unless there had been at least two visits by those Portuguese speakers, who I had decided were Brazilian twins because it was faster, the walls must have been scrubbed down by some earlier party. It was a very popular office to visit, I was beginning to see.

And standing in the middle of the room, not glowing, not covered in mysterious *dominion,* not hovering was not Samantha's ghost. There was nothing in the middle of the room. I frowned, probably, and sifted my mixed feelings. I'd been expecting a ghost, I realized. Expecting a ghost. It was confusing.

There was no ghost of course.

Maybe there never had been. Should you be glad if the thing you convinced yourself was real turned out not to be a hallucination? Which one was worse?

I stood in the hall, and pulled, but Samantha's door refused to shut, and then I stopped trying because I remembered it was broken. The lights were bright in the hall. The silence was everywhere. I stepped to the window to peer down at my car. It was the most comforting habit I had at the moment.

It took me a minute to get it figured out: the two forms well concealed in the trellises to either side of my trunk were shaped like violent kidnappers, although that might just have been my imagination. They'd made a good bet. My hood must still be warm. It was the only car in the lot. Why not wait for me to deliver myself? More darkness out there. If they hadn't been painted up like bike reflectors with glow in the dark Higher paint, it might have worked.

I'd been at the window too long. They'd spotted me. One shadow left the trellis and came creeping back toward the building. Maybe he still thought he was hiding. Somewhere, far off, I felt the *Gray* waking up. I needed some other kind of solution. I pulled out my phone.

"911. What is the nature of your emergency?"

"A break-in rampage."

"A rampage."

"Multiple break-ins. I don't know what that's called. I'll just report the one on the top floor if that makes it simpler. Also, the perpetrators are here, they might be violent. Anything else? I'm not really a 911 person. You can probably tell."

"What's your location, sir?"

The dispatcher took my crime location and gave me advice about waiting and staying safe, which I said I was doing. I hung up. I hurried down to the stairwell door and cracked it. I listened down the tube. Very faint, stories down, I heard another door, and footsteps coming.

"I called the cops," I echo shouted. Then more footsteps and the door again, and after that silence. I listened, but I was alone. Even the ghosts were gone.

When the sirens approached I ran back to the window overlooking my car, where the twins did not lurk. Soon there were boots in the stairway, and a police presence in the hall. Several officers. The last one up the stairs was one I knew. I heard his voice while I watched two other cops push into Samantha's office.

"Well, if it is not Asher Gale *Investigator.*" I turned, since it was.

"It's two in the morning, Hennessy. Do you ever sleep?"

"Yeah. When crime sleeps. What's your excuse?"

"I'm here following up for Waylon Goodman." It was a very accurate small percentage of the truth. "That's his daughter's office down there, though I don't think he knows about this. Someone tossed it."

"Tossed it. Nice. How about you stay out of the cop business?"

"Oh, believe me."

"No. I do not. Following up for Goodman, who doesn't know about this place, that's right? So. Here you come." He worked it out in bold strokes for both of us. An air movie. "You arrive. You come up to the girl's door. And how exactly is this version of you expecting to get in? Knock, the dead girl comes to answer?"

"It's funny you'd put it like that. But no. I have a key. It's part of the Waylon follow up."

I showed him Samantha's key. He politely told me to give it to him immediately. I fought it off my ring. We walked down the hall so he could satisfy himself at Samantha's broken door, and then he tossed the key back. Like baseball buddies. His fifty-pound eyebrows moved around his face.

"Keep the father out of this. Give the key to him. That's all there is?" he asked me.

"That's all there is," I said. "Except the other room downstairs with the same treatment. And all the paint everywhere."

"The same treatment? Downstairs? Did I not just tell you stay out of the cop business?"

"This was before you said anything," I assured him.

"You have a key to this other room?"

I told him I did not, did he think I was a janitor?

"And you're connecting the two rooms, random rooms on different floors in this big building," he mused for me, "with your mind powers. Is that it?"

"I'm connecting them using the two Brazilians who went past on the stairs coming from this floor, and then waited to jump me out by my car, who were wearing paint they might not have seen, probably picked up tossing the downstairs room. It was a lot of paint the Brazilians were wearing."

He took a minute to run it up and spread it out.

"So two Brazilians with spilled paint. You knew they were Brazilian because they showed their passports."

"I know some Portuguese obscenities."

"Portuguese obscenities. A little here, la ittle there—this story's coming out pretty slow, isn't it?"

"Is it? Honestly it feels kind of pacy."

"You could identify the Brazilians?"

"Sure. Anything I can do to help. That's my motto."

"I do not care about your motto. Anything else? Signed confessions? Is it all videotaped?"

"If I think of anything, should I call you?"

Along with instructions not to leave town, he gave me a card. He already had mine. Like we were going steady.

So then I went home. On the way I stopped to cash the Stipend check I had pocketed for a week. They still came, though I hadn't hung a canvas in ten years. Someday they might stop—who knew? Then maybe I'd take fifty bucks from Waylon whenever I found a fake Monet. Probably I'd just get a job at the Shrimp Shack. I got Mexican after the ATM, and at last I dribbled back into my house, the Higher borealis streaking pomp through the stars above me. I felt like a river that can't quite reach the sea. I stood in my living room, near my stool and easel and canvas, then sat on the stool.

For fifteen minutes I painted with nothing because that's what I have left. It's not that bad, simulating the thing that will break you to pieces, if you do it in short enough spurts. As I did, I thought about Samantha and the mural she, or more likely someone else, had painted. Roman had told me I was walking a dangerous path. Now I was starting to wonder, dangerous for who?

CHAPTER ELEVEN

For confusion, the driving cure is my favorite, second only to the vodka cure. Any road that winds will work. Ocean views help. You set off one morning down the highway, spin the car one way then the other. Your thoughts want to go straight. The car always turns. Do that enough times, your brain surrenders from exhaustion. And voilà, confusion clears like breaking dawn.

I'd driven all the way to the other side of Skysill Beach the next morning, and nearly out of the city on the winding Pacific Coast Highway, when I saw Samantha's ghost again, on the sidewalk in front of some shops.

I saw her from a distance. She looked like a Higher *light* totem pole. A tall rod of *dominion* stretched off the crown of her head into the clouds. My new least favorite Higher color. I eased over and parked a block away, and watched her, vaping away there on the sidewalk. My driving cure hadn't worked this time.

A place called The Empty Nest Furniture Store stood between Samantha and me, and I sat chewing a knuckle and deciding. The Empty Nest had put some sensible decorating options onto the sidewalk, as an enticement. There was a blue carpet under a love seat beside a 50s coffee table, and there was a lamp, and a bookcase. A sidewalk living room.

Samantha was doing nothing on the far side of the living room, but doing it in my direction: straight down the sidewalk at me. She was a ghost compass and I was north. I slow slipped the driver seat, squeezed over the front grill, stepped onto the sidewalk. Samantha just sprayed Higher light diamonds around, shifting a quarter-inch to keep me oriented. In sunlight she was prismatic. She just blew Higher color everywhere.

When I came to the Empty Nest sidewalk sectional I stopped. Samantha star-spangled me across the lamp and the table, from the other side of the room. A transparent room for a girl of light. Her left arm hung at her side and her right extended with her goblet of holes.

I crossed our room to meet her. I wanted to ask a few questions, friendly things, but my problem got obvious as I got closer, and I hadn't solved it by the time I stopped a foot away: the problem was that people who talked out loud to other *invisible* people in public were crazy. A self-identity problem. Because imagine any blistered hell creature you want in the privacy of your mind—believe your monsters are real and talk in there—but the minute you ask them anything out loud on a sidewalk, you're crazy.

What was I supposed to do, though? The girl was a prism. I had my list of questions.

"What the hell?" I cried, spreading out my arms and taking my understated approach. "You *wanted* me to find that key! Didn't you? God *dammit,* what do you *want from me?*"

Talking to nothing starts to feel normal pretty fast. Normal's a very plastic barrier. I pointed my finger straight at Samantha's transparent human looking face and ripped a few off my list.

"Why?" I shouted. "Why'd you get me to your office? I'm not an investigator! I mean why are you following me? Who am I Asher Gale *ghost whisperer?* I'm crazy, is *that* why you picked me? Is that the idea god dammit, *Asher Gale lunatic?* What are we doing on this sidewalk?

What the fuck am I supposed to do with your *cup*? I need an *explanation!*"

A part of me understood I was shouting on a public thoroughfare and that for all the other people, barbers and dog walkers and that kind of people, I was addressing a wall. But it was actually small potatoes compared to some of my *chroma storm* behavior. And what I've done in the *Gray*.

Samantha just sparkled nothing at me.

When you really looked at her, you appreciated how busy *dominion* was. It rotated down from the sky on long tendrils—or up from below—onto the ghostly form and went to work, making her glitter and puff coronas, making sure she stayed the right shape. Who knew if she even wanted to be here? *Dominion* was pulling all the strings here.

A thought wisped up, kind of weak, but the only thing going in my brain, that's why I noticed it. I wondered, what would a crazy Higher Colored ghost look like in the *Gray?* They wouldn't exist. There's no color in the *Gray,* not visible spectrum, not Higher. Maybe you perform a home exorcism that way. It made a simple kind of sense, and that's not usually even one of my criteria.

Where was the *Gray* when you needed an exorcism?

Celine's suggestion went past inside, on the long tail of my exorcism idea. Celine wanted me to have control. Control of the *chroma storms,* control of the *Gray.* Was it possible? Would the *Gray* come if I called? I filled my mind with the concept. *Gray.* Spread out around me. Worn like a shadow robe. I dial the colors down, as far as they'll go. As far as I could. Until they were almost gone. A blush of hue still lay atop it all. It wasn't the *Gray*. The *Gray* was more than just no colors, The *Gray* was the opposite of colors. A color antagonist.

I strained. I felt myself grow a little heavier. I felt myself tip a threshold. It wasn't that hard. Then the blush went away.

Instinctively I speared my fingers, like fending off disaster. I felt a cool wave wash me. I held up the fingers toward Samantha, palm out. I tried flexing them. I couldn't. Statue spears. It felt amazing.

And the *Gray* swept up around me, a cloak of shiver and delight.

I gave the ghost girl a smile. Oh. Sunlight was astonishing and warm on one side of my face.

"We're going to my world now." I smiled to Samantha. "Hold on."

In a moment she would be gone. Then I'd see what it felt like to throw that lamp off the Empty Nest coffee table out into traffic.

Everything was made of the space between black and white. The infinite greys. Everything *else,* that is. But not Samantha. The rest of the world had greyscaled, but she still fountained *light* like tinsel off a window fan, holding her goblet. Her pinchers of *dominion* were twisted an inch, bent sideways, but they still gyroscoped liquid light.

It wasn't an exorcism. It was just making her look more fantastic.

And suddenly I *felt.* I felt in the *Gray!* I never feel in the *Gray*. I do when I'm *chromatic,* that's what's so bad about *chroma storms,* the intensity. The *Gray* had always been a refuge. But instead of the splendor of zero consequences... I felt severed. From life. Severed from warmth. From empathy. I hadn't even known I had that. I felt very bad. Like lost bad, like losing your family bad, everything worthwhile far away out of reach.

And all the while this splintered, numinous, lit-up girl glowed *dominion.* I blamed *dominion* for forcing me full of this pain. *Dominion* had pulled ultraviolet color into the *Gray.* And it was battling to keep it there. Fighting, its *dominion* tendrils bending back. Enduring pain on its own. That's the thing I felt certain of. *Dominion* was suffering as much as me.

My *Gray* is made of a million billion trillion greys blending endlessly. It's *seamless Gray.* But it's wide open, inclusive, and anything goes. So inclusive, this thing floating in front of me had room to manufacture light.

But I'd wanted an exorcism, and I was going to get one.

I just needed the *Gray* to be *Grayer.* Less inclusive. It was going to hurt me. But I really doubted *dominion* could take as much as I could. Not bragging, just from the standpoint of so much practice. So I started yanking out grey, and crushing us down in there. I started numbering the shades.

*Live in **this**,* I thought to *dominion.*

I'd never done anything like it. Had no idea I could. Who'd want to do it? It was horrible. But it turns out you can do it. I compressed the *Gray* in tranches, methodically, until there were only 4096 shades in the world, a convenient platform to stop and look around, a number from computer design. Here the world stretched in flattened bands, like a terrible streaming video. And it hurt. I groaned slow dislocation, and watched Samantha's pinchers of *dominion* twisting back. They fought and squirmed. I could break them. I was sure. I could snap them off. Compress the *Gray* far enough. Get rid of more.

Down: 2048 shades. Greys around on a color wheel, distinct, everything else bled out of the world. I heard whistling, pieces separating, high wind. She was coming apart. *Dominion* keened. The color *dominion* made an actual *noise*—metal lathes, sparks, cars skidding rims down.

Samantha twisted funhouse longwise, *dominion* screaming in coriolis spirals.

1024 shades. My eyes sandpapered agony. *Dominion* keening and thinning like gum.

512 shades. Banshee death! I threw up, fell forward.

256 shades. A wasteland down here. Deep bleak. Squeeze the world like sorrowing cloth. *Dominion,* threaded high as torn clouds, clinging to Samantha, away into the sky. I was almost done. My exorcism. *Finally.*

128 shades. Of *Gray* to build. The world. Bad. Huge sections. One tone shapes. A wall and a shadow. A street and sky. Nothing fades. Here. Edges. Isolate. Night graph. Chest fire. Let's break it. *All.* Tried.

The closer I brought us. To black and white. The harder. To squeeze.

And then. Physics. Who knows, but something. The world just squeezed back.

Everything snapped. Samantha swooped straight like Friendly the Inflatable Higher Ghost, *dominion* swirled back to busily keeping her whole, like it had never been screaming the heat death of the universe, while regular color swept in everywhere. I looked up from the ground. Normal colors. A normal afternoon. On a sidewalk of normal seaside concrete. You wouldn't have known a titanic battle had been waged and lost here, a moment before. You might have wondered about the vomit if you looked that close. I struggled to sit up.

"Let's not do that again," I told Samantha.

CHAPTER TWELVE

There was a man in my invisible living room. It was my landlord from The Empty Nest Furniture Store. He looked down at his crawling tenant, unhappy, and he couldn't see Samantha, and he'd had about enough of me. He was short, round, had his hands perched on his hips and a wedge of goatee. He wore an Irish tweed hat, though he wasn't anything Irish.

"Move along," he urged, shoveling his hips.

"Hey," came a different voice from the other direction. I shuffled around. Back and forth. That's easier to do if you can stand. I wasn't there.

"Get him out of here," said my landlord from behind me.

"Just go back in your store, Tim," said a girl.

She was very ordinary-seeming at first glance, for a girl I instantly couldn't look away from. It might have been residual vertigo. But it also might have been waving hair and cardamom eyes. Before I could stop myself I'd spread my color out, just to soak in it, because her sunflower curls were riveting with her small, full mouth and determined jaw, and I wondered why, for the love of god, am I looking to see if this girl's hair is dyed? And finding it isn't? I liked the informal eye shadow dusted behind her lashes. She had eyes that'd already seen enough. They'd decided what was going on with me. I wished I knew what it was.

She stood a few feet from an open doorway, and held a glass of water, and she examined me another few seconds then stepped in slow, bent, set the glass on the ground with both hands, straightened and backed away, and became the first girl ever to give me water like a feral cat. I was thirsty from throwing up and going *Gray*. I took what she left.

I tried to decipher her camp counselor smolder. Her powder blue tank top and warm denim. Mashed up with a cosmopolitan brow, it created a confusing mélange of information for someone like me, crawling on the ground filtering his mélanges through nausea. I watched myself notice her tan smooth over the shape of her, and the breath of ginger she left when she delivered my water.

"Come in if you like," she pointed to the open door.

My landlord Tim stamped. "Dammit Caroline, I have *my* reputation, even if - "

"Here's an idea for you, Tim," she interrupted Tim but watched me like I might roll off the sidewalk and injure myself, "why don't you go back in your store and mind your own business? And by the way, your blue carpet? Does not go with your love seat. If you're worried about your reputation start there."

She turned, heels in worn cowboy boots, and slipped into her store. I stood and followed, carrying my glass which I hoped to fill again, and while I walked Samantha rotated as easy as a rolling pin, keeping oriented. I was her lodestar. She jangled ultraviolet and made it even harder for me to balance, and I didn't appreciate it. Maybe she was getting back at me for trying to exorcise her. I was beginning to feel bad about it. I'd risked Brazilians and a police inquiry finding her, just the day before, and the first thing I do now is give her an exorcism. She had a right to jangle.

"Sorry about Tim," I heard as I passed inside. I wanted to understand what the big deal was—why I was so interested in the way this girl's hair swept over her shoulders, urging me forward? I didn't have my legs yet. Hadn't I been through enough already today? Now I was going to do infatuation with this girl on top of everything else? I had a lot of other things on my mind, and my infatuations can be a consuming distraction. This was probably still manageable, but a tendency toward inexplicable enchantments is one of the many things I do have to manage. For everyone's safety.

"I once knew an angry janitor like him," I assured her, coming further into the room. "He seems harmless."

"I think he's angry because he's underworked," she said, "no one ever comes to his store." She returned with water in a pitcher. She nodded. "I'm Caroline. Put that glass on the counter."

I set my glass on a sideboard and watched her pitch water, which she did the way dancers do, a lifted impulse rising through her core muscles, before I made myself stop looking at her core muscles. Instead I looked at her room. It smelled fresh as a basket of meadows, with confounding incenses, a little intoxication, and some other things. I couldn't tell what kind of business Caroline did in there. The room had a split personality.

From the front half the room looked out onto the sidewalk through a window where Samantha could be seen doing her star dance. In the front half the room wore black drapes on foresty green walls and rugs on hardwood floors, with a wide drape you could draw to isolate the front of the room from the back. Ornate hardwood trimmed everything here, glass balls and ornate boxes and little statuettes of archers sat on cupboard shelves. A stain glass lamp hung over an inlaid tea table with a set of opposing, deeply cushioned chairs.

That was the front half. The back of her room wore stripped bare linoleum on the floor and had a metal, fifth-grade science teacher's desk flanked by battered file cabinets, a pulled open printer, and a fluorescent light that flickered, all very back office. In fact, if you combined the front and the back of the room, you got a place where people could quietly grieve some loved ones, then change chairs and notarize their estate paperwork. Very compartmentalized.

She slipped herself into the deep seat across the little inlaid table, and I knew the other chair was for me. She made it look comfortable, but I felt like I wasn't going to like mine. I didn't want to like it. I wanted to stop being distracted by the curve of her neck. Look at her hands instead, I gave myself advice. Caroline had a glass of water in one of her hands.

"What kind of work goes on here?" I asked. It came out a little suspicious, I thought.

"What kind of work would you like done?" she asked.

"I don't know, what are my choices?"

"What makes you think I know your choices?"

I had an intuition where this might be going.

"What happens if I just keep asking questions?"

"Why don't you try, and find out?"

I was happy to find this style terribly grating—it worked against the draw of her voice, softer than you'd expect. Maybe she'd keep doing irritating things until I had my legs back and I could leave before anything more complicated happened. I caught Samantha gazing in the window from the sidewalk and I shuddered. I couldn't help it.

"Could we draw that window drape?" I almost pleaded.

She peeled up a frown and tsked her head. "Sunshine's good for you."

"Nice. So I guess that's it for the customer's always right."

"What? Oh, you're not a customer. You're just a boy who needed a chair and some water. You might get to customer. I guess. Time will tell."

I did need to sit. My legs made me do it. I found my chair comfortable, but she definitely did a better job in hers than I did in mine. I emptied my glass and set it on the round table between us, on a coaster. Caroline rose to the sideboard and brought the pitcher and refilled the glass. It was a very small glass. Her fingers were long and precise. She sat n her chair again. She took a sip of water.

"Might as well do it," she said, smiling encouragement after a moment.

"Do what?"

"Whatever you're here for."

"I'm not here for anything, I'm here..." I jerked a thumb at Samantha, then stopped myself.

"Asher, isn't there something you want to talk to me about?"

I felt grateful she'd given me more water. I still had enough for a casual sip. I said, "Have we met? Some other sidewalk somewhere?"

"Not that I'm aware."

"But you know my name. How's that?"

"Well. I'll tell you. But I don't know if you'll like it."

"Try."

"Ok," she said, and she was really considering me with her eyes, which made it hard to concentrate on her story, "I was listening when you were screaming your guts onto the sidewalk in front of my store and driving my neurotic neighbor farther past the edge. And I listened to you scream your name real loud. A bunch of times. Asher Gale! See? I know your name because I used my listening skills."

"Ok, I see, well there doesn't seem to be anything wrong with that," I admitted, and to prove I had listening skills of my own and to experiment with what it felt like, I finished with her name, "Caroline."

"I'm happy you're impressed. We've got a more important problem though don't we? Who's that waiting outside my window?"

She pointed. I refreshed my recollection of how good the water was, then I put the glass down and casually looked over my shoulder, where Samantha could clearly be seen evaporating Higher color, without providing me any satisfaction at all, and then I turned back to Caroline and cleared my throat.

"You can see her?" This time it came out smaller than I intended.

"What? *No*. God. Of course not. You can, obviously. Her, you said?"

I shut my bag, but the cat was out. It was shocking.

"What that... did you just... trick me so I admitted I see an invisible girl outside?"

"No I did not. Do you want to talk about her?"

"Absolutely *not*. She's a private problem."

Caroline shook her head, like she was breaking bad news. "She isn't, though, after the performance you put on, which isn't what people do with private problems. I think you really *ought* to talk about her, now that she's on the table. Or how do you think she'll feel? I'll get you more water."

"She's only on the table because you made me..." This was frustrating. I turned and watched this Caroline girl go for her pitcher. I was so far away from being at my best I was almost invisible to myself. The *Gray,* the ghost, the unwelcome confusion of meadow smells and the unwelcome intoxication of the girl. I felt anticipated at every crossing.

"Well," I called, which came out disappointingly loud and surly, "you *asked*, you know, so just be careful what you ask I guess. That's the only reason I mentioned her. You asking. Because listen, I'm not that guy, complaining about *apparitions*. Alright? That tiresome guy? Just to be super clear."

"Well I agree you aren't tiresome. Not yet, anyhow. You're just seeing an invisible person. And that's totally, perfectly okay."

That could very well have been condescension, and I decided to treat it that way.

"Look," I really snapped, "it's not like that's a ghost or something, I don't believe in... you know... "

"You don't believe in ghosts? Good. Me neither. So Asher, how can I help?"

"*Caroline*. Honestly what is it you *do* here? It's like a discount mortuary. I can't figure it out."

She tilted forward in her chair and suddenly I was looking at her bare neck, which appeared to be soft and strong, and she put her glass on the table and pulled up her hair with a clip, like she wanted to make sure nothing got in her eyes while she listened to what I was about to tell her.

"You don't know what I do?" she asked. "Really?"

"Really. I don't. I'm dying to find out. What is it?"

"I guess I assumed," she said, like a pleasant surprise.

"Really, what is it? What is it you do?"

"Maybe I got you wrong. That'd be real rare."

"I wonder—is this conversation a maddening circle for you, like for me?"

"Maddening's not a word I'd ever use so it's probably you."

"It's no picnic getting you to answer a question is all. Has anyone ever told you that?"

"Oh. Yeah, they have. I'm a psychic."

Many of the things that had puzzled me earlier suddenly made sense. The decor. Some details like the decorative crystal balls which could've also been crystal balls employed in the course of someone's work. The heavy curtain on a track to separate the back half of the room where they work even protectors from the front half of the room where they wore turbans. Caroline was folded back, one leg up in her chair. Now that she was a psychic she looked exactly the same, which was not at all like a psychic. She'd slipped her cowboy boots to the floor and revealed green socks where Marvin the Martian posed, his orange blaster covering me. Caroline seemed a little tense, suddenly.

"You're a psychic?" I snapped. Why snap like that? I had no idea. "I thought you said you didn't believe in ghosts."

"I don't. Asher, listen close. No lies." She leaned forward, put her elbows on her knees, and stitched another frown, just as small as the first one but more serious.

"I don't know what's going on here," she warned, and this part was to clarify something to herself, "you showing up on my sidewalk, an hour where I've got no appointments? With your... whatever, misplaced self-confidence and heartbreak smile—I don't know what this thing is, but I *guarantee* I'll never lie. Not worth the energy."

I nodded at her main point, which seemed to involve trustworthiness or something, but got stuck on her idea that there was a *thing* between us that she didn't understand. Caroline began to tap her thumb and index nail tips together, watching me. She didn't know she was doing it.

"So you're a psychic who doesn't believe in ghosts," I went in, tangentially, off balance.

"That's right."

"What about spirits?"

"What's the difference?"

"How do I know? You're the psychic."

"None of that's real!" Then she seemed to be overcome with irritation, or something deeper. Her tapping nails dropped to her lap and scissored into the hem of her tank top, precise little pinpricks. "There're no *disembodied human souls* who *wander the earth* and *reach out to the living, hungry to be set free.* Okay? I've known a lot of psychics in my life. Believe me. And absolutely none of the real ones talk to ghosts. It's nonsense."

"Ok, then putting aside the fact that one of them is looking into your opium den from the sidewalk right now, no offense, what is it you *sell* here if not the spirit and ghost gag?"

"Psychometry."

I was forced to watch her take in a deep breath, like a person putting a bad experience behind her, then forced to see her chest rise against the straps of her top, the muscles deliberate and confident but a little weary, and finally watch her whole chest settle calm. I was forced to watch those things.

"Fair warning," she said. She'd narrowed her eyes at me. "Psychometry is not a gag I'm selling." Then she began having a focused, internal argument with some preexisting life experience, right in front of me, and it was mesmerizing. She was talking herself out of something.

"I spent enough of my life dealing with people who thought being psychic was doing séances," she said, quiet. "Séances aren't real—I don't do séances, *ghosts aren't real,* despite what you might have heard on TV—I don't put up with it anymore. But sometimes I'm sensitive about what I do. And I don't want you accidentally triggering all my issues with one of your smart comments, because that would be a real bad start, and I can see smart comments are one of your top problems. I bet they get you in plenty of trouble. Where I grew up they'd probably get you beaten semi-regular, deserved and otherwise. I'm sure you've got good reasons for how you sound. It's just I like to have everything out in the open. It's better."

"No problemo. So what's Psychometry?" I said. In for a penny and for a pound.

"Officially it's the ability to discover facts concerning an event or person by touching inanimate objects associated with them." She recited a memory, which she had mixed feeling about..

"I have no idea what that is." I could have worked it out but I wanted to hear her talk.

"Object reading. You've got a problem. You come to me with an object related to your problem, I touch it and tell the stories I find."

"Okay."

She waited. She expected me to have more to say about Psychometry, but I didn't say a thing. It was the first time I'd done anything that surprised her, and I took an untoward satisfaction in it, and then I gave up fighting whatever was happening to me. Because now at least I could do whatever it was I was going to do with this beautiful, camp counselor psychic girl, but I could do it without feeling so utterly predictable. It was a one of my childish victories.

"That's all you have to say?" she tested. "*Okay*?"

"Sure. You do Psychometry," I told her, smiling and being generous. "I'm a live and let live kind of person. No judgements."

"Oh, that kind," she said, suspicious of my generosity, which was impressive work so early in our relationship. "And if you *weren't* the non-judgmental kind, what would you be saying?"

"Look, let's be honest with each other," I told her, "I'm a person who sees a sparkly lady floating on the sidewalk and I just rolled around in my own vomit. You're a person who tells stories from frying pans. So this seems like one of those fifty-fifty situations. Neither of us in a position to throw stones."

Her smile came slow, over a few breaths it grew wide, and turned out to have soulful dimples when it was really breaking out. Her hands drifted off the hem of her tank top, which had taken a terrible beating, and not for the first time.

"I like fifty-fifty," she said, putting her glass on the table. "Nobody throws a stone. And I'll tell you a secret. I don't believe in ghosts, generally, but I halfway believe in yours. Obviously not a ghost. But I halfway believe it's something."

We seemed to be past the water stage. I had no idea what came next.

"Halfway believing," I agreed with her. "That's great. I'll meet halfway on Psychometry too. I mean, who knows? It might be real."

"Yeah, it is. Plus halfway's the best you can ever hope for—meet somebody halfway, you can both jump from the same plane together."

"You put a winning spin on a figure of speech."

"Is that what it was?"

I found myself smiling back at her, which doesn't happen very often and made me very nervous.

It was time for me to leave. We both figured it out the same second, and stood, and I reached into my pocket for my keys, to foreshadow a few of my upcoming activities to her, like driving away, in case she was interested.

"Well, this has been a surprise," I said.

"I know. I enjoyed not having you as a customer."

And I turned to her door. I pushed it open. Samantha sparkled and rotated around.

"Asher?"

"Yes?" I turned back. I was happy to do it. But she wasn't looking at me, she was looking down at her feet. Just a few inches from her socks. Where Samantha's Higher coated office key lay on the ground.

CHAPTER THIRTEEN

"You dropped something," she said. Her smile was gone and I thought she sounded sad, and tired. I remembered I hadn't put the key back on my ring after Hennessy had made me take it off, and I'd only put it on in the first place because keys are exactly the kind of thing I regularly lose. If this had been 7 Eleven I'd never have gotten it back.

Caroline was definitely disappointed and it seemed to involve me. Somehow. It was a lot worse seeing it on her than on Lady Damely.

"Just a little accidental test, I guess?" she allowed, soft with disappointment.

"What, now?"

"Asher, if you want me to read something, please just say it. No need to be sneaky."

"No. I didn't do that, what you're thinking, I mean not on purpose."

"Ok. Well, tell your *subconscious*, there isn't any need for games."

"I don't think it was my subconscious. I think it was an accident. I lose stuff. I'm well known for it."

"There's no such thing as an accident in my business. But a key won't do it. You have to get me something better."

"Something for what?"

"Whatever's got you twisted in your knot. Honey, you're strung tight as—oh, lah. Never mind. But a key? It's too general. It can't be something that's *utilized*. It's got to be something valued. Or *cherished*, cherished is best."

"Okay, but that key just fell out of my pocket."

"On its own."

It seemed like a very petty position for me to keep arguing, considering how much water she'd given me, so I decided I'd be the bigger man. It was a new feeling. I wasn't sure how long I could keep it up.

"Someone's going to have to pick up this key," she said.

Samantha sparkled everywhere. She turned and watched me go back in the fortune teller's office and bend to pick up the key. I wished I could tell if Samantha had any opinions about this. From where I knelt I could see Caroline's feet, where even Marvin seemed to be unhappy about what I'd done. What was his problem?

I knew it would be better if I left, after I'd wondered about her sock that way.

But instead I lifted the key.

"Okay. Fine. I'm game," I said. "There's a ghost girl in peril, well, she may not be in peril but she won't leave me alone and she's making me very nervous. I've been trying to figure out what's going on. And this is all I've got. Just her key."

"So you admit you wanted a reading."

"Maybe that's the way it happened. Honestly I'm not sure anymore."

"I'm telling you a key won't be enough."

"But this is all I have. Will you try?"

Her eyes took a while getting back with the decision. They started out thinking it was a bad idea, but some other part of her really gave the eyes the business, and eventually they gave up and

Caroline sighed and nodded. I held the key out to her and she stepped back quick.

"Uh uh," she said, shaking her head. She got a napkin to pick my glass up off the table, her own glass in the other hand, and put them on the sideboard, then returned with a simple white cloth and draped it. Then she pointed, and I put the key on the cloth. She sat in her chair. I sat in mine.

"It will help me to have some context," she said. "When did you start seeing this invisible person?"

"I guess, sort of, the other day when I saw her body?"

"Her dead body."

"Yeah."

She took my dead body as a matter of no concern, making me wonder what sorts of things her other clients came in to talk about.

"And have you seen invisible people before her?"

"*Before*?" I started to pretend to think really hard about it, but realized it would look like one of my smart comments. "No. Samantha's the only invisible person I've ever seen."

"That's her name? Samantha?" I nodded. "Ok. Have you ever seen any dead bodies before?" Caroline really had a way of getting into the middle, with just a few questions. This was probably her whole game, she was really good at it. Already she'd helped me.

"No," I said. "You think I'm seeing her ghost, or whatever, because I saw her dead body?"

"I don't think anything. I'm collecting facts. Has anyone else seen her?"

"No."

"How did she die?"

"Suicide."

"And you want to know how to make her go away."

"Yeah. I tried a little bit of exorcism. That made me throw up."

Caroline seemed to have assembled the facts she wanted. She took a deep breath and let it out. I pointed to the tracks for curtaining the room in half.

"Should I seal off the tax preparers in the back?" I asked.

"Shut up, Asher."

I pushed back in my seat and watched her take another breath and close her eyes. Her body grew quiet, her back straight up, her hands, palms up on her thighs, graceful and still. She spaced breaths out. I liked watching that. After a moment her hands rose and turned over and hovered above the key. I saw her eyes moving behind their lids.

"Are you ready to hear the story in this key?"

"Yes. I am."

Her fingertips came down on the key, soft as dragonflies landing. She gasped and pulled away, though her eyes didn't open.

"What?" I asked.

"Nothing. Took me by surprise is all."

This time when she settled them, her fingers pushed down and her eyes began to dart side to side in their mystery caves, an escape kind of movement, but her breathing came in as calm as evening fog.

"There's something funny about the key," she said.

"What is it?"

"Don't talk. There's something funny, but still, it's just a key. I see... key things, darkness, door, lock. Darkness, door, lock. That's what you'd expect... mm, what's this... weird... if you get this door open—oh, shit, get out! Stop her! Asher, it isn't, not safe for—" and then she screamed and jerked sideways on her chair and knocked the key off the table. I flashed all the Highers up, as far as they'd go—was something in the room? But whipping around showed me nothing other than fantastical streamers floating on sunbeams, and a key, laser locked on the floor, and Samantha in full *font of light* regalia. Caroline recovered faster than me. Neither of us got back all the way.

"My god, Asher."

"You want some water? That's your thing, right?" I didn't see anything harder.

"I'll get it."

She did the clinking and pouring and napkin carrying and pretty soon we both had more water. Then I couldn't take it.

"Tell me what it was," I begged.

"What in the world are you mixed in the middle of?"

"Please, just tell me."

"I don't like it. I don't like it at all. There's... so *much*."

"Caroline, please. Get to the part where you say an answer. Can you jump to that?"

"Well, your key is up to its neck in *something*. Just by itself. I've never touched anything like it."

"I won't ask you to describe it." Because I already suspected what it was. The key was up to its neck in Higher paint. Which, I realized, meant that I believed her Psychometry, more than halfway. Which was a surprise and not a surprise. "Why'd you scream?"

"The only thing I should have heard from this key was darkness, door, lock. It has a job, darkness, door, lock. That's how people think of keys, if they ever think about them. But there was some kind of bleed over... I don't know how to describe this. Something else, from somewhere else, bled over into the key. And stuck."

"Is bleeding over a thing? For psychics?"

"There's no *things*. It's all real simple."

"So the part that bled into the key, that's where you screamed?" Two could play the leading question game. It was probably the only thing that would get us through this.

"Do you know anything about a man with a black eye?" she asked. I drank water. "And a big hunting knife? Whoever had this key was... she was terrified, Asher. She was almost... insane from it. She thought she was insane. This girl was, over the edge, out of her mind, petrified."

There was a long quiet year in Caroline's room. Then I spoke.

"The black-eyed man with the knife, that was on a mural in her office."

"What does it mean?"

"I don't know."

"I believe in your invisible person. I wonder what she is?"

"A ghost. And I believe in your Psychometry. You knew about the black-eyed man."

"Something's going on. I know that. You've got trouble. It's dark."

Over my shoulder Samantha was still going at it. She was never going to stop, that's what I was afraid of. But for all the problems she might be dealing with, her expression was nothing like the insane fear Caroline saw. Samantha's expression was nothing at all. There were a total of zero expressions anywhere on her eyes or mouth or cheeks, the usual places. Not even serenity. It was slick work how she managed to look like she had something she badly wanted to say. She'd brought me here. That much was clear. Apparently the rest was still my responsibility.

"I'm sorry I brought this to darken your door," I sighed.

"Oh, that's all right. My door wasn't doing anything."

I stood. I felt I should leave before I pulled Caroline in any deeper. Seeing her scream had been strangely horrible. I picked the key off the floor and pushed it deep in a pocket.

"How much do I owe you?" I asked.

"I only charge for problems I solve, Asher, not one's I make worse."

"You didn't make anything worse."

"No? But now you're worried about me, too. Aren't you?"

She was right. It was worse. I'd brought this alluring psychic-next-door girl down into my ocean of intersecting problems, and it was the last thing I wanted.

"How about an IOU?" I asked.

"Don't worry. Some people I never charge at all. Maybe you'll be one of those. I have a Stipend. I'm just fine."

A Stipend. Where was my water? Water was such a great thing, swallowing and wrapping your hands around a glass while thinking happened.

"A Stipend?" It was the best I could do without water.

"A few of us do, here in the psychic district. A Fenestram Stipend, it's called. Covers rent and crystal balls." She smiled again, and watching her do it was a little better than flying in a dream, which was annoying and distracting. Her voice got a *long time ago* sound. "I was so lucky to get it. That's what got me out of Carson City. I'd still be dealing blackjack at Caesar's. Instead I have my own business. The Psychic Touch."

"And you're a painter?" I was trying to put it together. "An artist?"

"No. I'm all psychic, all the time."

"But a Fenestram Stipend..." Could Roman have made some kind of mistake? It seemed unlikely. So she was a fellow *all expense paid* recipient of a Fenestram Stipend?

"I've got a Stipend, too," I told her. "A lot of us do, in Skysill. But I'm not a psychic."

She was happy about my achievement, but she didn't seem to appreciate the cognitive dissonance. Psychics and painters? Both? I hadn't even known there were psychics in Skysill Beach, and now I'd discovered there was an entire district. There wasn't an obvious way to explain my confusion, and I'd run out of energy to try.

"Well," I said, before I turned toward the door.

"Be careful," she stopped me. I really didn't like the front I saw this time. "Your thing, your key... it isn't a good thing. It's real dark. It's... evil? Which isn't the kind of thing I ever say."

"What should I do?"

She shrugged. I nodded. I'd liked it better leaving her place the first time, before the key, in the middle of some surprising flirting, when I still knew where to find my blissful ignorance. When I got back to my car I was still filled with ignorance, but none of the good kind.

CHAPTER FOURTEEN

So I gave up my driving cure. Winding down the Pacific Coast Highway in clear sunlight and balmy air was for suckers. I wanted shortcuts. I felt like I'd been letting it all come in its own time up to now. I've heard you do your best work when you're focused and receptive. But I just wasn't seeing the evidence. I was receiving nothing. If I received any less I'd asphyxiate from lack of answers.

I'd put off visiting Tobias. Even though Samantha's mural and his Subscription collection at the Nagato *seemed* identical, something had felt wrong about the comparison. Still, Tobias was the only direction I could think of to go, so when I'd got north as far as Fenestram Color I parked. Before I confronted Tobias I needed painting supplies. I climbed out of the car and found my strength waning, just at the wrong moment.

The ceiling fan spun inside, and cars shivered past out the wide windows, but the cashier desk was empty. When I came up I saw a bell. I pressed it. Nobody came. I did it again. Then more, to make sure the sound carried everywhere.

The door to *authorized access* opened and Veronica came out, pale as a roll of paper towels, and after her came an artist I recognized but didn't know. He was tall and hunched. His eyes were pinched close, it might have looked hawklike once but now it just looked like a bad mood. He carried a bundle of Higher paints.

"Oh, it's Mr. Gale," Veronica called, leading the tall man to the desk where I stood. I gave the bell another press. I don't know why. Something about the way she said my name. "Look at you, you pushed the wee bell, over and over. Very clever. I'll bring round the rattle and the little horn, do you think you can sit quietly until I've checked Mr. Keller out?" She looked back at Mr. Keller and shrugged. "Children, yes? Well. Will there be anything else, Mr. Keller?"

"No," he surled, like the question shouldn't have come up. I waited for Veronica to offer him a subtle remark, because obviously she had her subtlety going today, and Keller was asking her to do it, but she didn't. Maybe he paid protection. He didn't pay for paints, I knew that. They were all Stipend provisions, the supplies in his pile of free.

"Thank you for coming in today, Mr. Keller, we truly appreciate your patronage," she said as she marked his receipt.

"Hurry up," he growled. He made single syllables as unpleasant as I've ever heard. Veronica just nodded. He was standing there waiting for attention from her but she didn't lavish him. It was hard to understand. I stepped in to give her some ideas.

"Absolutely *fantastic* patronage, Keller," I told him, "I saw it too. Inspirational."

"That's a bit arch," Veronica arched at me. "I'm *so* sorry, Mr. Keller," she turned back to him, "you see, this is Asher Gale, well known disrespectful malcontent. He's sure to apologize. He once apologized to me. Just give him a moment."

"That's right, Keller," I nodded. "All I need is someone like you to give me a moment."

Keller wanted to leave, I could see it, but Veronica had basically told him to stay and listen to me appologize, and deep down Keller was the kind of person who did whatever Veronica's kind of person told him to. I checked my wrist and rang the bell.

"And there's the moment," I said. "Mr. Keller, because of all the respect I have for Veronica, and because I still have some questions to ask her, I want to applogize. I know I blemished your visit to the paint store. I'm leaving as soon as I can."

"There you have it, the locally famous Gale apology!" Veronica clapped for me, then turned to Keller, and there was a bit of ice in her eyes. "Now you've got everything you need. I look forward to your show next month, Mr. Keller. I feel as if your work has really gathered steam, these last twenty years. You seem now as eloquent with a brush as you are as a conversationalist! It takes my breath away. I feel sure that soon the critics will be clamoring, *clamoring*, to hear your paintings roar!" Keller seemed a little overwhelmed, but he nodded, it all sounded accurate to him. "Roar, Mr. Keller! Roar on to victory!" I saw it then. She was still in the game, just cutting deeper than the rest of us. She had more patience. She really enjoyed the taste.

After Keller went away Veronica crossed her arms and created a smile that refused to try to be winning, full of her happiness. I saw - I didn't understand - but I saw from the way she was standing, we were going to do more wordplay.

I tried going in humble, because the supplies I needed I could only get from her.

"Keller seems nice," I said to his back going out the door.

"Mr. Keller is one of Skysill's brightest shining lights."

"Sure he is. I bet he's beautiful from orbit. Like a global forest fire."

"Now. Have you come merely to disparage my defenseless customers? Or do you have some errand of your own? You enjoyed the wee bell, would you like to buy that? Ring ring, just like a grownup."

"All I want is customer service."

"Oh dear, do they not teach waiting your turn any longer?

Parents these days. Yours seem to have been *particularly* negligent. I'd be very surprised if you still talked to them. Bad parents. Naughty."

My colors flared. I gritted them into a corner. My parents are a triggery thing. Caroline has Psychometry, with me, it's my parents.

"How about we leave my parents completely out of the conversation?" I told her. It was surprising, I heard my voice break a little, like I was serious.

"Oh?" she said. "Yes. Noted Mr. Gale. Parents completely out."

I brought my palms to my eyes and pressed and felt slower every second. Diving *Gray*, attempting an exorcism, tearing *dominion* into taffy, vomiting on the sidewalk, it all took its toll. Talking to Caroline had bridged the toll over, but Veronica rolled me into it.

"You oughtn't rub your eyes," said Veronica, "that's the surest way to get sick. I'm surprised your mother—oh, forbidden. Is that right? Forbidden to mention your parents. Oh, I just mentioned your parents *again*. Oh!"

"Look," I said, "it's okay, don't give me customer service. Just give me what you gave me already. Remember the tube of *bleed*? I'll take that, then I promise I'll leave."

I saw what I'd done when her face changed. I'd told her what I wanted. It's not the kind of mistake I usually make. On the rare occasions I even know what I want, I never say it out loud. I watched Veronica slip her fingers under the counter and bring up the tube. She held it in her palm like her favorite half-empty tube of paint, or a diamond tiara.

"I wonder what you'd give me for it," she wondered.

"Can I just ask," I asked, "what you have against me?"

"Absolutely nothing distinct or original in any way."

"You hold back with some of them. Some people get to leave with paints and brushes, I saw it. Why am I special?"

"The illusion of *specialness*. It's so charming. But I treat everyone the same, with respect to self-absorption and hypocrisy. Each of you Stipend babies are equally special, to me. You see?"

"You think *I'm* the one with self-absorption and hypocrisy? What? No *you* all, you're thieves! With your *compulsion,* your forgeries, you beat me by *miles* as hypocrites."

Her eyes narrowed.

"I am no *thief.* And you do not know yourself as well as you imagine. You most certainly do not know me."

She gave all that a swift English snap so it landed differently than the other things she'd said. I knew it had to mean something. I couldn't figure out what.

"Look," I told her, "I'm sorry. I'll admit it. Everything you said about me is true." I was using my reasonable voice, which I saw I needed practice with. "What if I started over? I'll talk nice, I'll stand nice. Nice like a customer." I couldn't tell if I was reaching her at all. "Veronica, I'd really like to get that paint. How do I make it happen? I have a project, I actually need paint."

She stood a minute calculating the price she'd charge for her free tube of already opened paint. I stood watching the rich get richer. Finally she decided what she was going to say.

"Did you know that Mr. Keller came to Skysill Beach many years ago as a teenager?" she asked. I didn't see how it got me closer to my tube, but I showed interest just to be safe.

"Yes!" she nodded. "He was telling me, the little chatterbox. And for the thirty-seven years since then, he has never left this village. Not once. Not to go to Walmart forty minutes inland. Not on a biking excursion. Not ever. What does that seem to say about Mr. Keller?"

"I don't know. How many of these do I have to do?" She shrugged. I gave it a moment of thought. "I think it makes him pretty typical for a Stipend artist."

"Yes! I had the same thought! It's astounding how few of you ever leave, not one single time. Practically— and by *practically* I mean *literally*—none of you. Ever. Leaves."

I watched. "Is that a question?" I wanted to get through with as few mistakes as possible.

"Doesn't it seem in the slightest odd to you?"

"Artists are funny I guess."

"And *seeing.* None of you want to talk about it. I can *see.* I'd like to have a conversation."

"Honestly, I'd like it too."

"Yes?"

"But today I'm busy."

"All right, answer this: Mr. Keller can *see* three steps into the higher spectrum. He has *choke, wander* and *compulsion.* How do you think I know about Mr. Keller?"

I couldn't tell where it all was going. I watched her shift down the counter to where the fliers and posters were racked, and bend behind it to a sliding cupboard. She dug a cardboard box up. It had a cardboard lid. She slid it up the counter so it stopped in front of me.

"I inherited this," she said, "from Dedrick. And dozens more. Alphabetized. It's so quaint. Shall we look?"

She lifted the top to show me inside the box, where there were papers filed dense, divided by tabs F and G. She pulled one out and made no effort to mark the place it came from. I admired her disregard for her ordered system. She widened her eyes and held it, like she was about to put on her reading glasses.

"Here is one," she said. "Edgar Harrow Stronhiem. Wonderful name! And Edgar... was born in 1884. So we presume he is no longer with us. But despite Edgar's demise, his legacy lives on. Look."

The paper slid across the counter. It was old, many years pressed in a box, stock and printing from a different time. I learned Edgar's birth information to the second. I learned the place of his birth, longitude and latitude. That his parents had been German. His educational history, comments about his artistic proclivities, the Higher Colors The Test had certified him for. Dedrick had never mentioned these records. Our conversations had ranged pretty widely. It was a surprise. I pushed the paper back.

Veronica returned to the box, but this time she was flipping like she was searching for something in particular.

"I looked *you* up," she said as she flipped. "Your visit piqued me.

Don't you love that word? I can look up anyone. It's an awesome responsibility." She found the section, pulled the pages apart, drew up one, two, three sheets, and laid them on the counter. This time she did hold her place.

"The Gale family!" she announced. She arranged the papers so I could read without touching. I looked them over.

My own sheet was least interesting. I took a few seconds over the second one, Amelia's. The third paper was my father. Marlon Francisco Gale. And just like that, after twenty-six years of life, I knew my father's middle name. I learned his birthday and birth time to the millisecond, his birth city—Chicago—and birth longitude and latitude. His schooling: Art Institute of Chicago. His parent's nationality: Czech and Spanish. Some thoughts about his artistic proclivities: "A brilliant colorist, dynamic brush, technically masterful, emotional depth, breathtaking novelty in form and subject." And his Colors, which I already knew from looking at his painting, spanning the spectrum all the way to *bleed*. This was more about him than I'd ever known. It was more than I'd ever tried to find.

"Now," said Veronica, "I know I'm forbidden from mentioning the subject, but I'm forced to point out—your mother is not in my box. Every other painter in Skysill Beach for the last century and more, but not her. Can you tell me anything about *that* mystery?"

The small hope candling up in my chest fell flat and died. I slid the paper back to her.

"It's not mysterious," I said. "Papers are easy to lose. You leave one out, a breeze blows, a door opens, anything can happen."

"Tiny dragons come steal just *that record*. Of course, easy to picture. But. I've checked against all the records. Accounts paid. Stipend draws. Your mother appears in none of them. Every other Higher painter in this town is extensively documented. Look at Mr. Keller. Even you, Mr. Gale. But not her."

"Maybe she was a ghost."

"No," she sighed. She said it like she wished it could be true, but knew it wasn't. "Maybe all this is nothing. But if you should ever have an insight, I'd be interested to know." She offered over the tube of *bleed*. "May I ask what you will do with this single, solitary tube of Higher paint?"

"No."

"Do you have any questions for me?"

"Why'd Dedrick sell you the store?"

"Just a right time, right place kind of thing, for both of us. Well, Mr. Gale, as was our first meeting, this has been a treat. Please come back soon. I look forward to it."

She almost made it sound like she meant it. I slipped the paint away and did the same with myself. Out the door. In the car. Up the road. Farther and farther from anything uncomplicated. Ten minutes in, I found myself picturing a glass of water on an inlaid table. I smelled a spritz of ginger and took a deep, sweet breath, which just made the day feel more complicated.

CHAPTER
FIFTEEN

After a sandwich in downtown Skysill and a stroll on the beach to sort my options and finding that neither activity brought me any closer to a better idea, I took myself down the coast to Catalina Village. I'd gotten jumpy. Every flash of Higher color I saw—a gallery sign, some graffiti on a sidewalk—my first thought was of eldritch girls in gowns of light. But Samantha made no appearances. She was wherever you went if you were whatever she was, when no one was around for you to haunt. As far as I knew she was, even now, hovering in our living room in front of The Empty Nest.

Catalina Village draped itself on its slice of continental rise like an ancient curtain, dense with buildings at the top, but tattered and worn thin at the bottom. The lowermost homes, closest to the water, were the oldest, and widely spaced, on property that had fallen into a no man's zone protected from further development in the name of marine preservation. So far none of the developers in town had been able to bribe the coastal commission to change the zoning, though it was only a matter of time. Until then the plots remained as they had been in the 50s, with most of the houses built decades earlier than that.

The house I was interested in was perched on a bluff overlooking Mineral Grain Beach, a pocket beach favored by locals, where I'd spent many a summer night in my teens, in the heat of a bonfire, wrapped around one bad choice or another, usually deep in the *Gray*. Today I was headed for the Manders House, a little pup tent of a 1920s holiday home at the end of the bluff, that over the years had been washed and brushed and straightened up and had a copse of junipers grown around it to shield it from embarrassment. The Manders had run Skysill's grocery emporium back in the 1920s, according to the tour guides.

The house was built the way everyone did it back then, clapboard runners, river stone chimney, a couple of picturesque bay windows which had probably been added later. It was all faded, weathered yellow like a lemon rind. The windows had orange blinds drawn, and no movement showed through them. It was 700 square feet of keeping its business to itself. No cars parked in the dirt lane leading into the trees. I wouldn't have expected it. A car would draw attention, and license plates could be run. Or so I'd heard. The hunch I was playing wanted a little air, though, or it was going to pass out. I ran the Highers up a moment, just to see if anything shocking appeared, but that only made the sunlight psychedelic.

That did leave me fairly sure no one hid in the pampas grass or the coastal sage dotting the dunes on the little point. No one peered down from the juniper whisks encircling the place. Artificial colors, clothes and glasses and shoes, pop out pretty stark when you pump the saturation up. So I took a breath, in case some extra oxygen was going to be the difference, and stepped lightly over the little shale pavers to get up onto the wooden landing.

I knocked.

From inside came a sort of gasp, like someone waking from a nap who hadn't expected a knock. The house was small, it was hard to hide a sound like that. Running the sink here probably woke the neighbors, or would have if there'd been any. The house got perfectly quiet after that, which was also impossible to hide.

I knocked more. It got like meditation. Like one of the great percussionists of history, I could have gone all day. I mentioned the fact out loud to the door, calling out inquiries and greetings, and after that I knocked on the door again, and then did it more. Finally the door got fed up and jerked inwards, but only a crack.

"Look, what?" said the door jerker.

I don't know what I'd expected, but he wasn't it. He was very unlike Felicia. Samantha sure liked variety.

"Tobias?" I asked. "Tobias Singlebee?"

His hair was dyed blond and cupped his cheeks to his jaw in swanny disorder. He had exotic wide eyes that made you think of bedrooms. His shirt hung open, a beige ribbed painter's gi, and a *choke* and *farewell* tattoo glowed over his breastbone, just the ends of pinion feathers and the top of a sunset. There were surface piercings on his clavicle, studs through his cheeks, his tongue flashed me a ring. He had a gold ring on his pinky. He was my height but several muscles broader. His shoulders really had the shape. They were doing it to be impressive, and pulling it off.

"How did you find me?" he asked and pulled some blond hair from his teeth. Maybe it'd gotten there during his nap.

"You don't want to know *who* I am first?" He did not. "Ok. How did I find you. I found you from your gallery show."

"You saw my show?"

"*Subscriptions.* Yeah. I won't share any opinions on the work itself. My sister liked it, so maybe I'm missing something. One of your subscriptions was a painting of the Manders place. An AirBnB rental, week after week, that's a kind of subscription—I thought that. It was the only thinking I had to do at all, in there with your art. I spent most of my time keeping my hands from tearing my eyes out. And now here we are together. At the end of my story."

"Who the fuck are you? Fuck off if you don't like my work. I don't like how you talk."

He tried to close the door, but before he could finish I had my toe in. It wasn't much for someone with Tobias's shoulders, it just took him by surprise.

"Did you know Samantha Goodman killed herself?" I yelled in, while I could. The door stopped closing. In fact, it stopped putting up any resistance at all, and when I saw Tobias stumbled back I pushed it all the way in. When that worked I stepped through.

"Do you know about... the mural?" I heard him from the living room.

"I know what I saw. What do you know about it?"

He began talking, and he really, actually sounded broken up about something, but I suspected it was me not liking his gallery show of Constructivist paintings. I stood near the door and listened.

"Look, Samantha and I dated for a few months. I admit I thought it might turn into something. She was into my body. And, I know, she didn't like my painting. But she was an animal in bed. I asked enough times. What about my work don't you like? I mean, come on." He shook his head, it really bothered him. I came a little farther into his house and he looked over at me from his couch from behind his hair. "What did you think of my show, really? Did you like any of it? Just be honest with me. Be bluntly honest."

"Ok I will. Your painting's all form, no substance. All the thinking's on the surface, and there's not much of it, and what there is I've seen before. The colors are obvious and tedious. It's compositionally trite. You named each painting after a violent historical episode. The Netflix subscription is called *Armenian Genocide.* I can't go into *all* the different things that make it horrible. We've only got the afternoon."

He'd stopped listening. He sat on one side of his little living room and gazed at the other side where a window framed a deck and then dome dunes with seagulls and a cloud.

"I'm just like anyone," he told me. "I try to figure out what people like, then paint it."

"That's all? Just figure out what they like. And paint it. Presto, you're the next master of light and shadow?"

"If only. Would you say the Manders House piece was your favorite?"

"Yeah, they're all my favorites. Let's talk about your dead girlfriend."

He nodded, more polite now that we'd discussed some of his paintings.

"Ok, well," he continued, thinking back, "we were getting closer, it was hot and heavy. One night we made out in her office, then went back to my house, not here, and in the morning I took her back to the Klimt—and the mural was *there*. She couldn't see it. It was so horrible! All Higher, mostly *compulsion*, in my style! I didn't paint it. It just appeared on her walls *in a few hours*. Like magic. I'm telling you, it freaked me out!"

"You didn't paint it."

"No!"

"What happened then?"

"I ran! I know a setup when I see it. I'm being set up. That mural was *compulsion!* You saw it? Who *knows* what that could do to a person? And now she killed herself! The mural was in *my style*!"

I wanted to point out that it wasn't his style, it was some Russian's style, which was a lot of what was wrong with it to begin with. But then we'd probably get into a thing. I tried to focus on less important points.

"What about the black eye and the knife? They're so specific, they have to mean something."

"I have no idea!" He staggered over to the window letting in the seagulls and threw it open, then reached behind the couch to draw up a pack of thin Indian cigarettes and lit one. All that so he could tremble softly and lean outside and blow pollution.

"I'm not supposed to smoke in here," he said. "I guess you won't tell anyone."

The place was packed with canvases and not much else. A few sticks of furniture. An antique clock on the mantle. The canvases I thought might be the ones I hadn't seen in his loft at the Klimt. He'd moved all his materials to the beach, together a studio hideaway here. Laying very low, it seemed to me. Out of the public eye. I doubted the paintings could have been the object of the loft search, though. They were of the same quality as the stuff in his show, constructivist presentations of pop and meme images. Not something anyone searched very hard for. Not inside a tube of paint.

These pieces all had plenty of Higher color along with visible spectrum, the same as his work at the gallery. I decided it was time to finish what I'd come for. Tobias started a small stream of consciousness coming out of his mouth, and as he did I got over behind his work in progress, a painting of Andy Warhol as Stalinist propagandist. I stood there like I was interested in it, so it blocked me from his view.

"I'm telling you," I heard him muse, as I started to work on the piece. I peeked around, just to check in, to find him determining how well the light was catching the muscles on his forearm, and he looked back at me once over it, but mostly he wanted to leave me alone to admire his painting. "I didn't paint that mural. You said your sister liked my work. Lady Damely's my patron! I'm going to get my own gallery by the time I'm 50. Who's your sister?"

"Amy Gale," I said, into one of his pauses.

"You're Amelia Gale's brother? You were famous. What was it, something weird about your painting, is that you? You used to *rock* Gala Lumina, now I remember. You could have had patronage at eight or something."

"Right. And look at me now. It's a cautionary tale. So, reassure me, Tobias, all the Higher color on your canvases, all the stuff in your show, that's as High as you go, right? Up to *farewell*?"

"You used to be a star."

"Can you see *bleed*?" I lifted the easel holding his Warhol and turned the whole thing around so he could view it from his couch, which made him nervous because apparently this picture was a really good one. He glared at me, but was tied down by a cigarette requiring a window and the pose which showed off his calves.

"Tell me about the giant smiley face," I said, pointing at the sloppy smiley face I'd painted on top of Andy Warhol.

He squinted at me. He squinted at his picture. "What are you talking about?" He couldn't see it. I was very sure. Nobody's that good a liar. If he could *see* what I'd just done to his masterpiece he'd have gone ballistic.

"Did you notice the mural in Samantha's office were full-spectrum?" I asked him. "All the way to *bleed?*"

"No. How would I notice that?"

"Right. You can't see *bleed,* can you? I mean, you didn't use any in your paintings at the Nagato, but that could just have been cleverness. But now I've met you and we can rule out cleverness. And now we've ruled out *bleed,* and basically ruled you out for painting the mural."

I turned his painting back the way I'd found it.

"Be careful," he snarled, "that took me three days! It's my best one yet!"

"So who's setting you up, painting things to look like you did it?"

"How should I know? It could be *anyone.*" I really did get the sense that he suspected most of the people he knew of planning his demise. But also, maybe he had someone more specific in mind. His eyes shifted around to focus on the curve of his biceps. It was to distract me. I can't claim I minded, though this really wasn't the time.

"Someone searched your studio," I told him. "They went through everything. They looked inside tubes of paint. Do you know what they were looking for?"

"How should I know? It could've been *anything.*" It seemed to me he might have some more specific idea of what the loft searchers had been after, from how he worked the distracting bicep. And the muss of the hair. The slant of the firm buttock. He'd told me everything I was going to hear, and he'd moved on to seduction.

"If that's all you've got," I said, moving toward the door, "I'll let the police handle it from here."

"Are you going to report me? As a suspect? I didn't do anything! I really liked Samantha, she was going to help me get a gallery!" He narrowed his eyes. He undid his pose, since I wasn't biting on it, and he put bitter on his face. "I've been persecuted my whole life. But I'm not taking this from you, not you or anyone else, not anymore. Get out!"

I paused at the door.

"One last question," I said.

"No. Leave. No, wait! Will you join my email list? You can get the info on my upcoming shows."

"I have too much info already. But tell me this—do you know anything about a cup, with holes all around it? Something Samantha might have had?"

"What are you talking about?"

That was it for my questions. I threw out an observation, for variety. "And I bet you've never seen a ghost."

"Oh man, I *wish*."

That much was true, it seemed to me, though I bet he'd change his mind if it ever happened to him. I left the tube of *bleed* behind, mostly empty now. It was more painting than I'd done in ten years, and it'd sickened me.

CHAPTER
SIXTEEN

I put a few twenties on the bar and Serena started a seltzer and lime. The arrangement was, unless I asked for something else, I got water, to prevent accidental alcoholism. Finger painting with Tobias had left something in my mouth wanting carbonate to wash away.

Serena's tailored yellow top worked pretty well with some patrons to encourage tips, but that was her only concession to the pleasantries of bar commerce. The half of her head that wasn't crew cut wore its hair kelp green. Her fingernails were many colored organizations of maximum discord. She wore an apron with a drunken parrot and she was tired of everything you were about to say but if you forced her to, sure, she'd listen, which usually kept you from saying it. But I'd had a long day.

"You like your job, Serena?" She put the seltzer in front of me.

"Joy overwhelms me sometimes."

"Well, you're here bartending, not fishing or driving a school bus. So."

"Are we really doing life stories tonight Ash?"

"People have mysteries. Not me. But everyone else, unexplained things. Like Stipends for instance. Does everyone have one? Listen, Serena, you're not in Skysill Beach on any kind of Stipend are you? A secret bartender Stipend?"

"Sure. In the bartender cult we call it *minimum wage* because we've got no imagination."

"So let's say you were a psychic girl, dealing blackjack in Carson City, and someone offered you a Stipend to come live here and do it, be psychic... would you?"

"Ask the girl. Leave me out of it. It's better for everybody."

"I understand. Have you ever seen a ghost?"

"Ash, I'm getting you a bigger lime, you need vitamin C."

Serena sliced one and dropped it, good as her word, then left me. I watched new bubbles gasping out of my tumbler, the jukebox played a hit, I drew out Samantha's green-tipped office key which I'd last seen pressed under a set of smooth pink fingernails, where it looked much better, and also got out Samantha's keyring, where it usually lived.

Setting simple goals encourages a healthy self-image. That's what I've been told. So on my way from Tobias' beach shack I'd set myself a simple goal of seltzer and slowly working a Higher painted key back on a coiled ring so it hung alongside the other keys, and later getting the entire collection back to the father of the dead former owner.

I did manage to get the key back on the ring. Then I lost track of my goal. I got more seltzer. I felt confusion. Then my phone rang. I put it on the bar and stabbed the call open.

"What?" I complained. "I'm kind of in the middle of something Amelia."

"You're at The Charles," she said. That was true. I had nothing to add. "How *is it?*"

"Yes, look, what do you need? Because I kind of have my hands full right now." I lifted my lime with both hands to stay technically between the lines.

"You're not doing anything important." I could see her picturing me in her mind. “You just lifted up a glass with your hands didn’t you?”

“A lime. God damn it what do you want?”

“Asher Gale, you watch your mouth!” I couldn’t tell where she was, but nowhere public. She wasn’t using her compassion-for-Asher voice, which was the one I preferred. “Did you or did you not come to *my opening* the other night freaking out because you were seeing *ghosts*? Did that happen? Because, sur*prise*, it’s a concern to me. Considering your history. So I, your sister, who loves you, and is calling to see if you are continuing to have a *problem*, and if there’s anything that needs to be *done* about it!”

I tried doing unspoken apologetic shame by not speaking, but she wasn’t interested.

“*Is* there anything that needs to be done?” she insisted.

“No. I’m sorry, Ames. You know how I get at the bar.”

“You’re a shit.”

“I’m sorry. I know. Hey, I think you’re a *brilliant* painter by the way.”

“That makes you a shit with decent taste, that’s all, but apology accepted.” Ames never freights the anger around to make a point. She likes accepting apologies as soon as possible, keeping our relationship perfectly balanced.

“Listen,” she said, “something funny happened after you left my show. There’s this lady, I guess you met her, Veronica Night—”

“Yeah. How do you know her?”

“I’ll tell you later. She was asking about Mom and Dad. Mostly Mom. And she said she talked to you. I probably... look, since *you* were asking about Mom and Dad, too, I wondered if it was connected. To your ghosts. Because I’m worried about you seeing ghosts.”

“*Ghost.* One ghost, Amelia. Veronica Night just has too much time on her hands, and blood too probably if you checked under her fingernails, just ignore her.”

“Ash, you should give her a chance. She can be sweet.”

"What? Like a Snickers with a razor blade. How well do you know her?"

"You're so *judgmental.* Give other people a little room to swing their elbows. No one's perfect."

"Well that's true, and here's a question I didn't ask the other night—why don't you hate Tobias Singlebee and everything he paints? Or even, just, everything he paints?"

She gave the question more time than I thought it deserved.

"Maybe if you knew his story. The context," she said. "He doesn't like to talk about it."

"Context is not going to change his paintings."

"Asher, the world's not black and white. Oh my god! You're impossible. I have to go. But I want you to call me if you see a new *something* that's not really there. Do you promise?"

I promised with a clear conscience, since technically I hadn't seen a new ghost just the same one a few different times, and then I was cast free into the land of *brothers who are a lot of extra work.* I took the chance to listen to more jukebox, feel air on my neck from fans, the buzz of human industry around me, and get another water and more citrus, and eat some peanuts. Finally I looked at my keyring of accomplishment on the bar and I dialed Waylon.

"There you are!" shouted Waylon. I tried putting the phone farther away on the bar but the effect wasn't better. "Do you know how many times I've called?"

"No. I have your number blocked."

"Answer when I call!"

"Waylon."

"Come up to the property! Who do you think you are?"

So many answers for that came to me so tightly grouped that I almost fainted, but Waylon was still a grieving father who I should feel sympathy for, even if I didn't like him, so I skipped his question.

"Waylon," I asked him, "did you ever see Samantha with a cup that had holes in it?"

"Is this a joke? I don't have time for your god damn - "

"Fine, okay," I interrupted, "then tell me about the man with the black eye and the big knife."

That was just blind arm-waving in the dark. It was all I had left.

"What man with a black eye?" he demanded. "What are you talking about?"

"What did the man, with the black eye, have to do with Samantha?"

"How should I know? Is this something you found? Asher? Did your investigation find something?"

"Just grief so far."

"The police called! They broke into my place on Bluebell Lane last night!"

"Who did?"

"How should I know? The police asked about *you*! Something about, there was an office of Samantha's, and you were there—why are they asking *me* about you? What are you dragging me into, Asher? What—"

Amelia would have been proud of the elbow room I gave Waylon as I hung up on him. My plan to give him Samantha's keys got rescheduled. I thought I'd keep them another day. But I was really just arm-waving again.

"You doing all right?" Serena asked, toweling around me and nodding at my water.

"I'll need more carbonation and lime," I said. She lifted my tumbler and pinned down my napkin, and I said, "There are true things, and *not* true things. Am I right, Serena? Context is bullshit."

"I'll bring you *three* limes. And a little umbrella. That's all I got."

An actual investigator would have had all the pieces they'd found puzzled together by now, but all I seemed to do was add puzzle pieces. Unfortunately I seemed to be the only person on the case. Selected by ghostly decree. I sighed.

Samantha had committed suicide, I felt confident about that piece of the puzzle. She'd probably done it because a *compulsion* mural had appeared on her walls—in just a few hours time, according to Tobias. I had no clue how the mural had gotten there, since Tobias hadn't painted it. I had no clue *why* it was put there. But Samantha had died because of it. And then *dominion* had turned her into a ghost. I had no idea about the ghost either.

Maybe the ghost had painted the mural. Except that the mural had basically brought the ghost into existence when it had made Samantha kill herself. This ghost didn't seem like a ghost who moved enough to pull off a mural anyway. And I wanted to stop calling it a ghost but I couldn't think of anything else.

And then there was the problem of fitting the Brazilians into the puzzle. Why break into Tobias *and* Samantha's rooms at the Klimt?

And Caroline. With her Stipend. And how I kept picturing her standing close to me, a very suspicious and pleasurable thing to picture. Something irregular was going on there. Just like everywhere else.

CHAPTER SEVENTEEN

The Bradley Building had grown on me by this time with its practical red brick and glassed great lakes facade, encouraging me to come and go as I pleased because that activity was clearly none of the Bradley's business. I enjoyed pressing up one and then another and the last broad flat step before its door, the sensible lobby with mirrors and hydrangeas. I liked everything except the office in it, wearing my name, but the office had things I needed.

While I stood at the elevator I read the push board to see who Asher Gale shared his floor with. There was a financial consultant, a tea importer, a shoe distributor and a Hawaiian travel agency. Skysill was a strange town for an agency doing fruit drinks and beaches, Skysill had too many of those already. Why not specialize in mountains or caves? Maybe the owner was not a person who liked anything different.

As I reached that conclusion the elevator arrived, and at the same time across the lobby the front door opened and Phil, in different Hawaiian shorts but the same eagle forehead as before and the same glasses, eased in, butt first. He balanced a tray of pineapple wedges with toothpicks, and the tray was covered in plastic wrap which was lifting away in the breeze of turning to see me.

"Hey, hooo-old that!" he yodeled. He kept the wrap down with his extra hand and tilted the tray toward me across the lobby as the pineapples shifted and the plastic wrap danced around. It had a lot of drama. The only thing missing was a unicycle. I held the door to see how it was going to end.

He was out of breath beside me as the doors closed, and didn't seem at all daunted by the leg of the journey still ahead. A line of perspiration came off his temple.

"Asher Gale, authentication and investigation, right?" he said.

I nodded. "Phil. Skysill's Only Hawaiian Vacations?"

"Yep," he said.

"How's the Bradley family today?"

"Excellent," he held his thumb up to show me, and his tray tipped since he'd been using the thumb to hold it up. A pineapple wedged to the floor. Phil didn't notice. He thought things were still going his way.

The doors opened, I stepped onto Asher Gale's floor and I held the door for Phil. He charged out. I thought he should give up the cellophane, for the good of the pineapples, but he thought he had it covered. I stood and watched as he bobbed toward his door. He was ninety percent gangle, but it looked like he was going to pull it off. Then he turned.

"Hey," he called, "there were two homeless guys waiting outside your office earlier. Just loitering."

"Loitering?" It didn't sound good, when Phil said it. "Did either of them have a black eye?"

"No, they were Mexicans or something."

"Two?"

"Yeah. They looked like they smelled."

"Looked like it. But you didn't get close enough to be sure?"

"Yeah, they looked like it, why would I get close?"

"Did they both wear suits, by chance? Tailored to fit them

because they were wide?" An Investigator thought. One of these was going to pay off.

"Oh yeah."

"What were they doing while they waited?"

"On their cell phones."

"They were two homeless men wearing suits and using cell phones waiting for me?"

"I chased them off."

"I'm not surprised to hear it. You know, they might have been customers? Not mine, since I don't take any. But customers sometimes have suits and phones."

"Oh, you're so naive," he said, quietly disappointed, so at least I had something familiar, "these homeless guys are all foreigner looking, just like these two, and they get suits from the shelter, and then they try to go into our restaurants. They come in and use our bathrooms. These two weren't customers. I did us all a favor, you should pay me."

"My sister has a theory," I told him after a moment's thought, "but I don't know. Do you think there's some context that explains you?"

"I don't follow."

"I know, right? I'm trying to put your behaviors into context. Explain to me the homeless thing."

"It's not a *thing*. They'll take everything we have if we let them. You watch."

"And what's the context that makes you say that?"

"The context is they're *failures*, the context is it's *obvious*."

"And scene. Thank you for your participation."

"You're welcome."

He lurched back down the hall and at his door he yelled and kicked and it was opened from the inside. The next time I talked to Amelia I'd be sure to share my examples of giving people room to swing their elbows. I turned back to Asher Gale's door.

Seeing Phil kick his door made me think of the wide, wide Brazilians and their propensity for kicking. I dialed up the saturation. The green of the carpet pulsed microbe-orange-green, and showed a million stains, splattered watermelons, filth and sun, which would take very special janitorial services to *see* and clean. And when I looked at Asher Gale's door I saw heavy boot prints around the knob; big, rat-black skids where someone had failed to shatter the lock, and then decided to loiter, and make a few innocent phone calls. Maybe Phil had something after all.

I didn't know what it meant, other than pointing to Waylon spending a lot of money on quality front doors. I keyed myself into the office and closed the door and locked it.

It was all the same in there, gentle sunlight bouncing off coastal hills, chairs patient in the sun, a glass and steel desk where my cards had scattered the time I'd proved my identity to Felicia. I took a few of the cards, in case I needed to convince any of Hennessy's friends about me. Unused space stretched back behind the desk to the back of the room. Asher Gale could generate extra money holding yoga classes back there. The room felt lopsided, from an empty/full perspective, but what held the entire space together were the forgeries hung along the walls. Two dozen or more. Asher Gale might not have accomplished much in his life, aside from occasional feats with keys, but what legacy he did have, it hung in that reception room.

Felicia had closed the frosted door to the main office when she'd left—assuming she had left. Who could take anything for granted these days? When I looked I found the inner office empty except for built-in cherry bookcases and an admiral's desk and an admiral's globe and the millionaire rugs and chairs where people like Felicia could cry and wait while the admiral thought about things.

The envelope was where I'd repacked it. It lay full of pictures and notes and cards on my desk. I undid the brads and emptied everything across the admiral's deep olive blotter. I used my fingers to push the papers around. All I had was Felicia's first name, but there were new questions to ask her, and I didn't know where to find her. This pile of Samantha Goodman had seemed like my best bet.

In no time I raised a page from a calendar book, by a corner, and found a Felicia contact. Felicia Su.

Felicia lived a short way up Skysill Canyon, and I planed up from the ocean toward her, a day at the edge of autumn, of high sun but ready for cooler weather. When the weather got wet the houses in the Canyon drained the surrounding foothills into the Pacific, washing our coast away. If you went all the way to the back of the Canyon it turned into a nature conservatory, where endangered grass and an endangered lizard lived, and hawks to eat the lizards, but closer to the sea in Felicia's neighborhood the trees were imported and flowering, and the lizards were replaced by many, many dogs. People walked them, they announced themselves from porches. Felicia's place was squirreled up a little lane stabbing the canyon wall called El Toro Way.

Realtors listing the place would show it nestled under its elms, behind leafy lawn, against a hillside, and include the tin windmills and hummingbird feeders. But I doubted the realtors would mention the fire terror chaparral dry-packed onto the slope directly above the house. Felicia's place on El Toro struck me like a fresh match in a smoker's lounge. It was only a matter of time.

I pointed my car back down El Toro, in case of conflagration, and followed the brick walkway toward the glass-paned front door, and ducked a wind chime to get to the doorbell. My fingers did a job crushing Felicia's envelope. I crewcut my color and it made me grimace more than many people would call typical. But I would ask them, typical of who?

There was nothing to see but dim shadow through the panes in the door so it shocked me when the door swung in. I saw Felicia, alone in the dark, more face than body, seeing herself answering her door from somewhere. Her forlorn deluged out the doorway, like water from a broken dam.

"Hi, um, Felicia," I said. It was worse than I'd expected. "Hi. You left these at the office. My office. I'm Asher Gale."

I held the envelope. She wasn't blinking, I thought we could drift into a silent standoff unless one of us did something, then she seemed to realize she was standing in her open door and I was outside. It surprised her.

"Leave it," she said and pointed at the ground. I set it down. I could see behind her a dark living room where large furniture pieces, with lace on cushion tops, grazed motionless. There was a grandfather clock, without lace, against the back wall, ticking dust.

"That's not the reason I came," I said. "I have a question. It's about Samantha." At the sound of Samantha's name Felicia came back to our conversation.

"The thing is, Samantha's father had me checking on what happened, and now something's come up a few times. So, did Samantha ever say anything to you about a man with a black eye? With a long knife, like a hunting knife or - "

She threw the door behind her and stepped up close so I was looking down onto her pale, damp forehead, at her eyes, and she spoke.

"How could you possibly know about him?"

"So Samantha knew him?"

"Knew him?"

"I mean... did she?"

Felicia went back into her house and flicked the door all the way open, so I went in. I brought the envelope because it would never get inside on its own, I saw that. Felicia stood by the standup clock and started speaking, though not in my direction. She gave her furniture the soliloquy it'd been asking for.

"I was in Italy when I met Sam. In Rome. Teaching English. There was a show at the Palazzo dei Conservatori, I don't usually go to museums. I did that time. I'll always remember, it was a showcase of ancient glassworks. I heard her talking. She had the most perfect accent." She looked away from her couch, which had heard it before, to me. "Did you know she was fluent in Italian, French, Russian and Latin? *Latin*. Do you know anyone who's fluent in Latin?"

I let her know I didn't by saying nothing.

"I guess it was love at first sight. It was the last thing I was looking for. That's when you find it, that's what they say, isn't it?" I nodded that it was, exactly. "We spent six months in Rome while she did post doc research on her Diatreta. In the evenings we drank, and ate, and went for these walks together, there was a park in the Monteverde Vecchio... then there came a day when, where she had to go home. You see, Samantha had nightmares."

"Nightmares," I encouraged, if you could call it that.

"Yes. Almost every night. Though not at first. That's what made her fall for me, I think. I used to be... I used to be funny. I made her laugh. When she first stayed with me in Rome the nightmares went away. So I didn't even know she had them. But it wasn't long, then they started coming back. She'd struggle, yell in her sleep. Finally she left her research, and we came here. To Skysill where she grew up.

"And it took her two years to tell me. I'm the only person she *ever* told. The *only* person, not even campus police, *nobody*. It happened when she was an undergrad. She'd been at Stanford a few months. It was late, she'd been at the library. She was walking across campus, and was assaulted, she... she told me about it finally. Once, when she woke up screaming and tearing her skin. Afterward I asked her to talk to someone. I wanted her to get help. Sometimes I think that made it worse..."

"Did she know the man who assaulted her?"

"No. Just a man with a black eye. He had a serrated kind of knife, she said... it was an image that almost never left her mind. The image of that horrible man."

She leaned back, she hoped the wall was behind her and it was. She was tired. I guess she hadn't slept. She let the wall slide her down, so she was hunched on her heels.

"How could you know about him?" she said. She wasn't crying but she was still making tears, rivers of tears that she seemed not to notice, and I felt the room was getting dense with dangerous triggers. I was ready for Felicia to stop talking, but she wouldn't. "I feel like, if I hadn't asked, if she'd never told me, maybe she'd still be alive. She wanted us to fit together. She wanted to confront it, for me. But I know she only told me. How do you know about it? How?"

Her eyes were hollowed remorse and accusation. And I saw it was such a bad idea, why I'd come. I felt something coming up in me, the *Gray* or a *chromatic* mania. I staggered back, forgot what Felicia's question had been. I still wanted to ask her about goblets with holes and about Tobias, and painting, and find out more about the black-eyed man and maybe even ask about ghosts. But instead, because I'm prudent, I fled.

In my car I sat garroting the steering wheel and I grappled myself and got in deep breaths. I took a couple minutes doing that. Then, when I thought I'd squeezed myself together, I went to turn the key, but found my fingers wrapped on the steering wheel, refusing to open. They tightened.

I sat in front of Felicia's tinderbox of despair and pulled every trick I knew, but the *chroma storm* rolled me over. This one felt different. Thicker. Empowered, purposeful. Slow and gripping, like syrup, something sticky covered it all. *Dominion.*

"No, *no,*" I heard the words grate out. The Higher color came in streamers. The giddy breeze of it. The beginning where passion burned, where color spread and was amazing. *Fantastic.* But quickly there came the fear, Felicia's despair and mine and the sadness of the ones you loved going away, those feelings were vast and various and they came in battering winds right alongside the Higher rainbow, from under me, filling the car, the air. The rainbow expanded, tore and *stormed.*

Don't go away, stay on the street, here in the car, I told myself. Make normal stay real. Stay in the car. The backs of my hands—I *saw,* I made myself concentrate, the backs of two hands on a wheel, with the veins pulp blueberry jam in ribbons under knuckle dunes of wheat yellow ocher peach flesh and a mind-stretching thin, it made me laugh, so *beautiful,* and a mole, on my wrist, crystal wheeling hungry shades of brown chocolate rotting lemon and the *sorrow.* I felt myself sob, belly to lips, blubbering.

Dominion ruled it all. I was, myself, made of color—I was *not* made of color—I was made of color, made of it over and over and *dominion* ranged in all the spaces between the other Colors. Created the Colors. *Dominion,* the canvas and the painter and the viewer, wanted me. It wanted me to come somewhere. I wondered, was it getting back at me, for the exorcism I'd tried with it in the *Gray?* I had a wild thought that *dominion* knew about the *Gray.* And didn't like it.

cross your eyes

Far away from where I was *storming* deep wild, lost on journeys unlike any before, I heard *cross your eyes, cross your eyes.*

It was me. I was saying it. My eyes didn't want to. They wanted to *see.* They wanted to *see* everything, because *dominion* wanted everything *seen.* Outside the car it flashed and ran in cascades off the roofs and fountained out of trees and then I was afraid and I had a premonition. An Investigator idea, that if I went all the way and *stormed* to the limit and passed out, I would never be the same. There would be terrible consequences *storming* to the end of my mind, very very bad. *Dominion* yearned for something.

But you can't yearn something out of me. I'm a person who doesn't have anything. That's well established.

On my right were a thousand horses. I had to pull them with the strength of that eye. On my left were a thousand more. My left eye pulled those. It wasn't impossible. Humans built pyramids and shot people to the moon. *Dominion* didn't like me even trying. *Dominion* surged. The car, full, the steering wheel glowed like 4th of July sparklers, my hands were in it, my body a conduit. But microns ticked, an eyelash, a milli-fraction, I squeezed both pupils toward each other. There came the sound of screaming. It might have been me.

Suddenly someone turned off the color TV. The *storm* cut out.

How about that? A *chroma storm* with Highers where I didn't pass out.

I couldn't have said how long I sat in my car with my head back and my jaw locked and my eyes crossed, but I kept it up, just for safety, just to make sure the *storm* was dead. Maybe only a few minutes. Or maybe twenty-four hours plus a few minutes. I got my colors down, streamlined and boxed in. After that I was a little trembly, but I thought I could drive.

My throat hurt, possibly from shrieking. But emotionally the stakes were Sunday morning placid because I held the colors flat, and I planned to keep them that way. Later I'd sit on my stool at The Charles and decide if this new style of *chroma storm*, where *dominion* seemed to have a hand in the outcome, meant anything. I took a slow drive out of Skysill Canyon and distracted myself from my achy throat by poking at the ideas I'd gathered from Felicia, while at the same time I avoided thinking about Felicia at all, in her house bent in sorrow on her floor. Sometimes it gets very finely calibrated in me. I don't know how I do it.

So Samantha had told someone about her long ago campus assault, despite what Felicia thought. And that someone, or someone else, had somehow painted those images on all four of her office walls in the space a few hours, in *compulsion,* to backdoor them into her brain in a nightmares feedback loop, and finally drive her to suicide. That's how she'd gotten Higher paint on her hands. Under her fingernails. She'd been rubbing the walls, unable to see, unable to know, but still, somehow, *knowing.* Knowing hadn't helped.

It was pretty straightforward as an explanation, but I knew it left a lot of questions, like *how* the mural had magically appeared, and *why* someone would want to do it to her in the first place. I thought it might have something to do with the goblet she was holding. That goblet had to mean something.

And my straightforward explanation didn't come near the really important question. The personal one. So far, no one else had admitted to seeing ghosts. The psychics in town denied ghosts existed at all. Tante Celine would have told me if my parents had passed me ghost sensitivity, she'd love to help me explain my insanity. So. What was left? There was the city itself. Maybe Skysill Beach was haunted. I knew next to nothing about the town I'd grown up in.

I'd skipped high school civics classes so I'd have time to throw up and lose consciousness, which really needs plenty of time. I never made it on the Historical Society field trips.

The Historical Society was still there though. On PCH, where the tourists could see it and lose interest. Maybe the society had dioramas of famous Skysill apparitions haunting their victims. Veronica had made me think about the history of the town, and my questions about its *sighted* population. What was Skysill Beach the capital of? I tried to remember. Not authenticity or self-awareness, not honesty. Maybe ghosts.

The slope descending the Canyon was gentle. My car had begun making strange noises when I went around corners, so I took it easy. The places I still had to go would be no better than the place I already was, so there was no hurry. I played a game pitting friction and inertia against the stop signs, and I took time to appreciate the settled conventions of the homes I passed. The car slow-rolled a succession of dogs on the lookout, then slipped me past a bike tipped onto the sidewalk in front of a white picket fence. Behind a little gate in the fence were rose bushes circling a sweep of grass, and in the middle of the grass was a tree with a swing and on the swing sat my friend Peter.

Finding a shady parking spot was simple. Once the car was off I peered back through the rear glass, then stepped out and onto the sidewalk. The air smelled like summer fruit, the breeze sweet mint, and along the fence fell a waterfall of shade. It wasn't hard to see why Peter might drop his bike here, push on a few gates, and wander into the first yard with a tree and a swing.

He looked peaceful and I stood and watched from my side of his fence over the top of a spread of pink roses. Peter spoke to his hands in a gentle voice while they listened on his lap, and he twitched his toes up and dragged them through the grass as he swung, a little in the sun and a little in the shade, not breaking anything or threatening anyone, just trespassing. A porch overlooked the swing, and behind that scowled a split-level ranch house that was pretty certainly going to want its unobstructed view back, sooner rather than later.

"Hey Peter," I called, pitching my voice low. "Hey."

His head came up gracefully, but very slowly, like a man pulling his long hair from the tar pits. "I might have gone to Rio," he told me in his basso profundo. His beard strings shifted a little in the breeze of his swing. His eyes were caramelized yellow. He looked at me like I was the first other person on his island in many years. "It was dinosaurs and mud, and then," he looked up, into his tree, "they talked about the monorail."

"Peter, come out of there," I said. He held his palms toward me.

"I want to wash windows."

"Yeah. Okay. Come out of those peoples' yard."

"Let's all get drunk on the past, where our mothers are living rain dancers."

Sometimes my conversations with Peter went like this, like lighthouse poetry in luminous circles, round and round, shining up ragged landscapes of true. He contributed all the true, I was nothing but an audience, but he seemed to value my contribution. Still, there was a time for poetry and a time for not having the police take you out of a stranger's swing. A path of pavers ran from the gate over to the swing. It kept me from getting lost as I crossed to Peter's tree. I cast a quick look at the disapproving roofline above us, and waved Peter toward the street.

"Come on, someone might take your bike," I motivated him, pointing.

"Do you live here, here in these ballroom laundromats?" he asked.

"I'm just passing through. Come on.."

"The dead eye is here, please eat my swing," he said, but he didn't get up. Maybe he wanted me in his lap. I took him by the arm and urged and then semi-forced him so he got started toward the gate, and once we were both on the sidewalk I latched it shut.

"You have someplace you can go?" I asked him.

He smiled, a sudden and genuine grin. "Oh, man," he said. He nodded. I grinned back. It was okay.

"Good," I said. Then I remembered. "Wait," I pulled one of Asher Gale's cards out. "Here's the address I was talking about, the office you can stay in. Hold on."

He drifted along with me as I got to my car, and from the passenger seat grabbed a pen, and on the back of Asher Gale's card wrote my own cell number and crossed out the office number so there'd be no confusion. He put the card in his pants without looking at it.

"Call the number on the back, call me anytime. Let me know if you want to stay at... " Peter never stopped smiling as he lifted his bike and put his leg over the seat. He started to laugh. He gave me a thumbs up then wheeled away down the street, out of shadow, into sunlight, then back, whisking toward the beach, cackling.

CHAPTER EIGHTEEN

Skysill Canyon Blvd dropped after that, in a twisting line, enjoying its final slalom to the sea, which soon glittered into view. PCH formed the intersection. The Historical Society building was less than a mile up the coast, and Mexico was ninety miles the other way. Me in the middle, with a car I suddenly felt very nervous having to turn in *any* direction. The noise was like bad karaoke now, a loud, enthusiastic drone. I couldn't just roll the car into the ocean, though, so I babied it right, and it screamed that it was being murdered. People looked. Between me and the Historical Society, I noted Arroyo Automotive.

Bill Andrews at Arroyo has a showpiece mustache that puffs when he's disbelieving you about maintenance you claim you've done to your car. He has bad knees and one speed, but he has the immaculate fingernails of a concert pianist, because he's religious about his latex gloves. When I crash landed my car in his lot he used his single speed to ease out under his bay door and stare, then start his mustache on me.

"Bill," I said, coming out of the car.

"Ash," he nodded, skeptical. "What'd you do to my car?"

"Nothing as far as I know," I told him.

"Em hm," he said and wandered near. He ungloved. We shook hands. Then he turned and looked at the hood. He did not move to open it. He did not look enthusiastic.

"You heard it?" I asked.

"Yep. I got a Canadian brother heard that. You missed your oil change."

"That's not true. And this noise just started fifteen minutes ago."

"Em hm."

"Can you look?"

He pulled contemplative air in above his mustache and it made a cavernous whistle, and ran mechanic calculations through his mind he didn't share with me. Then he said, "Yep. Leave it. Come back in two hours."

Two hours was an hour and a half more than I'd need to rule out ghosts at the Historical Society, even including ten minute walk each way. So since Bill had no magazines for me to read while I waited, I thought I'd go up, but walk very slowly.

The Skysill Beach Historical Society was kept in a little adobe hall peeking out behind a drought-tolerant plant scape; crushed granite, giant aloe snarls, cactuses and serrated palms within a grass fringe and separated from the sidewalk so the snakes and tortoises in the neighborhood could have a park. The building pushed out a portico and a medieval wooden door with a grilled speakeasy. A fortress door, to fend off the tortoises.

Inside it smelled like historical oxygen and lemon and terra cotta dust. When the door closed it was silent and gave the impression of a place surprised to have a visitor. I guessed history wasn't as popular as it had once been. Immediately to my right an alcove asked history seekers to sign the visitor registry. I fingered the pen, just to look like I wasn't doing what I was doing, which was casing the place for mannequins draped in sheets and other ghost paraphernalia. There didn't seem to be any.

Beyond the alcove the hall split into three little arched doorways, with elegant script above each. One read, *The Fenestram Legacy,* another read *Skysill Beach - A Planned Community,* and the last, *The Gala Lumina.* I could see into each domed room from where I stood. Nothing even remotely ghost themed.

I checked the open registry, where tourists had provided names and places of origin and dates of visits, and there weren't many. I began to think this visit was not the wise use of time I'd hoped, when a thin throat cleared behind me—someone had gotten behind me?—and I turned.

"Welcome," said an elderly man of mouse bone wrapped in a half ounce of flesh. He wore a tailored cranberry shirt, a violet tie, buckled pants the color and texture of a Van Gogh sunflower, which set off skin the black of a raven's shadow. If he'd only had an apple pie and a hat he could have been a complete county fair. He smiled a smile that seemed genuinely happy to be used on me, though that almost never lasts.

Under normal circumstances I'd have flipped on the Highers to see if he was one of us. Makeup, a tattoo, a glowing ceramic tie clip. We like our little fetishes. But I'd had enough of Higher color for today.

"Are you interested in signing our register?" he asked. He had a funny way of barely moving his jaw when he talked. I got the idea he was saving energy.

"Not interested," I told him.

"May I ask why, young man?

"You just did."

I've always had a way with strangers. Not a winning way, I've been told. In my defense at that moment I was still fighting the effects of going *chromatic* and had mostly lost consciousness and bodily control less than an hour before. Even for me that's unusual.

The cranberry man laughed, like the two of us were sharing a joke. The laugh was pretty good. I heard the sound sail in from far away, and when it arrived I felt like I'd been embraced by bells. I wanted to hear it again.

"Very well," he said. "You will not be a part of our history. That is your absolute right."

"It's a paper trail thing. Identity thieves."

"Please say no more. It's the historian in me. We do like our records. I apologize for asking. I'm very rude."

"No, I'm the one who's rude."

"Whatever do you mean?"

"You have a nice museum but I'm not going to sign your book. It seems rude."

He nodded that it was a crystal clear explanation, maybe because he recognized a lost cause when he saw one. When I'm going around disappointing people there isn't any single clear explanation that accounts for it. I usually don't even look. I do know, from experience, that the best thing for everyone under these circumstances is a change of subject, then a quick escape.

"So..." I searched for a new subject, then pointed to the arch above the middle door, "Skysill Beach was a planned community, is that right."

"Oh, yes. Oh, indeed. From the very beginning. Come this way. Welcome to Skysill Beach, by the way. I hope you're enjoying your visit to our city. My name is Shelby."

"I can't stay. I'm Asher."

Shelby took me through the middle arch and started in on the Skysill highlights. The room was full of sepia photos and framed documents and a model of City Hall under glass. I wanted to put in four or five minutes demonstrating social grace before taking an emergency text and leaving without saying goodbye. But pretty soon Shelby laughed again, and after that he told me a joke about the mayor's wife from 1947, and then we just fell into it, like a couple of happy old historians watching Rome burn.

And *then* I realized the room was absolutely fascinating, despite a single mention of ghosts or hauntings of any kind.

If Shelby was to be believed—and by this time I had absolute confidence in everything he said because I'm given to wild swings like that and also because he answered questions with confidence but was happiest admitting things he didn't know, since those were things he could look up in his tomes some midnight—the Skysill Beach of present day lay exactly the way it had been conceived when it was incorporated in 1832 by Cosimo Fenestram. Commercial districts, gallery districts, residential districts, the way everything radiated out from the Skysill Civic Auditorium. One wall of the room had overlays of old planning documents superimposed on satellite images, and they cohered street by street, down to the yard.

He took me on a few historical side trips while he coached me through Skysill's history. The Fenestram Foundation that sponsored so much of Skysill's art, Fenestram Glass and Steel from which the Foundation sprang—one of the world's ten oldest companies, in existence since 400 AD in some form, now isn't *that* a fascinating tidbit young man? But I had to tune him out at some point, to turn an idea of my own in my mind a few times. Then I interrupted a story he was telling about the first Gala Lumina being held in a rainstorm—he really made you feel like he'd seen it all himself—and I offered my idea out loud.

"Shelby, sorry to interrupt, but this map," I said, and pointed to a photo where the Gallery District in downtown was merged with a historical planning map, which lined up exactly. "You don't have that original planning map around here, do you? That Skysill map?"

"Oh no," he said, showing off a little horror, just between us historians, like I'd asked if he left children locked in cars during heat waves. "That document is in a secure, climate controlled vault. Scholars can petition the arts committee to view it. They usually decline."

"No chance to see it?"

"It is being preserved."

So much for bright thoughts.

"Did you have a question about it?" he prodded.

"There was something on the other end of town I thought I'd check."

"Why not examine a *copy* of the map?"

I eyed him.

"You do have a copy?"

"Well of *course*."

I decided historians must have a blind spot around the reasons normal people valued maps, which was for help finding things—buried treasures, Home Depots—where historians apparently valued maps for their state of preservation.

"Shelby," I said, "could you share your copy of this planning document with me?"

He walked with me into his office and sat me in front of a broad, laminated white desk with an articulated lamp hung above, while he pulled out one drawer from a set of wide, thin trays, and slipped out a square yard of white paper which he laid in front of me and lit it with the lamp. We were historians right away.

The copy was of a hand-drawn, topographic city outline, in a precise architectural style, dated 1822, entitled SKYSILL BEACH MASTER PLAN *Aspectu Prime*. I oriented myself by finding my own street, Alta Loma Lane, exactly where it was today. Two hundred years ago someone had decided where Alta Loma Lane would go and what it would be called. Neighborhoods were labeled, Catalina Village and Skysill Canyon. The Stipend Houses were marked. From the Civic Auditorium radiated the labels of other sections, *Arts Districts* and *Commercial Tracts,* all chartered in 1822, all as currently and accurate as google maps.

My finger drove south along present-day Pacific Coast Highway, past where Asher Gale's office was, past the studio of Light and Shadow and Fenestram Color and Candy's Diner, and stopped where I'd last seen Samantha, out in front of Psychic Touch. It sat in the middle of tracts labeled *Mixed Use,* among a few *Residential* tracts outlined to the east and northeast. But the tract containing Psychic Touch was labeled *Sensus Simul (Viaticus)*. The tract Caroline had called the psychic district. There were no other *Sensus Simul* tracts in the city.

"What's *Sensus Simul?*" I asked.

"I'm the wrong historian for that question," he apologized, and seemed a little sad.

"Do you know any another historians I could ask?"

"At this point, there is only me," he said. "But these old maps are full of misspellings. It may be a mystery now, but someday, the meaning will be clear."

He seemed very certain. "Why do you say that?"

"It's the historian's viewpoint. That nothing is ever lost. The past will not stay silent forever. It wants to be heard." He tapped his chin then, remembering some more history. "You know, it's curious. You are the second person in a year who has asked to see this map. She was also interested in the *Sensus Simul* tract."

Now that *was* curious, I agreed, to myself. I wished I had a glass of water in my hand. Caroline had absolutely ruined me for doing this kind of thing without water.

"Who, now?" I grunted, in my way. "Who wanted to see the tract, the *Sensus Simul?*"

"She never told me her name."

"Could you describe her?"

"I excel at dates and times, young man, stories, relationships—histories, you understand. But I don't tend to remember things I see. Perhaps because appearances, historically speaking, are never relevant." He shrugged. I wanted to argue that appearances might be a big part of history, like the face that launched a thousand ships, it must have appeared fantastic, but arguing with him felt ungrateful.

"How about her date?" I asked. "Any idea, sort of, how long ago it was?"

He closed one eye and pointed the other at the ceiling and nodded his head a few times like his memories were a pleasant song he sang to himself. His violet tie bobbed.

"It was September 6th," he sang. "Of last year."

"Shelby, you're a prince. I think I'd like to sign your registry."

He walked me back out of his office and down to his alcove,

where he lifted his pen and gave me a gracious smile, and smoothed his tie. I took the pen down to the first blank line and signed and dated myself. Then I gave the pen back.

"Can I look at your book?" I asked. Shelby beamed. Nothing could have made him happier seeing a fellow researcher consulting a historical document. I flipped back through pages, checking dates, until I got to September, then to the beginning of September where I found the visitor on *6 Sept.* The entry was signed: *Veronica Night.* I looked up at Shelby. The scholar's connection we shared made him cast a quick glance down, where my finger pinned Veronica's signature.

"What does it mean?" he asked.

"I wish I knew. I'll admit it. I'm in over my head."

"Oh? I think not. No. A historian learns to trust his hunches." He then took a moment to hitch his cranberry pants up and settling them around his hips, then showed me his unblinking eyes. "And my hunch is, your head is very much above water."

"It's pretty vague, Shelby, isn't it? For a hunch?"

"That's how they come sometimes."

"Okay. You're the historian. Now it's time for me to go, I'll get my car from the shop, I'll arrange my hunches in a startling historical insight. If I write a paper I'll mention you."

"You know, you don't speak like a historian, but you would do well in historical circles."

"I don't know. I wear my welcome out pretty fast."

"You value the revelatory, and meaning, which are the historian's purview. Every generation's historians take the truth, and give it meaning anew."

"And is this still part of the hunch?"

"It is."

"And you're going to forget my face the second I leave, but remember when I came?"

"Yes. I hardly recognize you now. I have very bad eyes."

I reached to shake his hand and he returned me a studious grip. I rejoined the tortoises and lizards and went through the unkillable front yard, then hurried across the street. I held down an impulse to see if I was being followed, because that's the way Veronica was starting to make me feel—no, not followed; preceded. Was that better or worse? We seemed to be interested in too many of the same things. My mother. My town. My psychic friends.

More than two hours had passed while Shelby dissected Skysill for me. I realized I'd never even asked him about ghosts. Maybe it'd be worth another visit later, but it was time to get my car back. I had one more visit I wanted to get out of the way before the day got dark and other, better things occurred to me to do.

I saw that bay One held my car high on a hoist, and Bill, faced away from me, looked up at it on his craned neck, standing near the front tires, hands on hips and gloves pasted with grime. Just staring.

"Birds nest?" I asked, coming up beside him.

"Ash," he said. He pointed up past the driver's tire with one of his latex fingers.

"Did you find the problem?"

"The problem." He teeter-tottered around on his bad knees to lift five fingers. He folded them in succession. "No brake fluid. No steering fluid. No water in the radiator. Tranny oil tapped. And that." He pointed up over his shoulder, back under the driver's side tire.

"What's that?" I asked. He was going to make me ask everything, I saw it.

"Steering column."

"So something's wrong with my steering column?"

"Ash, a Plymouth's not an off-road ve*hi*cle."

"So something *is* wrong with the steering column."

He turned and pointed and I crowded beside him so we both looked up at the pipe connecting the back of the steering wheel to the axel and the wheels. The steering column. A straight three feet of steel tube, or that's how it had been designed, but even I could see the problem: the column was buckled like a frozen slinky. It curved and rippled. None of the surrounding supports or mechanical elements were warped, but the steering column had run like wax, then hardened.

And it glowed *dominion.* The entire shaft. I had my Highers off, but the shaft was *dominion* and I couldn't block it out.

"Don't know how you steered this car," Bill said, skeptical that I had, but unable to account for the car's presence in his lot any other way. He turned to give me the opportunity for explanation.

"What causes that?" I asked, staring at the *dominion.* Bill didn't see the *dominion.* But he saw the curled steering column. Which meant that I might be crazy, but I wasn't insane. One piece of our realities overlapped.

"Nothing causes that," Bill told me. "Maybe collisions, if the front of the car was crushed. Which it's not. No damage anywhere else on the frame. Plus there's this."

He reached to his bay wall and flipped the hoist down, and didn't speak as the car settled onto its own haunches and squeaked in an ugly way on the bay floor. He pulled my driver's side door open and pointed to the steering wheel.

At ten and two, where I'd been holding the wheel, just like they taught in driver's ed, there were melted finger slots of two tightly gripping hands. All the slots glowed *dominion* too, the whole wheel did, but *dominion* razored up off the hand prints like midnight high beams. The steering column and the steering wheel, both deformed. And Bill saw it too. I kept repeating that to myself.

"That's funny," I told him, and shut the door, attempting to keep things in perspective and take the long view, where none of this was a thing.

"Sure. Funny."

"So how much to fix it?"

"No one fixes that."

"Well what are my options, Bill?" I felt like I was doing all the work here and he was the one making seventy-five dollars an hour, and I already had my hands full working on the long view.

Bill pointed at his lot full of used cars.

"Buy another car," he said. "Keep the fluids up. Stay off the rock fields."

"Are there rock fields in Skysill?"

"No."

We walked to the office, and Bill slipped off his gloves and we filled out paperwork. His nails were still impeccable. He ran my card. I transferred whatever flotsam I needed from the bad car to the less bad one. Bill passed the key. I drove off, watching Bill in my sideview, speculating with his mustache. And I saw, behind him, in the dark of Bay One, the glint of *dominion.*

I'd had a return to Waylon's Bluebell rental on my to do list after the Historical Society, because I wanted to double check the break-in Waylon had complained about. But Bluebell Lane was the place I'd first seen *dominion.* And *dominion* was showing up too frequently as it was, bending things in my world, making me buy new cars. The timing of a Bluebell Lane return felt questionable.

Timing is my most impeccable deficiency, however. I sighed, babied my new old car out onto PCH, and went upcoast, once again, to return to the scene of Samantha.

CHAPTER NINETEEN

Standing at the open end of Bluebell Lane, palming Samantha's keyring, which I'd failed to return to Waylon the night before, shivering just a little in the dark half of a California beach sunset, I thought of the many good reasons not to be where I was. Some of them were: it was dark, I was tired, Bluebell Lane was where *dominion* had first appeared, it was none of my business, and Bluebell was where *dominion* had appeared.

The spilled margarita had evaporated but the cup still lay in the alley. Some other things in the alley were garbage cans, some Audis and BMW sedans, some light from a garage too far away to help, and lots of shadows leaning in from what might have been plants and redwood fences but could have been anything. The hiss of distant waves beaching and the hiss of distant cars on PCH made a sound like gas in a distant kitchen.

Dark alleys, I found, suddenly made me unhappy. So many things and people could hide in one. This particular alley was also a crime scene twice over— one break-in and one suicide, which isn't a crime but bleeds like one—so I was extra unhappy. I wanted to flash Higher and peer into the dark, in among the shadows and the Audis, in case there were men in Higher painted silk suits lurking at the scene of their break-in. But I didn't, because I kept thinking about *dominion.* Lurking out there. I didn't want to *see* any more of it.

I couldn't decide what to be more unhappy about, violent stalkers or rogue Colors. And what do you do when you can't go forward but you can't go back and standing in the same place won't work either? You speed dial a call, and try not to sound sheepish.

"Hey baby brother," answered Amelia. "How *is it?* Everything ok?"

I didn't feel qualified to answer. I wasn't *storming,* but I *was* infusing a Higher color into cars and plastic bottles, which seemed like it might be important information she'd be interested to hear. But I didn't want to mention it. I didn't want to mention anything, really, which made me wonder what I'd expected to gain by this call.

"Ash?"

"I'm here," I admitted.

"What's wrong?"

"Nothing. Nothing's exactly wrong."

"Ash."

"I just wanted to call you. Hello, Amelia. Is that allowed?"

I pictured her, probably in her studio, maybe with a glass of wine, listening to her crappy stereo, singing, painting. But not doing that right now. Right now she was paging through all the *dealing with Asher* strategies she'd worked out over the years.

"Ok. Hello to you too." I heard her return to her canvas. I knew she'd gone back to it because of her humming. Around me, all around me, a potential hidden sea of color percolated. If I threw on the Highers, would it be there? Was *dominion* my freshest and most dangerous debility? Had I really needed another one?

"Remember that night we camped out?" I asked, after the far off waves had beat a little on their sand. "Maybe I was ten."

"I remember. Behind the round house. Celine found us a lantern."

"I'd been awake a couple days, right? At that point?"

"Yeah. We were taking turns with you. You wanted to paint in a tent."

"I was going hard that night. I was pretty gone."

"I know."

"But I fell asleep. You did it. I listened to everything you said, I was painting and listening and then the *storm*... faded away. Do you remember what you said to me that night?"

"No, Ashy, what did I say?"

"No, I mean I want to know what you said. What did you say that made it go away?"

I heard her put the wine down, and turn off the stereo, and stand in the middle of her space with her hands on her hips. "Ash. Do I need to come get you?"

"It's fine. I'm ok. Go paint."

"Asher Gale—"

"Oh my god, I'm *fine*. I was just... reminiscing, like normal people. Ok?"

"You know you and Celine are all I have?" she told me. She listened. "Right? You know that?"

"You have painting."

"Screw that. I have you."

"Message received. Happiness commencing."

"Ok Ash, you're obviously fine. I'm going. Let's have lunch this weekend."

I agreed to her plan, and I hung up and congratulated myself on generously offering my dysfunction around so other people could share it. Maybe I'd get set up as the patron saint of that someday.

Fuck it, I thought. I faced down the alley and flipped Higher.

At first, everything was normal. And then, to my surprise, everything stayed normal. Where I'd expected *dominion* to surge up, bouncing off car windows and out of manholes I found just exactly the right amount of naturally occurring Higher color, shining on flowers in the dark and coming off minerals in the ground and from the borealis screening things on high. The night flared to life with no sign of skulkers, or any other danger.

And into the shadowy block I scampered, which felt a little out of character, but got me to Samantha's front door without being spotted. It was locked tight as a Tupperware, no broken entry there. On the left side of the house a failing redwood fence separated the lot from the next house over, overrun with ivy in mounds. On the right side of the house there was space, and a line of pavers in lava rock led toward the back of the property. I shot a look over my shoulder. I felt a clear sense of being watched, but no one stopped me going down the lava rock, checking each dark window I passed, confirming darkness inside the house. I had the Highers flowing. I was just steering my eyes around, hoping to pick something out, skittish and rabbity.

The back yard hardly had room to hold its two potted palms, its covered hot tub, and its sealed BBQ. The room where I'd seen Samantha before, covered in blood, looked out into this backyard. One of those slider windows was covered with plywood. I assumed this was the break-in. I assumed by the Brazilians, since they'd already done it to her office. I prowled a quick, unsatisfied circle and hurried back to the street, fishing Samantha's keys up.

My hands actually trembled. I felt the cold night damp pressing closer on my back. I wanted to turn and look. But I forced myself to focus on the lock. The third key up, the door pushed open, and I jumped inside and shut it behind me.

It dripped with quiet. There was suicide in the air. I eased up the dark hall past the apocalyptic kitchen and followed the trash toward the living room. I went slow. But there was shit everywhere. A bottle fell, and rolled when I kicked it, and I froze and waited for my chest to stop thumping, and I took in the smell. Long weeks past putrid. Cats, trash, clothes, blood, a potpourri. I breathed through my mouth and soft stepped toward the living room.

In the deep shadows I saw the same stratified piles of split boxes on clothes on wrappers on sundries. Some of the furniture had been knifed open and turned upside down. I couldn't remember if it had been like that, but it seemed new. It looked like it could be the result of a search, but it blended into the larger catastrophe.

I had my own searching to try, but no clue how to start. I'd come looking for ghost clues. Goblets with holes. Anything that might help rid me of my haunting. It started to occur to me that the Brazilians might have been there looking for the same thing. Maybe they'd even found it. Maybe this was all a waste of time. I decided it might be a good time to beat a fast retreat, before the oppression I felt around me turned into something real.

But I didn't. Something kept me. Some fractional sight, or smell, or idea, some leftover remainder of a thought kept me, for just a minute longer. Outside I heard a cat scream. Then more silence. I felt there was something I was missing, and I had to see it before I left. I goosed the Highers so they surged, just for a second, then pulled them back when nothing glowed out.

I found myself staring back at Samantha's collection on the walls. Really staring. The darkness in the room pushed me closer to the wall. A thread of a memory tantalized me. Just out of reach. Something about Samantha's collection. Something I'd seen. Or *seen.* What had I *seen*? A vestigial ghostly blur. A smear of nicotine down the walls, a missing picture which convinced me the smoker had been a previous tenant...

A missing picture. She'd laid salted waste to her house, torn and piled and pushed and then, finally, settled back into suicide, but through all that she hadn't touched her collection. Except for one missing picture?

My foreboding was pushing up the back of my throat. I felt sure I needed to get out, and soon. But I didn't leave, I stepped to the living room wall, where the missing picture had hung, and saw again what I'd noticed without noticing the first time—the frame had been ripped from the mount, the hardware jerking plaster from the wall. Long before the Brazilians had come, someone had ripped a painting off this wall. Samantha.

I had cut my hand. I had fallen in her hallway, going for the glint of the key as I started *storming,* cut my hand on a broken picture frame. Hadn't I? And washed the cut in The Charles bathroom. I took a few steps back down the hall toward the front door, and pushed my toe through piled misery and booze rot on the floor, searching. I saw it slow. It revealed itself in shards, splinters, the wood brittle with age—a priceless antique frame like all the others.

The frame fought when I pulled, then came up in a tangle of binding and tiny pins and wire. She'd smashed it to pieces. Maybe started smashing in the living room and just smashed away until it broke apart here in the hall. I looked down, bled bright into the scene, dug with my foot but couldn't see a canvas. So I flared Higher, and I almost dropped the frame.

There was *compulsion* all over it, and judging by the pattern, the *compulsion* had been smeared from the inside—from the painting, out onto the frame, as if someone, rubbing, smearing, screaming and never knowing why, had attacked it, again and again.

I really wanted to see this painting. I dropped the snarl of wood and wire and bent to my knees, with the Highers working hard, and began digging in earnest, pushing and overturning, and I'd worked a ways back toward the living room before I stopped.

If *I'd* hated a picture this much, what would I do? Beat up on it until the frame was shards, then drop it in the hall to get on with my fabulous dinner with my cats? No. I'd rip it out, I'd dispose of it.

The front door hardly slowed me. I rushed out to the trash cans sitting along the ally. Collection came tomorrow so there was a week's worth of garbage here. If I got lucky she'd done her smashing recently. I might still be able to find the painting. Four plastic bins slept in a corral, and I pulled one out, because apparently I was really going to do this, and I flipped it open. Empty, as was the bin beside it. The third bin was organized in bags of plastic and paper and metal, and the fourth had square little bags from a trash compactor. Not Samantha's style. These belonged to the upstairs tenant.

So, nothing. I didn't want to go back into the house. It was creeping me out. My hands were coated with filth. No goblets, no picture, no answers. I slid back down the lava rock to the back and found a hose, and twisted the spigot, then stood with the hose and my disappointment, staring into the yard. I looked at the yard—and then, very slowly, I reached and turned the spigot back off.

What would I do with a painting I couldn't stand to have in the house? A painting driving me mad, suicidally mad? Would I maybe... burn it? It only took three steps to reach the BBQ because it was a small yard with a big BBQ. I gave the handle a pull. The hood was gritty, but it wasn't greased closed. Inside, on the grill, I saw it. The soft remnants of a full sized canvas, burned to grey ash, sagging between the spokes.

There'd be no knowing what this painting had looked like. Only bits and pieces had come through unburned, around the edges. Some of it still effervesced Higher color. I tried to lift one edge and the whole canvas collapsed.

I thought of Caroline then. I wondered if a piece of this picture would be something she could read, if I could salvage something. I remembered she'd told me *cherished* was best, however, and I doubted this painting had been anything near to cherished. If a tiny bit of blowback on a key had shaken her the way I'd seen, I couldn't imagine what an actual object of hatred would do to her.

But a wispy little thought came up, the kind that had been coming up so uselessly ever since Waylon had pointed me down here to his cottage of doom, three days before. It was more speculation than thought. The fringes of the picture were the least burned. I took the grill off its mounts. Very gingerly, from the accumulated ashes at the bottom of the pan, I lifted the least burned pieces. I was looking for the lower right hand corner of what had once been a painting.

A few scraps fell apart in my hand, a few others held themselves together but didn't have what I was looking for. And then, there it was. The signature corner, blackened with soot, the swirls of a faded signature visible like faintest silver, deep under muddy water, through the soot. I twisted all the dials, all the colors, up, full-spectrum, to grab what light I could. And I read the signature.

Roman Sutherland, I saw, past the grime, the heat, the Higher color, and a sudden knot in my stomach.

CHAPTER TWENTY

I spent the night sitting by my window watching front yard moonlight in simmering Higher color, wondering if the fact that the Brazilians had found Asher Gale's office also meant they knew how to find my house and if I should go to a motel, and thinking about Roman's burned painting – and how his painting had ended up in a dead girl's BBQ. And as soon as the sun rose, I bagged my little charcoal-fired trophy and headed out. Roman Sutherland more or less lived at his gallery of light and shadow. I steered myself that way.

Skysill Beach looked different this morning. I'd seen its plans. Now when I passed the Chevron on the corner, where the houses morphed into restaurants and sunglass huts and chocolatiers, I pictured a dividing line drawn on a map nearly two hundred years ago. I pictured zones. Psychic districts. The city I'd grown up in felt at the same time much clearer, and murderously distant. There were things I'd never noticed before, and all the things I knew I must still be missing. The imposed, homogenous design of banks and stores and offices. How beachfront properties had such symmetrical facades. I noticed the views of the hills, and the way the Point appeared and vanished past successive corners, and I finally figured out I was supposed to notice it. Or someone was.

I drove slowly, noticing, until I came to a light and rolled to idle. Then I found myself noticing something else on the sidewalk out the passenger window—a pair of Brazilians. They loitered by a trash can, sharing some gum. Fear tightened my back. They hadn't seen me yet. I glared at the stoplight. Nowhere to hide. Should I run it?

One of the twins looked in my direction, and at that moment green came. I started to roll forward, but something was wrong. A corner of my brain noticed it. I couldn't grip the wheel. I really wanted to grip the wheel and steer myself away from danger but I couldn't. It's not impossible to steer a car when your fingers are flared out straighter than salad tongs, but the strategy you have to use is different.

The *Gray.* Cool and soft and astounding, the *Gray* poured in, and my fear of the Brazilians went away. Suddenly I felt full and empty, hard and soft, big and little, no meaning or consequences, and it was *brilliant.* I noticed a knot in my lower back and smiled and worked my ass around and passed the twins on the sidewalk by their trashcan—it felt so good to get that knot out. My smile spread. I slowed the car, and used my palms to U-turn. The honking and brake screeching made me smile too. I parked, half a block from the boys, and jumped from the car and jogged across the street. The anticipation I felt. *Breathless.*

The people on the sidewalk fascinated me. I wondered what it would feel like to push one of them over. Pretty good? A day like this was for strolling. A day like this you just sat down on the sidewalk and took it all in, if you weren't really curious about the pair of gangsters you were strolling toward. I wondered what would happen when I got to them. The chances were high they had weapons. What would that be like, getting shot at? Maybe there'd be a brawl and I'd end up with a gun and I'd shoot them instead. What would *that* be like?

One of them left the trashcan for the driver's side of a car, and the other stepped to the passenger door, and I began to hurry because it seemed like my chance to shoot someone or get shot was setting up to drive away. I raised my arm and took a deep breath and shouted, and the people around me looked up, but the twins had closed their doors, and they were too far anyway. I ran, but I didn't make it in time. Their car pulled off.

No matter. I felt fine.

And that's when I wondered if it really had been a fantastic idea to call attention to myself like that, since I'd been hiding from them before, and I thought that maybe I should leak a little color into the air and get myself—

Oh shit—I came back up in a rush, and my knees went weak. I backed up against a wall and tried for inconspicuous, which is the most conspicuous thing you can do. I felt exposed. I clamped down. Just a narrow trickle of color. I grabbed my phone and wallet, and pawed for a number. I dialed.

"What?" said Hennessy.

"It's Asher Gale," I told him. I thought I sounded a little breathless.

"Here I was, afraid you'd never call."

"I saw them again."

"This was who?"

"The two, the Brazilians."

"The two Brazilians."

"From the Klimt."

"The ones you told me about, the night you were mysteriously found at the scene of several break-ins."

"Those."

"For that, try 911. Should I spell it out?"

"Isn't your number for, you know, when I find more information, you can hear it?"

"No. My number is for saying how big my Christmas tip is. Or congratulations on retiring. Do not call with petty crime." He sighed. I could tell he was going to be big-hearted and make an exception for me and do his job. "So, exactly where did you see these two?"

"By Sandals 'n Such on PCH."

"And they were doing what?"

"Chewing gum."

"They threatened you?"

"No, they didn't see me."

"And then what happened."

"They drove off."

"What did the car look like?"

"It was grey."

"Make? Model?"

"I'm not great with cars, I don't really understand them."

"But you know one when you see one. So two men chewed gum, drove away in a car, which was grey, and you would like me to do what?"

"Arrest them."

The pause was just long enough.

"This is the least useful crime report I have received in twenty three years of law enforcement, and I've had them from kindergarteners and mutes."

"You don't have to be like that. We're both on the same side."

"No. We are not. I am on the side of order. You are on the other side. That is our relationship. Do not call here again."

"Unless I have something to report?"

"No. Never call."

Hennessy ended my crime report without another word, and I put my wallet and my phone back where they'd been. I felt exposed on the sidewalk, and it got me to thinking. I revisited my plan to confront Roman. It looked different. I wondered if Roman and the Brazilians might possibly know each other. Why this just now occurred to me, I don't know. I'd had all night to fixate on Roman. In the sunlight, on a sidewalk, I thought Roman and the Brazilians were somehow connected with some of the same mysteries, like Samantha, and possibly Tobias. If Roman was acquainted with the twins, I wondered did I want to disappear all the way back into Roman's pitch dark gallery slot to question him about criminal behavior?

I did not. I did not.

Roman's number was in my phone. Roman's number is in every Fenestram artist's phone. My fingers were steady as I dialed. The *Gray* leaves me pretty even-handed.

"Asher!" I heard. "My friend! To what do I owe this tremendous pleasure?"

"Me wanting to talk. Let's talk, Roman."

"But of course! Please, come see me, I will have a cup of coffee waiting."

"Not at your gallery. But can you meet me at the Bayside?"

"What—wait, can it be? Have you decided?"

"I go back and forth. On everything. I'm like ping pong."

"Of course, very funny! But you want to speak to *me* about it?"

"I think I do."

"This is very exciting."

"I'm glad you feel that way. Get over there fast, before I change my mind or decide I know what you're talking about."

"Oh Asher! You do make me laugh, yes, of course! I will meet you at the Bayside, I'll be there as soon as I can."

The Bayside glinted at the north end of the Beach, above tide pools and rocks on its ruffle of coastal cliff. If you preferred your buildings round, and pretending they didn't have walls, you were sure to like the Bayside Grill. You knew there had to be walls. Something had to be holding the roof up. But everything was a view at the Bayside. Anything that hadn't been a view had been shortened waist high or pushed over the cliff for the sharks.

I got in, and took a table. The grill in the dining rotunda was commanded by chefs as coordinated as fish in a school, whose hats were the only things blocking out all the Pacific scenery. They tried to keep their heads tilted to maximize the sightlines.

I myself did not prefer my buildings round. I did not like them without walls. In the case of the Bayside I disliked them serving forgettable food at unforgettable prices. But I did like watching the chefs, who seemed to enjoy each other's company and shared their seasonings gallantly. And I liked how hard it would be for assailants to hide at The Bayside.

"Vodka, rocks," I told my server. He specialized in all the things a waiter is supposed to, but doing them just out of sight so you could enjoy the horizon. It only took a few seconds for the drink to drop above my salad fork.

"I'm Jander," said a voice behind me. "What can I get you today?"

I turned and looked at him, which I could see made him uncomfortable. He had moussed hair, exhausted being propped so straight. His skin showed surfer sun on the outside, but on the inside I thought it was really struggling. He needed more sleep and less liquid in his diet.

"I'm waiting for someone," I told him, shooting glances. I wondered what Jander would do if a fight broke out in his section. Did the busboys like him enough to rush in?

"Can I get an appetizer started while you wait?" he asked me.

"If you're hungry," I said. It confused him. I don't know why I do it, that tone doesn't make my world any rounder. It's just me pounding nails. I tried something friendlier, in case there was a man with a gun and maybe Jander would give me hand signals to warn me. "Late night, Jander? You look a little roughed up."

"Oh, yeah." It came out a moan, but laughing. "You could say rough."

"You get discounts, drinking here?"

"Here?" He bent closer. His hair considered spiking me but didn't have the energy. "I can get three times the buzz for half the price anywhere else in town."

"But other places, you don't have this nice cliff to fall off afterward."

"I can't afford this cliff. I have some stairs."

"You ever lose any customers over there, after they see their check?"

"Sure. Dine and dash your brains on the rocks." We laughed. Jander was ok. I wouldn't pick him for a foxhole, but I wouldn't pick myself either. I wished imagery like that would stop occurring to me.

"If you're ever up past Point Marshall," I told him, sociable from anxiety and throwing glances around like a horse in a branding stall, "you should try a spot I know," but I got the brakes on just in time. The Charles didn't need the business. I didn't need the company. And that's what comes of conversations, which is why I try to leave them for other people.

Jander didn't mind.

"I do my damage on the other end of town," he confided. "You know The Baja? Longboard Larry plays every Thursday. You should try it. Down in the psychic district."

"The psychic district." It shot from my mouth, trumpeted, I thought, louder and more surprised than I'd expected.

"That's what they call it," he shrugged.

"Did you ever try any? The psychics?"

"Hell no." He squinted, headachy, and sighed. "My girlfriend goes. Madam Thomasonian, spirits and ghosts." Then he thought about his girlfriend. "I should probably break up with her."

Before I could conduct the subject of psychics around with Jander, I saw Roman sweep through the side of the building where a door should have been, spot me, and come at a very subdued gallop over to the table. My shoulders stiffened. I shot my vodka.

"My friend!" Roman cried, one man arriving like a complete horse drawn carriage with jangling and extra footsteps. He turned to Jander, now resigned to being visible to everyone at my table. "I will have one very strong coffee."

Roman never took his eyes off me, which added to my tension, as he gripped his chair and pulled it out and stepped around and settled in, and then reached under to scoot forward. He placed his laced prayer offering on the table. And after that he took a deep breath. We both knew he deserved it after all his work.

"I do love the Bayside," he said after Jander had dropped his coffee and my new vodka, and Roman had taken his smallest spoon to stir cream in, still without lifting his eyes from me. He said it to fill our silence.

"But it's all light here," I said, "and no shadow. Kind of off-brand for you, isn't it?"

He sipped his coffee and smiled. He made it look delicious, like coffee from a dream or a commercial. I tried the same thing with my vodka but it was just vodka. I scanned the room, peered behind him in case there were suits drifting up in his wake. I flashed Higher and stared around the room, but only saw old ladies eating brunch and some tourist families getting ready to regret their meal.

"Are we expecting anyone?" he asked, following my glances.

"I was going to ask you the same question."

Roman's eyes are a blue you only get sacrificing dolphin souls, and he poured that ultramarine down on me and dimpled his precision beard shadow in a whirl of charisma and confusion that was just breathtaking.

"Whatever do you mean, Asher? Is something wrong?"

"Oh, god damn it, Roman, cut it out."

From the table at my right I lifted the piece of charred canvas in its freezer bag. I pinched it out, delicate as a vein surgeon, and laid it on my bread plate, then lifted my plate and took Roman's and switched courses on him.

"What's this?" he asked, looking down.

"You keep beating me to my questions."

"I don't understand." He cocked his head. Something was dawning on him. "Are we not here to talk about my patronage?"

"Tell me about this picture."

"But what can I tell you? It is burned."

"Okay. Anything else?"

Roman made a decision then, to humor me. I saw it. He put his napkin in his lap and picked up his knife and fork and brought them down to the crisped leftover on the China. He poked it gently. He seemed to enjoy himself. It was cute. I wanted to throttle him.

"Well, this is definitely my signature," he nodded at last. "There is not enough canvas left for me to say which series. The Higher paint makes me think it has been altered. The work I sell, as you know, is not Higher. Was this yours?" He looked up and speculated, then back down, and turned the shred with his knife. "From these marks on the back, I would say it had been... put in an oven?"

"Good guess. I found this at Samantha Goodman's house. In her BBQ. Higher color and all. Do you want to explain it now?"

Roman set his knife and fork slowly onto the table. I could see him decide it was time for an important statement. Either one of his speeches, or I figured he was about to deny everything. I pulled up my phone and set Samantha's picture where he could see her.

"You told me you didn't know this girl," I said.

"No. You asked me if she was *sighted*, I told you she was not."

"But you know her."

"I don't. I know she killed herself. I'm sorry, was she a friend?"

"I never met her. But *you* did. Am I right?" Just a guess. But I saw it hit the mark.

"Must we do this?" he sighed.

"Let's do it, just one time. Let's just see what it feels like."

"Well. Yes, then, I have met her. I don't want there to be secrets between us Asher. I should have told you long ago. Back when you were first getting involved. But patronage is sacred, and I didn't know if it was my place."

"I'm not here to talk about being your fucking apprentice!"

"My apprentice? I'm speaking of Waylon Goodman, of course. Your patron."

That was a pretty sharp right turn. I tried not to let it slow me down.

"Waylon has nothing to do with this," I said. "Quit stalling."

"Oh, I'm afraid he does. Some weeks ago, you see, perhaps a

month? Samantha Goodman came to my gallery. I knew of her, of course. The writer. Investigative journalist. She said she wanted to interview me about Skysill Beach's art community, which I was happy to agree to. But her story was not a fluff piece, I soon understood: she was doing an exposé. An investigation of money laundering in the art world. Money laundering here in Skysill Beach. I agreed to tell her what I knew, but off the record, you understand. I wouldn't want my brand associated with a story of that kind. And there it is. That is how I know her. She came to me."

"And Waylon?" Why ask? Something made me. My dysfunction, probably. "What's he got to do with this?"

"Asher, Waylon Goodman is the most infamous money launderer on the West Coast. If you have money you need to clean, or art you need to place, you go to Waylon. He is connected to a Brazilian cartel, and please, you did not hear this from me. Samantha would have blown it into the open. And so it is too bad she killed herself. It would have been a fascinating read. And, of course, suicide, such a tragedy." Roman reached out to put his hand on my shoulder and it didn't even occur to me to shrug him off.

"Asher, my poor boy," he said soft. "I assure you, I never thought you knew of Waylon's crimes. Or were complicit. You're too innocent. Too wonderfully naive. That is the reason I felt so conflicted. Your patron is a *crime lord*. But what was I to do?"

His face was so filled with concern I almost believed it. That made it worse.

"He's not my *patron*," I snarled. "Stop saying that!"

"Oh?" Roman shrugged. "He provides your *extremely* expensive office space. You authenticate his inventory. Everyone simply *assumes*."

"I never took a dime from him. And who's *everyone*?"

Roman held his hands up and looked around, as though the dataset was too big to fit in one restaurant. It was all getting worse and worse. I had the feeling I was being handled, that I wasn't as smart as I thought I was, and I don't have that high an opinion to start with so it was a pretty bad feeling.

"So you're saying... Samantha... he killed... Waylon *wanted* her to kill herself?"

"I suppose he might have. It was certainly convenient."

"Why should I believe any of this?" I wanted to know and also did not.

He shrugged. "Why would I lie? If you, his apprentice, confronted Waylon, I doubt he would deny a word of it. In some ways he is very open about his operation. And if he refuses to admit it, then believe me, it will not be difficult to corroborate what I'm saying. Just, leave my name out."

I was spinning. I tossed the last of the vodka back. Roman concerned himself with me.

"So what does your painting have to do with any of that?" I asked, a last weak jab.

"But I have no idea, Asher. Nothing, as far as I am aware."

Jander came back to take our order. I surprised myself by being hungry, but decided I didn't want to eat at the same restaurant as Roman. I didn't want to give everyone the wrong idea about our relationship. I dropped Jander a tip and left.

CHAPTER TWENTY-ONE

I wove my way up Skyline Drive, headed for Waylon's place. Waylon Goodman, money launderer. It fit him like one of his tight plaid shirts.

I worked on Roman's thoughts as I spun my car up switchbacks, and for part of the trip Roman's thoughts tracked my new induced-suicide-by-mural theory with grisly perfection. Samantha had uncovered her father's crimes. She'd prepared to write an expose. Waylon discovered her project, and to stop her he engineered her suicide. But by the fourth hair pin, it stopped making sense. I started driving slower.

Samantha might have told Waylon about the black-eyed man, despite Felicia's claims of exclusivity. And it was possible Waylon knew about the knife, so he could have used that fear against her in a painting.

But could Waylon *see*? No. Or why would he need me to pick out his forgeries? Did he hire someone *sighted* to paint the mural? That would fit his pattern. He liked spending money getting other people doing things. But he'd have to know about *seeing* to do it, which I was convinced he didn't, and he'd have to talk about *seeing* with a

Fenestram artist which is a conversation I'd been trying to have for years.

By the sixth switchback, the induced suicide theory was shot. Not the whole theory. Just Waylon as inducer.

I slowed just below the ridge where Skyline topped over into Waylon's dead end. I pulled my car out on three feet of dirt overhanging the face of the hill, and sat for a minute with the engine off.

Waylon the money launderer. Really? I was taking Roman's word on that. Supposedly it wouldn't be hard to confirm. I realized I didn't even know how money laundering worked. A quick google on *waylon goodman money laundering* got me nothing, despite Roman's opinion. But I did learn a little about money laundering in general and in the art world. There were New York Times articles—the FBI was "seeing an uptick." The whole scheme was just adding hidden wallets for the rich and it fit what I knew of Waylon like a driving glove.

But I couldn't fit the mural.

I stood, failing to understand, which is not actually that bad when you're as used to it as I am, pointed away from the road out over Skysill Beach. Below me the town slipped off the hill toward the sea. I might have stayed like that, facing Japan somewhere, if it hadn't been for the car I heard come over the saddle behind me.

I turned. The car came fast, but in horizontal slices; first the slice with the antenna top, then the slice of thin metal roof, and the slice with two visors blocking the sun, and the slice with two heads with black slicked hair, starting to look familiar, and the slice with eyes and two Brazilians talking to each other without, for that second, looking ahead at me.

I thought I could dive back into the car and hunker. But I couldn't get the door open. My fingers were doing jazz hands.

When the *Gray* comes, it comes fast. My world turned to chalk and powdered concrete before a single new slice of car or Brazilian became visible. There was time for me to set my rear foot on the ground and flex to push myself out into the road, because of how fast I am while *Gray,* so I could leap out and have a conversation with them or get hit by their car, which was something I was curious about feeling. But there wasn't time for solid footing. My shoe slipped back, I fell behind my hood, the car and the Brazilians continued and passed without stopping.

It was funny. I laughed, on my knees, then pulled the grey driver's door as soon as I could finger it open, and sat. I shut the door, twisted the key, backed into the street, enjoying the pain in my palms from falling, wondering how it would feel to have your hand cut off, enjoying the wind which blew off the top of the ocean and in through my passenger window to hit my cheek and pass out my driver's window. I turned and headed up over Waylon's saddle. I could have gone after the Brazilians. It was a pretty delicious thought. But I thought it would be even more enjoyable to ask Waylon about knowing them, and see what it felt like to tell him about Samantha's suicide blood and how she went insane and stayed that way, and then I'd go get pie. Apple à la mode. A perfect day.

A part of me began suggesting it might be advisable to surface from the *Gray*. But this time the *Gray* wasn't interested, and I couldn't blame it. I felt clear, cool, unstoppable. Well, not *unstoppable*, that's crazy. The feeling was more, interested in seeing what I would do before someone or something *did* stop me. Like the old days.

I parked near Waylon's devil-grey steel gates and got out because I was interested in feeling the shade from the palms on my head as I walked under them, and also from pleasure, because leaving my car off Waylon's compound drives him crazy and it's funny. He likes people to use his parking area. He built it for parking.

The palm shade was *extraordinary*. You couldn't ask for more arbored and silky-hot and breathy-cool shade. I shivered with goose-bumps. I picked up a rock the size of a baseball which I wanted to feel, and continued toward the compound. I reached the garage. I saw Waylon's five convertibles taking the sun. The sun broke sheets of grey light off their windshields. I came to the grill of one and looked over the hood and wondered what it would feel like to shatter a collector's edition windshield with a rock when the sun was so perfect and I'd just walked through prefect palm shade, so I wound up and hurled and hit the first windshield exactly where I aimed, of course, and it wasn't even safety glass! It was too antique for that! It went a thousand jagged pieces like sheet ice breaking. And the way it felt was *good.* A really good feeling. So I pitched the rock through the other four windshields. It was *fantastic.*

Damien was still down at The Charles, but he'd dug a few more feet of his invisible room. His soil was soft. I liked it. It was funny to wade in pulling the strings and stakes out so they trailed behind me like I was a fly in a web, it made me laugh. I saw Damien's shovel, I wondered what it would feel like to chop down the sides of his burrow, and after I'd done it I thought it felt fine, though nothing special.

The front door was unlocked so I went in without ringing the octopus to see what trespassing felt like, and once in the lobby I listened to see if I could tell where Waylon was but didn't hear anything. I yelled his name but still didn't hear anything, so I dragged my shovel behind me into Waylon's atrium of amazement. I found myself wondering if Waylon had a gun. Of course he had a gun. It had been a few years since I'd shot a gun but if I stayed *Gray* long enough guns almost always came up. I wondered what kind of gun Waylon had and if he'd kill me or if he even had a reason to kill me, other than him being curious what it would feel like to do it.

In the atrium I stopped. Here were the pictures. All Waylon's treasures. They looked different *Gray,* not nearly as impressive, though still more impressive than real life. I stopped before a Vermeer, from 1658, where open stained glass windows cast strong light across a table into a room with a checked floor while a man in a pilgrim hat filled the wine glass of a woman in a bonnet. All grey. Something about Vermeer's composition had always felt too static to me. To formal. If Vermeer had cut the people three-quarters of the way down their legs, so the man and the woman were torsos, viewers would be *forced* to ponder their static, puzzled faces instead of the overly formal room—and what would *that* be like? I lifted my shovel and sliced the canvas, which was old and ripped easily, so the people were parsed off, along with the rest of the room, then I peeled that section down and ripped it off like a roll of toilet paper.

It didn't look great. Vermeer had probably had it right. They were just two people. Dead people, the least interesting kind.

I'd been looking forward to hearing Waylon's alarm screaming after the picture was torn and had wondered what *that* would feel like, but the alarm was missing. I dropped my shovel and wandered into his living room with the open doors which owned the view of air above the Pacific horizon, and maybe out beyond the horizon to the other oceans attached to the Pacific. No telling how much air Waylon owned. I took a deep breath, since the doors were bucketing so much in.

In front of the big fireplace, sprawled below the Hockney, I saw Waylon's dead body with stab wounds in his belly, and beyond that, outside the open swung doors, the grecian patio gathering sun. I walked out to the little scalloped table and sat in one of the metal chairs. Here outside it smelled like jasmine and saltwater and the sun felt *beautiful* on my chest. I closed my eyes, I soaked in it. So amazing. After a minute I wanted a drink so I went back in, past the Hockney and Waylon, over to the bar, where I tweezed ice with tongs and poured a drink of vodka. It was the good vodka. So good.

As I swallowed there came a little twist of Higher color in the air, near Waylon in his dark grey blood, and at just about that time my gut wrenched to the side of my stomach where it wasn't supposed to be, then back to the center, then started churning, and I started to feel sick, and afraid, and sad, and confused, all the things I never feel in the *Gray*. And I remembered.

The color swarm did a dizzy loop-de-loop in the living room, from one *there*, to another *there*, like streamers tied at the end of a wand. In the middle of that was a tiny bead of *dominion*. It made me nauseous. *Dominion* obliterated everything good about the *Gray*, like when I'd tried snuffing Samantha's multicolored ghost out. I didn't know if *dominion* was stronger than my *Gray.* I thought one day I'd like to really test it. Like really. But not today. It was too hard. I was tired. It was *excruciating.*

I let color flood back in.

Even without being open to the Highers I saw the ghost shape form over Waylon's dead body, because *dominion* didn't care if I had the Highers up, it made itself seen. And suddenly I really had to look at Waylon, on the floor, cut open, gruesome as discards from a butcher shop, flesh from his stomach, face beaten red, guts exposed. There was no way to stop the ghost.

It only took a second, and then Waylon Goodman hovered, in plaid and khaki and a crest of tumbled hair and every Higher color, strung by tendrils of *dominion* at top and bottom. My breath came in ragged bursts. I drained my drink and slid the glass away, while Waylon did the same ghost dance Samantha had—he refused to move, while holding out his right hand, in which there was a photo. He rotated so he remained facing me if I moved.

The couch stood between me and the atrium. I took the short route, past the body, and the ghost of Waylon incremented around, following me. I turned the corner of the couch. I stopped when I came to the blood spreading away from the body. Now I was closer and I saw the picture the ghost held out. It was the framed photo of Samantha in her graduation gown that he had first showed me.

Straight through the ghost I saw the real picture on the mantel below the Hockney.

I pulled the photo off the mantle and backed into the atrium. I saw my handiwork with the thirty million dollar Vermeer, which was far from the worst thing I'd ever ruined in the *Gray.* I took the shovel outside with me into the trench and rubbed the handle with soil where I thought I'd touched it.

When I'm *Gray* I'm nimble as a lynx. I can do pull-ups with my fingertips. I sometimes think I might be indestructible. But dealing with the consequences of the *Gray* when I'm just Asher can be physically humbling. It took me five tries to get up out of the trench, dragging stakes and strings. When I reached the convertibles I found my stone in the front seat of the last car. I tossed the rock as far as I could into the agave forest.

When I reached my car I popped the trunk and put Waylon's photo in a bag, and left it there and closed the trunk and walked back until I stood again by his body, near his kaleidoscopic ghost, and I took out my phone.

"Go make a friend," I heard Hennessy snarl, "and stay off my line."

"I'm afraid I've got a body this time."

"Can you move it?"

"I guess."

"Make it move its finger up to the phone in its other hand and delete the phone number it just called."

"No, it's Waylon Goodman's *dead* body. I have that. I'm in his living room."

There was a heavy, heavy sigh. Hennessy sounded like a man trying to breathe a mountain of rock instead of air. After he did it, he did it again. I watched Waylon's ghost while Waylon's ghost watched me.

"Dead you say?" Hennessy verified.

"Knifed to death."

"Knifed. To death. And you know it's a knife because you have forensic expertise?"

"Just from the way the intestines pour out. It might have been a sword."

I heard another sigh.

"Is there have a suspect you have in custody, by any chance? Maybe charged and imprisoned, so we can all live happily never speaking again?"

"It was the Brazilians."

"The grey car Brazilians. The gum chewers not threatening anyone."

"I saw them fleeing the scene."

"Fleeing the scene. Is that right. Like an attorney."

"So what now?"

"Remember 911? We talked about it before. The number to call for murders, and pimples, and policemen who are not me."

"What happens after I call?"

"Don't leave. Don't touch, don't breath, don't move."

The police arrived soon after that, as I suppose they do when millionaires are murdered. They screamed down the drive and skidded while orders flew, leapt from their cars while I listened to it all from the living room. I hadn't done exactly what Hennessy instructed. I'd gone to sit at the bar for another vodka. A squadron came in, guns out, found me and we spent a few moments negotiating my presumption of innocence and settled on me being guilty. Then some detectives arrived and we did the same thing again, and then a few more times.

I hardly noticed any of it. I told my story but got more and more disoriented, vodka hitting, detectives with the same questions different ways or not different at all, while the ghost of Waylon Goodman steamed off ultraviolet color and spun out color and fogged color out into the room, an endless mist stitched in *dominion* that only I *saw*. Under the circumstances, I think I did pretty well.

Finally they were done, and none too happy, and I didn't blame them. All I could manage were stagger steps out the atrium, through to the courtyard, and toward the cop cars and the lights.

The day was heading for afternoon now. Sitting on the hood of one car and losing a game on his phone was my favorite patrolman. He pushed his arm up into the air and froze me in place while he lost the rest of his game and then put his phone in his shirt. He motioned me close. It wasn't so bad, puppeting. Less to think about.

"Let me tell you about my disappointment," Hennessy began.

"I know about all that," I assured him. "Are you Skysill's only cop? You're everywhere."

"Yeah. There's been a rash of crime, maybe you've noticed."

"It's been harder to miss than I'd like."

"My instructions to you were leave cop work out of your life, but this seems like you did the opposite. Or you killed him."

"There's no blood on me. No motive. I'm free to go."

"So it sounds like cop work somehow just *finds* you, is that right?"

"That in there wasn't cop work, okay, that was a murdered money laundering crime lord who was dead already when I got here. But as far as I'm concerned, the world's a better place. I'm sorry to have to say that to you, since I know you were *his cop*. What'll you do with all your free time?"

He sucked his teeth. I looked up at him and wondered how they found a bullet-proof vest wide and deep and tall enough to fit him. When he crossed his arms his chest creaked like a saddle.

"Do not cross the very thin line I allow you to stand behind," he advised in a soft voice.

"Honestly—I don't know what I'm saying. I won't come near your line. There was a dead body, I'm all disjointed."

"Joint up fast."

"Listen, I honestly think Waylon might have killed his daughter. Or had her killed. Does that mean anything for you?"

"Killed her. By *suicide*? See, that's what I'm saying about cop work. It's complicated."

"Ok, you're right. Anyway look, the detectives said I can—" I started turning toward the house to show him which detectives I was about to talk about but I jumped and shrieked because Waylon's ghost was boiling and bubbling two feet behind me. Just motionless. Just following me while motionless.

"What is the problem that you have?" Hennessy demanded, unhappy because he really didn't know.

"Hennessy, I wish I could tell you. It doesn't have a name. I'm leaving to go mind my own business, I hope for the rest of my life. Can I do that now? Is it time?"

He jerked his thumb up the driveway after his brain metabolized a decision, leaving me with the understanding that he'd somehow expected more of me.

I started up the drive, thinking how the photo in my trunk almost qualified as cop work. It really did. Technically it was evidence, evidence of a world no one but me *saw* or admitted to. I knew what Waylon's ghost wanted me to do with that picture. That turned me back to Hennessy.

He'd already pulled out his phone. I hated to interrupt.

"Do not interrupt," he confirmed.

"Don't stop playing," I softball in, "I just wondered have you ever, or has anybody ever, seen Samantha, when she was alive, or in your investigation, with a cup? With dozens of holes bored in it? Holes the size of a dime, maybe?"

I felt suddenly like I might swoon. I reached toward his car.

"Do not touch my car," he said, playing on. "Think of someplace new. Go there. Now."

They were pretty clear instructions. And honestly, that's all I'm ever really looking for.

CHAPTER TWENTY-TWO

I didn't go straight to my new destination after I left. I'm much too crafty and unpredictable and disorganized in my thinking. Who can ever tell what Asher Gale is about to do—light a fire, swallow poison, shovel masterpieces in half? I put my colors on a diet of slim and slid forward, pretending I didn't know where I was going, through downtown, seeing if any new sunglass shops or sandal stands had opened, then past The Charles, because maybe I was out for a drink. By and by I found myself entering Skysill Beach's psychic district, entirely by coincidence, just the way I liked it.

From there, just below the foothills, I looked down over the roofs of all the psychics, toward the beach. According to the historical society map the *Sensus Simul* tract started at PCH and rose six blocks toward the foothills. It was bounded by Horizon Parkway and Seaward Parkway, a rectangle of paranormal storefronts and adobe cottages washed in the late afternoon sun, so it all glowed grapefruit red.

If you knew to look you saw the storefronts. They appeared where hair salons or payday loan shops do in other neighborhoods. My muted colors and I went for a sightseeing crawl, down to the highway, and found along the way Spiritual Mediums, Psychic Mediums, a medium called Medium Rare, some healers, some futurists and a handful of astrologists, and then I found what I was sightseeing for. I pulled to a corner, where *Madam Nikita Thomasonian: Guide in Spirit* had hung her sign. She kept two pots with geraniums by the front door. I flashed full-spectrum, then stood from the car. I got the bag with Waylon's picture from the trunk and carried it between the geraniums.

Walk-Ins Welcome! read the sign on the door. I pushed into a little hall with a low ceiling.

"Enter," called a voice of glottal stops.

I heard it from the end of the hall behind a curtain of hanging beads. Parting the curtain got me into a spooky gumdrop of a room. The lights were dimmed halfway. There was lavender wallpaper and purple drapes, but the windows had been painted over and scenes from the zodiac blacked the ceiling. In the middle of it sat Madam Thomasonian in a red dress-shirt that didn't compliment the wallpaper, with a face someone had squeezed on a bookshelf between two graveyard dictionaries until it was very serious and tall. She nodded and turned sideways in her wooden chair so she could look at me over one shoulder.

"Come in to me," she said. "I am Madam Thomasonian."

"A waiter I know told me about you," I said, while I turned my bag in my hands. It felt as big as a baby. It felt very conspicuous, but she didn't want to look at it.

"Stop," Madam Thomasonian said. "Do not say anything about yourself."

"I wasn't."

"What is your name?"

"I thought we weren't going to do that."

"You may call me Nikita. I sense... a dark presence."

"I have that effect on some people."

"You will soon inherit something unexpected."

"You move pretty fast."

"Someone associated with... your... family is in danger."

"My family?" My pulse raced suddenly. It's sad. I'm a conditioning test case. Ring the *family* bell, I start salivating grief.

"Yes. You have a question. I see. You have a question about the spirit world. What is it?"

I stepped into the room. She seemed to be moving pretty fast.

"I'm actually interested in Psychometry," I said.

She twitched. I thought she gave me a sharp look. Then she shrugged.

"Object reading. Yes. What will I read?"

"So it's real? Psychometry? I mean, I saw it. A girl, she read a key. But you do it too?"

"Yes. It is real. More real than you can know. What is your question?"

I thought about my question. But another question kind of bumped the first one out of the way.

"I just don't know," I said. "I mean, if Psychometry's real, what about ghosts? Why aren't those real?"

"They are, around us swirl endless realms."

"So ghosts are real?"

"They are everywhere," she gave a short shrug. She closed her eyes and they rolled up, then rolled back down.

"Where is everywhere?"

"Here, there," she pointed, "I am a sensitive. The spirit world. I am a sensitive for ghosts, here with us, they contact us, warn us, tell their love for us. I sense you have lost someone. I am sensing a great heaviness here? On the heart? In the lungs? Is this right?"

Beside Nikita there was a second wooden chair. I pulled it to me and sat backward, facing her, and I put my paper bag in my lap. I'd been struck by one of the brilliant ideas I'm becoming known for.

"I do have a spirit question," I told her. "About the ghosts. Do you ever see them... holding things out?"

"Yes. I see them. They hold things out."

It might be real, there might be real answers. I thought that, and

I dove right in, no breaks, because why pretend to be someone I'm not? Careful and credulous?

"Look, Nikita," I ordered, "did you ever do something like a reverse lookup? Have you ever done a séance?"

"I have done many, many, many. Once, sixteen in a day."

"Ok. If we tried a séance, let's say, but we didn't find the spirit we were looking for, could that mean the person is alive?"

"Yes. It could mean they are alive. Who?"

"It's an old... " I used my hands. I cleared out my throat to get it working. "I was... "

"Say it. Who is dead or not dead that we will reverse lookup? Tell me now. Everything."

"My mother." I watched Madam Thomasonian.

"You are wondering if your mother is dead or alive. I sense her."

"Can you contact her?"

"I will. Put my chair here." I did. It wasn't comfortable anyway. "Sit."

"I don't want to."

"Yes." She caught my hand as I dropped the chair. She was fast. She closed her eyes. "You have a sad hand," she said.

"It's just not sure what's going on. It probably needs coffee."

"Think about your mother."

"What about her?"

"Her face. Her voice. Anything about her."

"I don't remember much. She used... she sang to me."

"Yes. Sing. Like she did."

I cleared my throat, and reminded myself that Asher Gale was unpredictable. Who even knew what he was going to do, or say, or feel? Who even knew what he cared about?

"*Mommy's got three,*
Daddy's got four,
But little baby Asher,
Has got one more."

The words fell out into her thick purple air. Madam Thomasonian put her forehead on the back of my hand and her fingers locked my wrist. She breathed on me and I felt a wisp of warmth.

"Your mother is alive," she whispered. She opened her eyes.

"For sure?"

"Yes. She gave me a message. An important message."

I waited.

"What is it?" I asked after the waiting ran out.

"That is all I can tell today." Her lids fluttered. She let go of my hand. "I am strained. You must wait exactly three days, and come back to me on the third day. I will reveal your mother's message."

"How important is this message?"

"Very, but like I say, I am strained. You must come in three days. In the meantime, join our email list. We have a drawing on Tuesdays. Also a subscription plan. If you want to come back before three days, that is fine also."

"Ok. I see." I watched her being guileless. She looked really good. I checked my hand to be sure I had my fingerprints.

"I am the *only one* who can help," she warned. "Contact your mother. Find true love. Travel in your future. Also you may be inheriting something soon, of great value."

"I see. You saw me coming when I got up this morning, didn't you?"

"Eh," she said, palms up, "I have good days and bad days."

"I should really trust my instincts. I know it's true. That's what everyone says."

"Now you are talking to yourself. What are these instincts?"

"It's a complicated world, Nikita, that's all I'm saying. The *real* psychics don't believe in *ghosts*. I don't understand it, but I'll have to live with it."

"What do you mean real, I am real. I know your problem. You do not ask your real *question,* that is your problem." She looked at my bag. "What is there?"

There were too many ways to answer. I picked one at random.

"Something I saw on a ghost. He wanted me to take it."

"Ah. You are a sensitive. Which path are you on?"

"The beaten one," I told her. "I get lost otherwise."

Her bead strings did some deboning then let me out, and I got into the hall and out the front door to my car. Not much time had passed while Nikita upsold me, but the temperature had chilled five degrees and now the sun rode the horizon, a nuclear penny waiting to drop. A half dozen stars spread above my head. Not a ghost was visible anywhere despite the spiritual expertise around. I had a pretty good idea where I'd be able to find ghosts, though, and an idea whose responsibility they thought they were. I turned my car and set it drifting down Seaward Parkway. I was in no hurry.

At the coast highway I pulled left, and one block down stood Psychic Touch, in front of which, a foot above the sidewalk, Samantha floated. Beside her hung Waylon. They were like statues at a specter fun park. Gyroscopes of light circled the evening sky above them and wove elliptical super orbits to light Caroline's street corner, a Vegas fever dream that only I could see. But it wasn't a fever dream, they were real. Depending on who you asked. It was almost too confusing to go park the car, but I did it, and got out and grabbed Waylon's bag of photo.

Empty Nest Furniture demonstrated some sectional loungers and an entertainment cabinet out on the sidewalk. Between those was a sculpture of a golden deer. It was all lit by ghost fireworks, which made it beautiful, but just to me. The ghosts posed, right hands extended, four eyes full of something that wasn't anything pressing on me. As I skirted them they pivoted. When I got to Caroline's door they'd rotated half a circle.

Caroline's store was the least psychic looking of any in the district. It was without tarot, astrology, star or pyramid. She'd hung a simple blue sign below the eaves, beneath which were the ghosts. Her door had a sign pressed on the inside by deep, folded curtains, where I read *No Walk-Ins, by Appointment Only!*

"Do I knock?" I asked Waylon, the closer of the two ghosts. "Is she with a customer? What do you think?"

He had no idea. We both palmed a picture of Samantha in her graduation gown. I offered mine out, then I waved it up and down through the Higher color version he held, just to have something to do while I thought about knocking. Nothing happened to Waylon. From Empty Nest stepped Tim in tweed hat pushing his hardball of belly. We both watched me wave my picture in the air, which was the only thing one of us saw. He convinced me of his disdain before going back inside.

After that I backed a few steps and bent and sat on the sidewalk, leaning against a car facing Psychic Touch, and there I stayed, motionless at last. This was a quiet kind of final resting place. The sunset finished in the sky over the roof of the shop. The car I leaned against was warm, but grew cooler.

More stars came. Then Caroline's door swung and Caroline stood in it. The light from behind caught her around the hips and shoulders. She was in the middle of some amused confusion. She did that while she looked at me and I looked at her, how her t-shirt rode along her waist, her belly, how her arms propped her in the door with delicate strength and it seemed odd that I was thinking phrases like *delicate strength.* Some hair escaped and she pulled it behind her ear.

"Asher," she said.

"Hello Caroline."

"You spend a lot of time on my sidewalk."

"I decided to wait out here since I didn't have an appointment."

"That's real sweet. How long were you planning to wait?"

"Until someone moved this car?"

"I see. How hard did you really try making an appointment?"

"Not at all."

"Well, now I understand everything. You should get in or Tim will blow a heart valve. He hates when people lean on his car."

It took more energy than I expected to climb off the concrete. Caroline watched, and in particular she watched the bag with Waylon's photo. Waylon and Samantha watched too, as I went toward the door. Caroline held it open and when I was closer she turned inside.

"Are you still open?" I said as she went to the sideboard with the tray and the glasses. My mind wandered, watching her back, her calves. It was a ridiculous mind.

"Was there something you needed?" she asked.

"I guess I meant are you still seeing customers."

"I might be. Is that what you consider yourself, a customer?"

"I don't consider myself at all, it's better that way. But I will say this, it's no easier getting you to answer a question than it was the first time. I thought maybe it was a psychic thing, but now I know it's not. For instance, I know another psychic, if you ask her a question she tells your fortune, just like that. Easy peasy."

"That sounds real convenient for you," she said. She returned with the small water glasses she liked and set mine on the table. As I drank some she sat down and watched me. Then she said, "Now. Who's this easy peasy psychic?"

"Madam Thomasonian," I told her. "What a marvel. I ask her a question, an answer pops out."

"Nikita?"

Abruptly Caroline pushed her chest out over her knees and bent forward, like people do on a swing, and just for a moment her body rolled and she giggled, then she sat back up.

"I bet Nikita gave you some real specific information," she agreed.

"Very good information, thank you, yes. I discovered that people are stealing from me. But I'm also going to get a large inheritance. I hope they cancel each other out."

"Did she sense a dark presence?"

"Absolutely, and I'd always wondered about that presence."

"Where was your heaviness? Was it the heart? Sometimes it's lungs."

"There was heaviness everywhere, but she got strained and couldn't talk anymore."

"Ah, Asher. Bless your heart." She seemed at a loss for words for me. It wasn't a bad feeling, which made no sense at all. "So why are you here? Just saying hi?"

She asked it like she knew it wasn't true, but wanted it to be.

"I have a new ghost," I said, surprised to sound defensive. Why would I sound like that?

"Ok. No such thing, but, lady or man this time?"

And we were off. She made it look easy, believing in so many different directions at one time.

"A man," I said. "He was murdered. I knew him."

"Oh. I'm real sorry, Asher."

"That's okay, he was just a millionaire."

"All right. Well, is he in front of my store?"

"Both of them are, the original one and the new one. I think the new one maybe had the first one killed. Or maybe not. It's complicated."

"Do they ever follow you anywhere else?"

"Not once they come here. They get attached to you."

Caroline looked at me, wondering if she wanted to take that further. She didn't.

"The new one appeared like the first one?" she asked. "With the dead body?"

I nodded. You couldn't talk about dead bodies in a room like the front half of Caroline's room without a pause afterward, to collect your thoughts. The moments went through her chamber, got used up, got replaced.

Finally she sighed. "Just so I'm real clear, there's no such thing as what you have. Once people die they are dead. That's all there is."

"So you say. But I've seen your psychic powers. How come those are real?"

"Some things are real."

"And also, you said you believed in my ghosts."

"I did say that, but believing *in* them doesn't mean there's such a thing *as* them. It just means I have a little faith in you. Which, if I'm being honest, raises more questions about me than you. I don't know what I'm... I mean look at you. Out on my doorstep, like a cat dragged you off a field." She followed her instructions. She looked at me. "I never saw a boy so comfortable on a sidewalk."

"Sidewalks aren't comfortable, they're just convenient."

Her tone shifted toward vexation. "I can't even tell how you're doing it."

"Doing what, now?"

"Staying like that, attractive, alluring, considering all your deficiencies."

"Yes, it's a puzzle. You should talk more about my deficiencies, in case I'm suffering any self-confidence."

"You don't lack self-confidence, I'll give you that. It's actually a big part of the problem. God knows what you've got to feel confident about, as much time as you spend laying in the street."

"You keep bringing that up. But I'm only out there because the ghosts bring me."

"Ghosts which don't exist."

"And that's a full circle. So look, if there's no such thing, what are those out in front of your shop, looking in your window?"

"I just don't know, Asher. They sure sound like ghosts. I'll admit I'm torn."

The photo of Samantha made a sharp clack as I set it on the inlaid tile of the little table where I remembered Samantha's key had ended up before Caroline had done psychometry on it.

"The new ghost," I said, pointing a thumb back outside and not shying away from the word, whatever she thought, "is holding this picture. The ghost version of this picture. You said a *cherished* item was good. He used to carry this around his house crying."

"Pick it off the table," she told me. I did it and she lifted my water back to the sideboard with a napkin and returned with her white drape, and shot it out to create a small pedestal of psychic possibility. She pointed, and I put the photo on the cloth.

She took a breath. That did nothing for me but call attention to her collarbones, under her shirt, and made me think of her shirt, and how it shaped so well to her chest. I was having a hard time staying on one subject. I wondered if all the real psychics were this distracting?

"Do you want me to close the big drape?" I asked, "like, hide the math teacher's desk?"

"No. Shh."

"I feel like Madam Thomasonian would want it closed."

"If you're going to act like a customer you have to follow customer rules."

"What are those?"

"Shut up."

All anyone ever has to do is give me clear instructions and I'm happy. After that I didn't say anything and Caroline closed her eyes. She took air in, which I watched with my heart sinking while it began pounding, which felt overly complicated, because I knew what was happening to me. I wished she'd get to the reading, so we could get to whatever came after. Minutes passed that way and then her fingers came out over the table, her arms straight, and settled themselves on the glass and the frame of the photo.

We waited a few more moments, then she spoke, her eyes still closed.

"Are you ready to hear about it, Asher?"

"Yeah," I said.

"Ok. Here's the story that's in this picture. There was a rich man with a daughter. He loved her with all his heart. There was a divorce. And the mother moved far away. The man and daughter stopped understanding each other sometime in the years after that. They couldn't figure out how to mean the right thing to each other when they talked, and they stopped talking, they argued. But the man loved her so much that when he started to think the life of riches was the worst thing for her, he sent her away. To a boarding school. He was proud how she adjusted. She went to university in Stanford, then went to study in Italy, graduated top of her class, and became a journalist, and was getting her PhD. Then one day she came home, and everything was worse than it had ever been. Something had happened. Finally the day came when she told him... she knew about his crimes... the man was involved in crimes with paintings. Money laundering. She wanted him to stop his crimes but he wouldn't. So she blackmailed his partners in South America. She even told her father she was doing it.

"He was furious. It was dangerous. She said she'd stop the blackmail when he stopped money laundering. For two years neither of them budged, while the girl kept squeezing more blackmail payments, cryptocurrency, a lot, and the danger went up, and her father finally couldn't take it. He gave up his criminal enterprises. He made a show in the news, there was a big story where one of his paintings was discovered to be a forgery. He used that as an excuse to cut off the... Brazilian partnership, but by that time his partners figured out it was Samantha blackmailing them. They came up to... Skysill Beach. The man had been very afraid for his daughter. He wanted her to pay these Brazilians back, but she told him all the cryptocurrency was stolen. He didn't believe her. She refused to leave town. Then she died by suicide. And then... "

Caroline opened her eyes. No blinking the way you'd expect after being so long closed. They just struck open pointed at me.

"You didn't tell me your new ghost was the father of the first ghost."

Before I could get a few words together in explanation a funny light, a whole cloudburst of *dominion,* came falling through the front window onto Caroline's body, and the dark wood chairs, and the filing cabinets, and made it all *bright.* The other Colors plowed through right after *dominion*, pulsing, dancing spots and whorls. Caroline couldn't see any of it. But I had to turn and look.

Through the front window I saw Waylon begin to stretch and waver, and get much—so much—brighter.

"Let's go outside," I said and I stood and left without seeing what Caroline did, and outside was even more a vortex, a counterflow of full-spectrum laser chaos, all orchestrated very carefully. I stood still, facing the building and the ghosts. Beside me I felt Caroline come and stand. She had nothing else to watch so she watched me. She watched my face. I felt it.

I watched the ghosts.

Waylon dropped his right hand to his side, and it no longer held Samantha's picture. It was empty. His face finally had an expression. It was as much of an expression as something could be, while still hardly being anything. He got hard to see fast, because his body was being pulled apart. He began spinning. The *dominion* above his head and under his feet twirled him. The faster he spun the brighter he got, as he got brighter he got more transparent, which didn't make sense, until he wasn't there at all and there was a titanic sluicing gyre of Higher color which contracted to a single ball and shattered a trillion motes, and was gone.

I watched the top *dominion* tendril rise into the Higher boreal storm riding the uppermost atmosphere, and vanish. And after that I looked up at dark nothing. Why, I do not know.

"That was real beautiful," Caroline said softly. She stood at my side and hadn't taken her eyes away from me.

"What?"

"What just happened on your face."

"I wish you could have seen this."

"Why? What just happened?"

"Waylon went away. First the picture wasn't in his hand. He put his hand down. And then he just... evaporated. Or exploded."

"And the other one?"

"Still there."

"The daughter."

Samantha hadn't moved. Samantha floated and watched me without watching me. It was a heavy way to look. I felt the weight. I felt I was struggling at the bottom of a pool, pressed beneath something that she insisted down on top of me.

I tore my eyes away, and I ended up looking down at Caroline, who watched me still. I hadn't realized anything about her height before, or her temperature. But I got those. Plus the ginger off her hair. The temperature was warm. The height was perfection.

"I couldn't see before, you have freckles," I said, because of my gift for oddly intimate small talk.

"If you can see those you're too close," she told me, but stayed where she was. Her eyes were focused elsewhere, on some pie chart or list of pros and cons, assessing. I watched one of her choices rise into her eyes and become a decision.

"So do you like freckles?" she asked at last.

It happens that I do. But I didn't have a chance to say that. An elderly lady, stooped like a question mark, appeared out of the night to stare back and forth between us. Her head hardly needed to move an inch.

"I hate to interrupt, Caroline," she said, which I had a sense wasn't true, and Caroline thought was funny. "But I have been waiting ten minutes already."

Caroline introduced us. "Asher Gale, meet Helen Forester. Asher, Helen's my appointment at seven. Helen, Asher's a boy I found on the street."

"He's disreputable," she advised, loud so I heard it.

"Go on inside," Caroline told her. "I won't be a minute." We watched her go and watched her stop to stare from the doorway and finally vanish. When Caroline turned back I couldn't see her freckles anymore.

"So, Helen... ?" I said.

"She put in the extra effort to call for an appointment."

"I'd like to try that."

"Yes, Asher. You try. You're welcome to attempt it. Here's a card." She took one from her pocket and laid it on the outer sill of her window. I took it. Caroline's tongue had got her laughter put away. Now she eyed me, and I was disappointed to see something very rational as she assessed me. I'd never hold up under that kind of scrutiny. "So, let me ask *you* something," she said.

"Ok. It's a psychic role reversal. You ask me."

"Uh huh. What do you actually do? Did you say you're an artist?"

It wasn't the reversal I was hoping for.

"No, absolutely not. I'm... in—it's very reputable, whatever Helen thinks—I'm an... authenticator. I find forgeries. That is it. The thing I do." It was technically true. Very true. Horribly true.

"Ok well, that's real weird, the way you just said that? But it obviously *is* true. You're the one in Waylon's story! The big news report, where he severed ties with those Brazilians, because of that forgery—you helped Waylon escape his life of crime. Asher Gale, I think you might be a very respectable person."

"Well, no. Not technically." Becoming an art authenticator so suddenly left me feeling skittish about taking on any more labels, like *respectable*. Plus I really do know myself, and all the things I've done—and, who knows, all the things I'll likely do again the second the *Gray* takes me or I go *chromatic*—so I know from experience I have to set reasonable expectations. That's how all the people end up disappointed. Unreasonable expectations.

"Waylon used me," I told her. "If I'd known the plan, I wouldn't have done it."

"Well, I heard what I heard. In the photo. You're actually sweet and decent."

"No. Look, trust me, I've been down that road. No one's ever happy how I turn out. You don't even know—what if I made a smart comment, right now, and just turned and walked away without saying goodbye? I'm more than capable of that. What would you think about me?"

"Maybe you have someplace to go."

"I don't."

"Then it's kind of petulant."

She turned. It was very entertaining to her. She didn't understand the danger. One trip into the *Gray*... I'd never killed anyone. There was that, at least. But someone who had a high opinion of me, that's the kind of weakness I always get around to exploiting. Not because it's cruel. Just out of curiosity. But the effects end up looking the same.

When she got to the door she turned back.

"If you come get your photo off my table, I'll just chalk it up to regular manners, not you being a superhero of decency." So I followed her in, took the photo, also took withering fire from Helen's scowl, and Caroline escorted me back out.

"Don't look so sad, Asher, I don't really think you're gallant. Honestly I don't know what you are. A boy with an invisible person problem. You're not boring, and you sure are pretty to look at. The jury's out on everything else." And then she smiled, and shut the door, and then I was just another art authenticator abandoned to his own devices on a sidewalk with a ghost.

A ghost with a goblet full of holes. I had some new theories about the goblet, after watching what had happened to Waylon. Suddenly I wanted a better look at it.

I leaned right to shift the view, but Samantha rotated. I tried a quick juke right then left, but she was too fast. I wanted to see the cup from behind, but apparently I would only ever get the straight ahead view. Along the lip ran the feet of a series of letters, poking under her curled index finger. When I stepped in very close, the whole apparition began to blur. Of course. The only reason I didn't complain out loud about the ironies of blurriness and clarity, seeing things and not *seeing* things, was because I was done talking to ghosts for the night.

CHAPTER TWENTY-THREE

I steered my car up the coast and arrowed it into a spot on the side of The Charles. This new car didn't turn its headlights off by itself, but I remembered. After I shut my door I did some cool sea-air breathing, then went inside.

The warmth and the jukebox and nobody paying any attention eased up around me. My cheeks felt like they had circulation, then things circulated everywhere. Damien sat in his corner, he hadn't moved in three days. Someday someone would tell him Waylon was dead, but I didn't have that job anymore. I was at The Charles to celebrate being rid of dead person problems, though I still had a ghost.

Near Damien a table of collegian tourists battered out pleasure, while Damien held them arms-length from his drunk, but only barely. They kept impinging with fantastic livelihood. You didn't see this type in The Charles often. Sometimes when you did, it was a good reason to leave, but tonight I felt tolerant. I was curious how long Damien would last.

I pointed at the shelves and Serena got to work pouring, and in moments, with my drink and stool and very limited understanding, I arranged my facts around me to review.

The mysteries with solutions: Waylon had *not* killed Samantha. Not arranged her suicide, somehow. Waylon, the former crime lord, had only loved her. Some parents do. Samantha had killed herself of course, from pain and crazy and *compulsion* as a chaser, and she might have been lucky, if she'd waited for the Brazilians to do it the mess could have been even worse.

The Brazilians had come to Skysill, breaking down every likely door, because they wanted their cryptocurrency back. They must have discovered where Samantha kept it, a computer, a flash drive. But now that I'd identified them in a book to Hennessy's co-workers, those two were on a murder list, with DNA, and maybe Hennessy himself paying attention. The cops felt certain they'd recrossed the border by this time, which meant very little, considering the cops in question. But I'd come to the same conclusion myself.

That left the mystery of the ghost and the goblet, which I had really no idea how to review, let alone understand, so I skipped it, for the mystery of the mural. I had a pretty good idea about that. Not an idea I liked, but that's true of most of my ideas, I just swallow them down as they come. I watched Serena coax my drink out, and ice it, and bring it.

The tourist drinkers hadn't gotten quieter by then.

"How long's the cheering section been here?" I asked Serena.

"I lost track—since time began?"

"Where'd they come from?"

"Universities? Cradles? They're cheerleaders, they're physicists, they're young, who can tell?"

She left, she had to make a drink for one of the physicists who'd come to lean against the bar on a bare midriff with many silver bracelets on her arms. She flirted with Serena and Serena took her money, and I returned to my review.

The mural.

Dominion had created the mural. That was my idea. When I saw

Waylon glow to oblivion, *dominion* controlled every Higher color. If *dominion* brought ghosts to earth, and kept them facing me holding their objects, and made them disappear when a psychic spoke, then *dominion* was my best explanation for the mural. It had ideas of its own. It was the only element I could see stringing the pieces together.

Dominion itself flashed that Higher art up on the walls of Samantha's office in a single micro instant, knowing it would drive her crazy because it seemed like it was everywhere, probably Samantha's mind and probably mine, and used what it found. I had a theory about why *dominion* would do that to Samantha, drive her to suicide.

It had to do with the goblet Samantha held.

I formed it in my mind. What did I know?

I modeled Samantha's fingers onto the rim, halfway around, which meant it was bigger than a shot glass. There were the holes. It appeared empty, though the ones with holes always do. And obscured on the rim the bottoms of letters, stamped or embossed, not English.

My tentative thesis was, people did Psychometry on things ghosts held, so that ghosts evaporated, so what if *dominion's* whole point was having someone do Psychometry on the goblet Samantha's ghost was holding? To get out whatever wild story was inside? What if Samantha had died, an innocent, because she knew something about a goblet, and was supposed to be found, and read psychically? What if *that?*

The speculating wore out my drink. I was ready for more but Serena was busy with a pair from the physics table. After a moment I saw all three turn to watch me. I didn't like the look. Serena pointed. The pair detached from her and began to slide my direction using the bar rail like a whiskey train, and Serena watched them and looked at me and flicked up her hands, *What are you going to do,* she shrugged. In some ways she was a bad bartender.

In a moment the girls reached me.

"Hello," said the one with huge blue eyes

"The bartender says you're an *artist*," said the other girl with perfect teeth in her smile. They chimed when they moved. Hanging charms swooped from their necks and arms as they both stopped, swaying, like jingling Christmas reindeer easing a sleigh home.

"Well, I'm not," I corrected Serena, who ignored my disappointed glance.

"Bartenders are *never wrong,*" gushed blue eyes, who was also long-black-hair, and small-black-dress, and not what people wore at The Charles.

"So just *admit it*," said her friend with teeth, whose plunging neckline had on a yellow dress and very little room for error. Both were less than eighty percent sober.

"Ladies," I said, "you got bad information. Actually, Serena's just a bad person."

"No," said plunging neckline. "She said *you,* were, *an artist.* We have a question. Just a teeny question?"

"It's super teeny," agreed blue eyes.

"If it's that small go ahead and ask, hopefully I won't notice."

"Who is, or was, the world's greatest artist?" Blue eyes said, slow, like she was on a sentence-making game show.

"You're right," I said. "That too small. Give me a bigger one."

"Don't be like that. We're stranded."

"Our van broke," said plunging neckline. She waved up the coast in an uncertain way. "We came for *art*. We're still waiting for the other van."

"Come on. Help us. We've in *distress*. Look!" The other one crinkled her forehead and showed her sapphire eyes and did the look of a girl in distress. It was terrific, but she laughed and ruined it and when her friend laughed neither of them was in distress. A cheer rose from their table, where someone had surpassed a drinking record, and I finally noticed that all of these physicists were girls.

"What are you all, a tour of lady CEOs? Cheerleaders?" I asked.

"Cheerleaders?" neckline challenged. "What are *you*, a misogynist pig?"

"I said cheer *leaders*. If I said cheer followers, that's misogynist."

"You're cute."

"It's our sorority trip," said blue eyes. "I'm a structural engineer."

"I'm an evolutionary biologist," said the other. She hiccuped.

"Who was the greatest artist ever," blue eyes pressed, "I mean, in history, or now, or any other time. Go! Drinking game! Go!"

"What's the criteria?" I almost protested, because it was almost a question I cared about. "That kind of—"

"No criteria! That's for pussies! The greatest one, *ever*, come on!"

"It's a horrible question," I said. "Look, could you say who was the one, single, greatest structural engineer? *Ever*? Not so easy, is it?"

"Pshh. Yes easy. Fazlur Rahman Khan," said neckline. "He invented skyscrapers plus tubular infrastructure."

"Yeah. Well, okay. But how about you?" I asked blue eyes. "Quick, name the greatest biologist who *ever lived*."

"Um—*Darwin?*" They frowned at each other like they'd stumbled into a land of mental midgets and wondered how it could happen to smart girls like them. Then they cackled and one of them slipped.

"Come sit with us," said blue eyes.

"You're cute," repeated the neckline one.

"I can't," I said. "You ladies are out of my league. Some mathematicians are coming later, I'll introduce you."

"This town *sucks*," said the botanist from the floor.

"I know, what a *waste*," complained the engineer. "All that driving and all we get is *this*?" She pointed to the walls of The Charles, where the rich pageantry of British peerage spread, the cream of the Empire at the pinnacle of sidesaddle smoke-stack landed gentrification, which is my preferred gentrification.

The botanist scoffed. "Why would anyone spend all this time painting a bunch of *English countrysides*?"

"This mural wouldn't have taken any time at all," I assured them, coming to the defense of my establishment, and these bygone painters, and the gentry. I wanted to leave the scientists with a sense of the art insight they'd miss, being so far out of my league. "It could've been finished, all this, in just a few hours."

"No," said the engineer. She ran the idea through the machine of her engineer brain. "How?"

"Well, back in *those* days," I allowed, in her direction, with authority, "a mural like this would be painted by a team of artists. They'd all be trained to paint in the same style, and so used to each other, painting together, they could do the walls of a place... this size... in a few..."

Amelia used to say I'm the sparkling intellect of the Gale family, but we're a very slow people so that means nothing. I saw it then. Nobody painted murals this way anymore. No one trained artists in teams with coordinated styles. Times had passed those draftsmen by —except, *someone* still trained artists in teams. Someone had teams of artists just lying around, waiting to do whatever they were told.

"Where are you going?" cried the botanist, as I stepped away from the bar. "You can't leave, you have to introduce us to the mathematics!"

I didn't have time to trade more smart comments. Not even one more. I had a Master of Light and Shadow to see.

CHAPTER

TWENTY-FOUR

It was 9 pm and Pacific temperate. In downtown Skysill Beach cars promenaded, shepherding locals and visitors to delicious sights and destinations. The closest I could park to the Studio of Light and Shadow was a fifteen-minute walk, and during that time I considered all my faulty reasoning and issues with common sense. *Dominion* as a mastermind. I blamed Roman because that was convenient and thematic. I was looking forward to doing it to his face.

The tourists I passed hugged canvases. A portrait here, a landscape there. Skysill was killing it tonight. These visitors always went home and told friends, who came to buy their own piece of freshly made art, *compulsion* in charge of it all, an endless loop of commerce. Nothing ever changed in Skysill Beach. We fleeced but nothing grew. No one went on to great things. No charities were founded here. No presidents went to our schools.

These were the thoughts I wasted while I walked toward the Light and the Shadow, until I heard it.

The Square on the Sea moaned up music from two blocks away.

When I reached the cobbled alley piercing the Square, the music ran in even throbs through the air, drumming techno-club, a stream guaranteed to stir a certain group, like a rabble of Fenestram artists, to rave. In the Square gyrated a multispectral pool of bodies. Faces up and happy. A miniature Gala Lumina. Some Fenestram Dancers must have come to town.

I dodged forward over the cobbles and stopped when I saw them. The pair spun through the partiers with lithe tiger arabesques. When you saw them onstage it actually diminished the brute force they tapped, but you saw it here, they arced air like pitched water. One boy, one girl. When they landed they gave out long kisses, and the crowd, artists all, tried responding, but were too slow. Two cats at play in a field of tripping turtles.

Skysill's finest were stripped to their Higher tattoos, draped in Higher textile, highlighting full-spectrum body paint, neglecting their propriety. When a couple of Fenestram Dancers come through, the news spreads electron fast, though this was nothing compared to the propriety that got neglected when the whole dance troupe flew in for the Gala Lumina.

I cast an eye across the crowd to Roman's gallery and saw the man himself, laughing in conversation with a familiar figure. Veronica Night.

A thick velvet cord roped me out, attended by a pair of *sighted*. They stood in front of the sign that read *Private Party. A* spinning platter mounted with a five fingered hand in *choke* waited on my side of the rope. The usual. I turned the disk while the two of them watched, lined the *choke* fingers straight up, then slid my thumb and fingertips exactly down to match, confirming my standing invitation. One attendant dropped the rope.

Cutting through the mob looked bruising so I skirted and circled right. All the gallery owners were out, in front of their own galleries, watching like Roman was doing, the satisfied and prosperous merchants of Skysill Beach. I got halfway around the Square when the mob burst open and Dancers flew out and played a game of *can you do this move* with a pair of our finest wholesalers, then kissed them, long lingering kisses, while the wholesalers stood and took it, knowing they deserved it. Then the Dancers turned for me.

You couldn't say how it happened, because of the way they moved, but the girl was behind me and the boy in front in an instant, and they didn't touch me but I felt them. The boy leaned in. His eyes were clear except for a fire, his face was young shelved cheekbones, an animal face without a flaw. He was engine warm. He smiled and his tongue was on mine, he wouldn't hear no and that's not what I was saying anyway. He was one hundred percent validation. I don't pretend I don't need the validation. Well, that's not true. I do pretend.

Plus there's no sense fighting it, they'll find you if they want you. He did, while the girl spun us—I felt, then saw—then both were gone. One moment to shake it off, then I lowered my head and forged around and started toward Roman, his back to me. Veronica spotted me over his shoulder and she was going to say something.

"Roman," I called, to get my conversation started before her. It didn't stop Veronica.

"Mr. Gale," she said. She seemed very happy, if only for herself. "Speak of the devil."

Roman turned, saw me, smiled, couldn't get one back, found me charming and hilarious, and spread his arms.

"My friend!" he said. "We were just—I was describing to Veronica the way you used to paint. And will again, god willing. And here you are!"

"I am. Do you notice, Veronica's very curious about me?" I asked. I looked at Veronica. "Every time I turn around. Like she's my unauthorized biographer."

Veronica shrugged. "You keep coming up. You and your *wild paintings.*"

"Why don't we ever talk about your paintings?"

"Oh, I don't paint, Mr. Gale. Not a stroke."

"But you *see*."

"I am a mystery, am I not, Mr. Gale? But you are too. I think you should come in, and we should have a talk, some time. What do you think of that idea?"

There was applause from the crowd and the Dancers broke out again, spreading cheer at the edge of the Square. Then suddenly they came for Veronica. The girl went high, the boy went low, he worked his way past her hips toward her neck until he looked down at her face. He pulled her in. Veronica held her hand up, over the boy's lips, and shook her head.

"Oh darling," she said, confessional, "I'm afraid I have a touch of the herpes. So frustrating. So. No thank you."

You don't say *no thank you* to a Dancer's embrace, or if you do it doesn't matter because they figure a way in. But a funny thing happened just as Veronica said *no thank you.* She turned away, subtly blocking Roman's view but not quite blocking mine, closed her eyes, and I saw, thought I did, *compulsion* wink among her fingertips, the fingertips she held over the boy's mouth—a static discharge of *compulsion.* And the Dancer smiled and turned away. The flicker was gone the instant it appeared. A reflection? The vodka?

Whatever it was took her out of the conversation at just the right time, and I swung back to Roman.

"Let's go talk," I said.

"I'm sorry about today, at the Bayside," he told me. "I hope it wasn't too shocking."

"Let's go inside."

We left the crowd and went in, then down toward the little coffee alcove at the back of the gallery of shadows.

"You seem upset," he sorrowed. "I hope it wasn't anything I said."

"No. I love hearing you talk. It sounds like angels making an illicit fortune."

"Asher," he looked back, with just the faintest exasperation, like we both knew I didn't mean the things I said. We knew I had nothing but affection for him. We came to his alcove and he urged me low, like a Maître'd, then slid after and put his prayer on the table.

"How good is your memory?" I asked him.

"Average, I think. Why?"

"Did you go to my sister's opening two days ago? At the Nagato?"

"No, though I find her work stunning. You must be proud. Is she looking for a patron?"

"Julian was there."

"Oh?"

"Earlier that day I met him leaving his space at the Klimt. Showered and sharp. Also full of smack, by the way. But later when I saw him at the Nagato, he had Higher paint on him. He'd washed, but he missed enough. Did you have him painting for you the afternoon of Amelia's opening? In dress clothes?"

Roman looked. He didn't bother to say, *Asher, what is this about?* He thought back with his average memory and shook his head.

"They haven't painted anything for almost a week, waiting while I finalize a hotel branding contract. I only started Julian and the others on a new assignment this very evening. That's where he is right now, at my studio. He was very unhappy to miss the Dancers, poor dear."

"Ok, then the night I saw him at Amelia's exhibition," I told Roman, "I think Julian had just come back from washing down a room full of Higher mural. He probably had help. Any idea where the rest of your apprentices were that evening?"

"No. Asher, I won't answer another question until you tell me what all this means."

I couldn't see I had any option but to tell him. I was out of rhetorical sleight of hand. So first I told him everything I *knew*. Not the ghost, or *dominion,* but the rest of it. I included the Brazilians, and Tobias, just to be comprehensive. Then I told him everything I speculated: Julian hated Tobias. Maybe envy. Julian hated everyone anyway and Tobias was a social climber. They met at the Klimt. I told Roman I thought Julian had been looking for a new patron and he'd picked Lady Damely for the job. So Julian painted the mural in Tobias's style, to ruin him.

"I saw him at the Klimt, he needled at me about picking his work out of a lineup. I think he knew what I was looking for, he hoped I'd find it. Some kind of test of wills. In the end, the plan didn't go the way it was supposed to, and Samantha killed herself."

"But you say this mural went up in the span of hours," Roman pressed.

"Right, no one person could have done it, but your team could have. Did you know about any of this, Roman?"

I looked to see what he knew. It was hard to tell.

"Of course not," he said. "What about *my* painting, the one that was burned at her house?"

"Someone here sold it to her, doctored with *compulsion,* probably in Tobias' hand. Just check, if we're going to play you didn't know any of it. The sale would be in your records, right?"

"Wait here."

Roman left for record-keeping and I remained, elbows on the table, without a coffee, just a whiff of Roman's dusky incense and the bones in my shoulders, fending off Roman's art. The formula of it, the waste. How you'd never find a monster in any shadowed Sutherland wood, because the shadows were just there to make the light sell harder.

Roman reappeared. He held a phone which he dialed as he came, then stood by the table, listening into.

"Julian, this is Roman," he said, in voice message tones, "I would like you to call me immediately. I will wait."

Roman put the phone in the middle of the table like a man unaccustomed to, and not in favor of, waiting on things he wants. We both looked at the phone, which didn't do anything.

"I checked," Roman said quietly, pointing lidded charisma at me, which had sadness and confusion in it along with anger. "Julian sold the painting to Samantha almost a month ago. Now, I have a hard and fast rule: I sign all statements of authenticity, which we provide for every painting we sell. In this case, Julian seems to have signed. Julian is headstrong. He can be difficult to control."

"You mean other than painting exactly what you tell him, exactly the way you tell him."

"The artists I'm patron to do have lives apart from my gallery."

"So did you know he was working on patronage from Damely?"

"Lady Damely would never sponsor one of my own apprentices. That's not the way it's done."

"What do you really know about Julian? Where'd he go to school? He didn't start in Skysill, you found him on the outside."

"I know he is immensely talented Asher, though given to grandiose... moods. It comes out in my art, sometimes he will simply waste a canvas. I know he is beautiful. His schooling..." Roman thought a moment, I thought he wanted to tell me the truth but probably pimp it to look its best. It was a lot like his approach to art, just make things easy to look at.

"Julian is self-taught," Roman decided to say.

The phone rang. Roman reached for it fast but stopped when he read the caller id. The phone rang again, but he let it. It rang again.

"Hello?" he answered finally. "Yes. This is he." He listened. His face grew hard by increments, like concrete drying. "Yes. That is my home. But... how could it? No, though there's extensive studio space on the ground floor... I'm sorry, but how did... how could... yes. Did you find anyone... oh. My god. I can, as soon as possible."

He stopped the call, then forgot the phone, and held it in the air like he was waiting for a waiter to get it.

"The fire department," he said. "My house just... burned down."

"Just?"

"They said... it was very swift."

The thing on his face could only be devastation. I knew it, even though I tried not to recognize it, and I felt the *Gray* widen under me, coming to suck me down from proper shock. People losing things, important things, essential things—it's a trigger.

"I'm sorry for your loss," I said, holding onto the color.

"It was my studio. All my work was there."

"Did they save any?" Please don't be devastated. Say they saved your life's work.

"I mean all my work was *done* there. That's where Julian and the others were working tonight. There's no word of them. I fear..."

He didn't have to say what he feared, it was the thing anyone would. It's what I would, and for a moment I did, accidentally, and then the *Gray* grabbed for me, it was *fantastic*, but I pushed against it, clawing for color.

Just before the *Gray* let me go, Roman asked, "Please, Asher, will you come to my house with me? I need... a friendly face."

And I heard myself answer, "God, I'll *totally* go to your place Roman! That's, like, *amazing*. I wonder what that'll be like?"

Then the colors were back but it was too late. Roman had my arm and we hurried out the rear of the gallery into his car. I'd never been to his house before so this was when I discovered that Roman lived up Skyline Drive in The Seacliffs, one or two switchbacks below Waylon's estate, though you could survey the same empire from either address.

I spent the trip imagining the best way to jump from a moving vehicle and might have tried my plan but I wasn't sure Roman's BMW would even let the door open without his permission. When we reached the feeder drive for Roman's row of mansions we saw emergency lights, and smoke, reflective clothes with wet charcoal grime. Roman stopped the car. He got out. A fire captain approached.

I listened to him ask Roman questions about flammable materials, fire suppression systems. The darkness felt cool, but it smelled dry and hot, like burning couches. I watched water cascade on what remained of Roman's house.

"Asher," said Roman, beginning to follow the Captain. "This way."

I got out of the car. That's when I saw the stretchers. Forms covered with sheets.

"Dead bodies?" I asked.

"They found, yes... five bodies, and - "

In the floodlights I turned. I turned and walked back down the hill. After a while I ran.

CHAPTER TWENTY-FIVE

The next morning I took my painting to the beach. Sometimes I like to see it in a different light. It makes the pain cleaner.

I set up the easel so eastern sunrise could freshen it, and the ocean west could frame it, and let it torture a little, for no good reason, while the morning dawned, and I was still among the living. The light was bright but had no weight. I drank a whole thermos of coffee. One job at a time.

It was a few minutes past ten when I bundled the canvas and walked it home, then started my car toward Mineral Grain Beach, and the Manders place on its bluff.

I clung to hope I could help Samantha. Somehow Julian had known to paint a single, precise horror on Samantha's walls, and drive her to kill herself. But I still didn't know things like, why do it? And how'd he known what to scene paint? And why had he picked Tobias, in particular, to frame? Just jealousy about Lady Damely, or something else? I hoped answering these answers could help me with Samantha problem, whatever it was, because despite myself her problem was beginning to feel kind of personal.

I left my car on the sandy shoulder of the Mineral Beach access road and started up the twin tracks that passed for a drive to the Manders place, where Tobias sheltered. The tracks led between small dunes and clumps of grass, and then the long-suffering yellow barbie box came into view, caged in its juniper windscreen. Tobias still had no car out front. I flashed the Highers: no paint outside, no ghosts. I crept closer. The windows gave nothing away. Orange blinds still hid the interior. I knocked. A moment passed, I knocked again. I listened. The air inside didn't stir an atom. I gave up knocking.

Around the back I found a cottony redwood deck with faded beach chairs and a doormat with *Whalecome* in white letters inside a green whale. The back door hung open, flung into the house. I knocked, but only as a formality—the door had been kicked. By this time I picked out the signs like a professional. I felt pretty safe stepping in. There'd been plenty of time during my front door knocking to close this and pretend you weren't here, if you were.

The door let directly into the little living room filled with Tobias' canvases, formerly stacked against the walls, and several of his easels, formerly upright and with works in progress. The place had been stirred like heavy cream. Another familiar scenario. I flashed Higher, saw pigment everywhere, leaking from tubes and bottles, and saw where shoes had torn through canvases and kicked apart frames and stepped in spilled *choke*. The glowing trail of those shoes went out the back door, off the deck, and out over the sand, where I dialed saturation high to pick out glimmers where they disappeared over the bluff and down toward the hidden beach.

I stepped out of the living room onto the deck. I went off the deck and between the dunes, following minuscule grains of Higher while I figured the odds that whatever had happened had happened long before I arrived, and was over. They seemed pretty good. After a few minutes of walking I crested the last sandy hillock and saw a line of horizon, the sea, the rocks of Manders Point breaking seawater to my right.

Before me a slope fell, in a series of hard sand moguls pinned by toupees of grass. At the bottom curved the gravely private cove. The rocks of Manders Point piled in a basalt spine on the right. The waves beat those rocks. The rocks loved it and asked for more. A broken pagoda hid away down there, near the rocks, where the Manders had sat many decades ago, contemplating groceries at the edge of the world.

Nothing and no one flashed up or stood out, and I'd entirely lost the track of Higher paint. But I'd come this far and I thought I'd check the pagoda. Then I'd retreat, use my Subway punch card, get one hole closer to a free sandwich, and maybe call the police about this new break-in, although the police had given me the feeling they wouldn't mind never hearing from me again. It was steep going down that sandy hillside, picking my way, then one of my shoes filled with sand and pulled off.

I'm not sure when the Brazilians came into view. I was looking at my shoe. By the time I got the shoe on they'd advanced a good distance up the slope. They came fast, like a pair of hunting dogs.

My insides tilted toward *Gray*, but I held it down, and one thought only filled me: *don't go.* Don't go confident and cool and carefree, and skip down to confront these killers—*don't go Gray.* I spun and dug my heel at the slope and angled up the way I'd come. As I scrambled I reached for my phone, for police. I got it out but couldn't get fingers on the numbers, and I shook sand—*don't go Gray* —I wanted to go *Gray—don't*—and the phone flew from my hand.

I grabbed a grass tuft to lever past a sandy shoulder and when the clump broke I tumbled backward, rolled to my knees, helpless for split seconds, then lurched back again, up-slope. Sawed up. A desperate climb. One of the Brazilians almost had me only three steps back, gaining and reaching and calling in Portuguese, but I got to the lip of the hill and monkeyed over, kicking down sand spray at him.

The other Brazilian hit me from the side—he must have circled around—he got me with his shoulder and we both went backward and slid down, separating, a few feet apart like logs in a sluice. He had a knife. I saw it was already dripping blood. Not mine.

A shelf hit us and stopped us and he staggered to me and stabbed and I kicked his leg - his knee gave way. His arm flailed, the knife flying, so he fell on me, a grand piano elbow drove through my stomach. I gasped. He rolled on my chest and reached for my neck. I hurled sand, caught his face, struggled free, he swung blind. I stumbled downslope, then stood.

If I hadn't forgotten the other Brazilian I might have gone upslope, but I'd forgotten. I had no strength for climbing anyway. His fist crushed me behind the jaw, and I spun, windmilled. Gravity took me sideways, where there hadn't been any. I folded on a mound of sage sand, lost track of the twins. For just a second.

They both came at me then. One still had a knife, a new knife clean and long. I saw this was the one with a scar on one cheek and a tattoo of a scar on the other. They split right and left, practiced dance partners. I tried facing the one with the blade but the other got behind and caught my arms. He knew what he was doing. I yanked but hardly moved either of us. The one Brazilian held me while the other stood beside me, lowered his knife, and brought it up.

Always bend your knees when you knife someone, he knew that. I felt it come in tip first, icicle cold, rib cage level, where everything's soft, which made him grunt. Frozen shivers went through me. You don't have nerves to register damage like that right away.

The blow jerked me into the air. He yanked the blade down. Then plunged in again. His breath was on my cheek. He grunted like Damien shoveling trenches. Out the blade came, one more time inside me then, where he left it while he wheezed and swallowed before he plucked it out. With a twist and a flourish he stepped back to look. They both did. All three of us stood and looked at my stomach for the time it took for a wave to beat the beach. We panted.

A hillock caught me when I fell and propped me on my back to view my wounds. The blood bucketed. I saw other things down there through my shredded clothes, sickening pink edges of things. The cuffs of my attackers stirred languidly on the Brazilians I had at each shoulder. They toed sand while not speaking English. I looked up. The light hit me in the face. The Brazilians seemed immensely tall, tiny heads moving in the sun. One of them held his hand out to the other because an abrasion stung him. He wasn't happy. He looked at me and cursed.

I coughed. My eyes closed. The fingers on my right hand spread open in a *Gray* fan. The fingers on my left hand clenched in a *chroma storm* ball.

The ball started to open. In a moment both my hands would be finger spines.

Ok, I thought, go *Gray. It's fine. In a minute everything will be gone. I will be. It's just pain management now. Go in peace.*

But I had another thought, and it stopped my *storm* clenched left hand from fanning completely out.

If there's only a minute left, I thought, *shouldn't I have the color experience, the full experience, just once? Isn't that something all people deserve, even me, to ride color all the way, wherever it takes them, at the end?*

Slowly I clenched that left hand back into its *chroma* ball. I held myself like that, balanced between my great deficiencies, while blood poured away.

Gray. Peace. No pain.

It was the humane, the merciful thing, to do for myself. Escape. But even dying, I discovered, I resist doing what's best for me. And so I took the *Gray* fingers of my right hand and... Winched. Them. Down. The world's tightest monkey trap.

Crushed fingers, black tight, so both arms on unseen sand wore fists.

Chroma storm.

It pounded down from the sky and instantly brought the Highers, it brought everything, and that's what I felt—everything at once. Everything in color: the sand on my back hot towel brown. Knifed open belly a paper bag crushed in cherry compote. Fear, dying tree char. Ecstasy, atomic pink cotton, sadness blue as arctic moss, regret worn parrot green. The Highers swooped and lifted me. I saw it all fully. They took me up a ladder, and every step Higher the *storm* pumped harder. I thought it would end but it didn't. It didn't end it got more, and, unbelievably, *more.*

I had a terrible thought. A realization. I realized I'd made a mistake.

"Help... " I pushed out my cracked lips, if my killers could only hear. *Help me go back.* No person should ever *ever* have to endure this. This. Would wash me away. *Help me,* I heard them talking. Far away. Farther. Yelling.

And then for a moment there was still me in the world, but the intensity vanished.

Color with no feeling. And silence. I found myself in a body or a version of a body made of Higher light, a floating billion billion, a color monsoon, a crayon gulf stream, prism shattered.

Something kept it all a yard from me, in a sphere. A tendril above. A tendril below.

The sphere coalesced. It knit me a form. My right hand extended. I held something. What? I couldn't look. Frozen. *Dominion* radioacted to drown out all the other Colors. I gasped, someone did, I screamed, someone did.

In the terrible distance still I felt the agony of eviscerated flesh, still sensible at the miniaturized end of the telescope of me. Underneath everything else, that pain radiated. Would I always have it? Wasn't there ever anything I could do to stop the pain? How can you die, if you still feel so much pain?

The answer is, you can't.

The agony lessened, as I, in my ghostly form, became more dream than experience. I was fading. Into nothing. The *dominion* sphere around me got white-hot and blinding. Everything went away.

CHAPTER
TWENTY-SIX

I'd done it a hundred times, so I knew—put consciousness back together from the outside in, a pair at a time. Fingertips plus toe tips. Wrists plus ankles. Elbows, knees. Find them, name them, hook them on. Do the list. Leave what, when, where and why for later. Maybe never get to those. They don't matter. Not like hips and shoulders.

I ended up with a body, though not a very good body. Usually after you put everything together you can move over to the toilet or the curb and throw up, and you feel better. I didn't have energy to move. Or do anything. All I could do was listen.

I heard a woman's voice. It came from a great distance. A voice from someone's past. My own past. Familiar.

"Who..." I grated out. Apparently I couldn't talk yet. "Wha... shuopipy..."

"Yes darling, very very good," said the voice. "Now keep quiet, this is a work call."

I listened harder and wished I hadn't. This was a light British lilt of a voice and had an undertone of ice. Well, not an undertone.

"Aspectu, a prime, yes," I heard Veronica ice off. "Yes, of course. Five kilometers, I should think."

I peeled my eyelids apart, surprised that I could, to see some blurry sky. I flexed my hands, pointed one leg, and some important pieces came back. I didn't use them right away. I'd been stabbed. I'd had a *chroma storm*. I'd... died? No. But. Become a... something? Where was the pain?

"The complete sensus lucrum," I heard her say. "Of course I have. Because I *seen the signs*! This is exactly what I have been telling you all for years. All of it leads back to Aeternus. He has been building...he has been preparing for a quorum... yes, I know—a thousand years but—no of course... well, if that is your position." A moment passed. "Exasperating."

I heard the ocean. Tobias' hillside? I opened my eyes.

I lay within a shallow, perfectly circular bowl in the sand, as wide across as my body, no deeper than my knees. The brittle surface of the tub looked like sand dried in syrup and was radiant with *dominion*. Because of course it was. I had no shirt, no pants, no shoes. Where were my clothes? I lay on my back, the posture I'd fallen into when my guts had been cut. Guts.

I gagged. I sat up. The surface of the tub was thin when I braced my hands behind me, I felt it snap under my palms, chunked like wet ice. I lifted a piece and stared while it shone *dominion* the way a yoke shines yellow. Then the piece fell apart into *dominion* colored beach. When I spun my head I saw grass, sand, sage, a slice of sea book-ended by dunes past the edge of my crater. No Brazilians.

"What happened?" I mumbled.

Veronica came to squat at the edge of my hole. She had a lot of blood on her hands and the sleeves of her white painter's shirt. She had tortoise-shell sunglasses pushed up on her head. She was starched and pale as usual, other than the sunglasses and the blood. The wind moved her hair off one shoulder like lady aviator hair, from long ago when they had lady aviators. It was old world, elegant subtly. I admit it when I see it.

The blood. There should be gaping cuts all across my belly, but I saw only blood, smeared and filthy, and healthy Asher Gale skin, with dainty, flinty grains of *dominion* sand mixed everywhere.

"Where's my stomach?" I demanded, not saying what I meant.

"Something has happened to your pants, Mr. Gale," she said.

I pointed out the *dominion* around me. I broke off a piece of the tub, and it rolled into *dominion* sand in my palm. I held it out.

"What's this tub of?" I demanded, still finding the range. She flicked a glance at my sand, then back to me.

"Sand, I should think. You ought to come out of there."

I noticed she looked a little punch drunk.

"Why's all the sand *glowing*?" I demanded.

She gave me a more puzzled squint. "What do you see?" I glowered and wiped my hands on my sides, which I knew looked primitive and confused, but I was stuck with it now.

"I think you really ought to come up out..." Veronica's gesture reminded me where I was. I stood. The rounded surface under my feet cracked. Blood pooled there, some of it dried, some seeping into the sand. It was my own blood. It had run down my legs, that blood, and dried. Blood on my belly, down my legs, but no gut wound. No knife work.

Someone else had already come into my shell, someone in bare feet, I could see the tracks from Veronica's side. And tracks back up.

"Why are you here?" I demanded.

"I was just passing. Is this your charming hovel?" She indicated the Manders' hovel.

"Where're the Brazilians?" I thought I'd keep demanding things, it'd gotten me this far.

"Brazil! Next question." She swayed, and her eyes rolled up for a second.

"Is something wrong with you?"

"No. By the way, have you seen these cut in half shoes? They seem to have bloody, cut in half feet inside them. But not your feet. I checked."

Still in her squat she pointed out the toes of a pair of Brazilian loafers. I remembered seeing a pair like these, beside each of my ears, as I lay looking up at the Brazilians. The shoes Veronica pointed to were nothing but slender leather tips and with laces on top. They balanced right at the edge of my curved tub, bleeding down the wall. Like a giant mouth had bitten down to take a mouthful of sand, and maybe included two entire Brazilians, except for the toes, which had been outside the scope of the mouth. I'd been in that mouthful, though. Why was I here, if the sand and the Brazilians were gone?

I knew I should have wounds. It's very traumatizing being knifed in the stomach, it's not the kind of thing you imagine happening to you. But my wounds had been erased, along with my clothes, a huge scoop full of sand, some coastal plants and two violent Portuguese killers. Those were the pieces of my working theory.

Veronica moaned, put her hand up, moaned again and left a palm print of blood on her cheek and she fell back with her eyes closed.

I chicken pecked up the crater wall. The surface snapped like pearlescent gingerbread. I stumbled up onto the outer sand, deeply unhappy, and made for Veronica, but she was back up before I reached her. Like nothing had happened at all. She did blink.

"What's wrong with you?" I demanded, a question that was getting to be our thing.

"Just a bit of unexpected exercise. And what of you? Did you know you have a birthmark on that buttock?"

I felt like I needed to take more control of the situation, to compensate for not having a shirt or pants. "I saw what you did last night," I growled at her. "Talking to Roman." I was going for menace, but I convinced neither of us.

"What did you see?" she asked.

"Your trick with *compulsion,* when the Dancer tried to kiss you."

"I don't do tricks. You may be thinking of a pony."

"I saw *compulsion*, but light, not paint. Then Dancer left you alone. And I also know you're checking out the psychic district.

Sensus Simul? What's that mean? How do you explain any of that? Huh?"

"*Sensus Simul.* Hm. Do you know the phrase, *Google is your friend?*"

"Veronica, no shit, what happened here?" I more or less stopped demanding anything then, and fell back on pleading, which came more naturally anyway. "What'd you *do*?"

"I had no part in whatever happened here. I was passing, I saw you in the sand, I wondered where your pants had gone."

"You've been asking about my painting. My parents. Tell me what you know!"

"So sorry. Forbidden to speak of Gale parents," she monotoned. I watched her interview different thoughts in her brain, which made her sway a little, hypnotic and disturbing. "Mr. Gale, I think perhaps you should come be my intern."

"Your *what*?"

"Oh, fine, what do you people call it? A patron? I should probably select you for patronage."

"That's like the surfer getting picked by the shark. No thanks. I have no use for a patron, I don't paint."

"Not a *painting* patronage," she smiled—the one where the person getting smiled at is a total idiot and the smiler is unbelievably tolerant. "You people. Everything is pigment. Painting this, painting that. But there is *pigment*, Mr. Gale. And there is *light*."

"So, if not a painting patron, what? Snake charming?"

"What indeed? Hello. Is that a friend of yours?"

She pointed downslope suddenly, and I turned. On the fingernail of beach far below was a walrus. No, a man. Lurching on his stomach, and big. The tide was coming in and the man, Tobias, I saw, had been hit by more than one wave so his hair hung kelpy and his clothes were sodden dark. His right hand was under his stomach, pressed into the worn rock of the beach, while his left clawed him toward the hillside. The left hand gave up as I watched, and then Tobias rolled on his back. Cut open. There wasn't much left.

"What do you say to an internship with me, Mr. Gale?" she asked, ignoring Tobias as soon as he stopped moving.

"You're the kind that needs to hear things more than once, I guess."

"There is some chance you might be part of something much, much bigger than either one of us. It's a horrifying thought, if true. Considering what I know of you."

"Nice. But also, I might be part of something that means absolutely nothing. Who's to say?"

She stood, her clothes blood smeared, holding two half shoes filled with half feet. She nodded. "Well. You know where to find me if you have a change of heart. I will dispose of these. You might not like the questions they raise. Or, I think, the answers."

She started back toward the Manders place. I noticed she had no shoes, and wore a flirty shade of *choke*-pink toenail polish. She stepped past my glowing cocoon. No shoes.

"You didn't just *find* me in that hole," I shouted. I looked down at my stomach. "Did you... fix me? Is there... some other thing... with Higher light? Other than *compulsion?* Something where you can... do disappearing stomach wounds?"

"I believe the word you are grasping for is *heal,*" she called as she walked off, very gay and infuriating, "*heal* stomach wounds, and as I said, you know where to find me, if you are interested. Who's to say? Maybe it wasn't me who healed you. Maybe you healed yourself. I've been waiting four years for something to happen. Wouldn't that be something?"

I remembered Tobias, and all the questions I had for him. He might be my link to the goblet. It had to be him who had known about the black-eyed man. I hoped he'd still be in some kind of condition to talk.

I slid downhill. I saw my phone, which I'd lost in the middle of failing to escape my pursuers, and I dropped toward it. I used 911 and called an ambulance. Then on toward Tobias—who kept raising one hand over his head as though he'd like to try more crawling, if only people did that in his condition. As I dropped I updated my theories about him. It occurred to me that in addition to being despicable artistically, though a competent draftsman, he was probably also a thief, and he might not know a thing about the black-eyed man. I passed the sandy, bloody knife the first Brazilian had lost. I guessed the blood was Tobias'. By the time I came to the stony beach, the waves had risen to his ankles. The smooth, wet clack of stones as I came toward him didn't draw his eye. He was in bad shape. I knelt.

"My raging eagle's ruined," he gurgled. He meant the unfurling wings tattooed in *choke* and *farewell* on his chest and, mostly, on his stomach. Tobias' stomach was a mess. He'd undergone a complete procedure. I agreed his tattoo was in bad shape.

"I'm dying," he said.

"The ambulance's coming." I showed him the phone.

There was no fear in Tobias' voice, and not much pain, so it was possible to keep the *Gray* or the *storms* or whatever kept wanting to happen to me from happening before I could interrogate him, and hopefully leave.

"I don't want to die," he said. Now there was a little pathos. It was horrible.

"Maybe you won't," I encouraged.

"Talk. Talk to me," he coughed. "I want to hear... a person, just..."

He closed his eyes. He only had a few moments. I didn't think he had until the ambulance. I wanted to be gone before he stopped breathing because my record with dead bodies the last few days was, one hundred percent of them produced ghosts. But I couldn't do it, abandon him on the beach, to die alone. I felt I should try some human comfort, for once. What was the worst that could happen?

My phone dropped from my hand and fell onto the smooth wet rocks as a wave rushed up. I reached as it fell, to catch it, but my hand was stiff as a coral fan, so I just batted it, then I groaned back onto the stones. God dammit, I thought. Really, now?

"Talk," Tobias whispered.

The *Gray* took me. The ocean soaked away to India ink and

turbulent film, a solid shale-grey sky washed in over that, peanut-grey rocks to my right blasting stork-grey waves into spray, over and over. It felt *fantastic.*

"Please, talk," he moaned.

"Once there was an artist," I heard myself start, stop, and I stared at Tobias' grey face.

"Keep talking," he begged.

"Sure," I heard myself agree. "Once there was an artist who wasn't any good. He was a decent draftsman, I guess. If he'd worked illustrating textbooks he could have made a decent living. But he wanted fame and money. And he knew he wasn't good enough to get either one painting alone. So this artist got busy, he climbed the social ladder, and the art ladder, and then the day came when he was sleeping with the daughter of the richest man in town and he'd been sponsored by one of the real mover and shakers in the art world. None of it because he was good at painting! That's the hilarious part, it happened because he was soulless and just took whatever he wanted, wherever he could find it."

Soulless? That's how I felt, right now, and it was beyond pleasant, it was *godly*. So it almost sounded like this could be a story about me. And that was very, very funny! I laughed and threw a grey stone at a seagull as hard as I could. The stone was flat and hard and though it was not large, it knocked the bird over. When I'm *Gray* I never miss.

"Keep talking," Tobias said, quiet as a tide drawing down. I remembered him.

"Okay. The story's sort of complicated here. I used to think it went like, the shitty painter got the rich girl to confide her dark secret in him, and he passed her secret to a painting team, so they could drive the girl crazy, but she accidentally committed suicide. I thought that was the way it happened because *somebody* had to tell the painting team what secrets to paint, and I just assumed it could only be this soulless painter. But it didn't make any sense why the rich girl would tell him her dark secret, since the painter was a scumbag and the girl was a neurotic psycho. And I should know! It also didn't make sense the soulless painter would cooperate with Julian—the leader of the painting team—because they were rivals. But I *knew* the soulless painter was involved somehow. He was scared, and people kept breaking in where he kept things."

I checked Tobias, to see what he looked like dying. His blood was bilge-grey where it leaked past his lips and down his cheek, and his cheek was long winter-grey, and smooth as a pearl. He had fantastic skin.

"I know this story," he whispered.

"I know! It's almost over. I figured it all out. Well not all of it. I still don't know who told Julian about the black-eyed man. But the painter story I figured out. See, there were some criminals who wanted their cryptocurrency back. The soulless painter had stolen a crypto disk from the rich girl he'd been sleeping with. I bet he wanted to make sure he could get his own gallery, that'd be hilarious! But when he saw the mural on the walls he thought someone knew he'd taken it and was setting him up, because the mural was Soviet constructionism, like he'd been painting. See? Being set up is exactly the kind of thing guilty people are afraid of. So he freaked out, and ran away, and the criminals caught him on a beach."

Tobias stared at me, and more blood came past his lips, but I could see in his eyes that he understood.

"His big problem was, he stopped noticing he was stealing things. That's my theory. This painter got a taste of success, patronage and a rich girlfriend, by painting in an artistic tradition that he *stole full stop*. The style belongs to a different people, who suffered, and a different time, and they came to their style because it was the only thing they could find to express who they really were. Their one authentic thing. But this soulless painter claimed it, just to make a few dollars, because he was empty. And after you steal something priceless like that, like someone else's style, it's really easy to steal *anything*. Cryptocurrency? That's nothing compared to a stolen soul."

"This story," he whispered, "is true... everything... but my style... it's *my style...*"

"No, Tobias. You don't have any. You're a thief."

Those were his last words. His chest heaved once, and stopped. His hands fell to the stones at his sides. A gull called the time. A wave came. I took a deep, immensely comfortable breath, and the day stretched out *Gray* and *wonderful* ahead of me.

This time *dominion* was the very first color I saw. It drew down from the smut-grey sky, and up from the beach, and between these tendrils it spun a Higher cage, a dream, 3D printed. It color-wheeled and fell inward softly, and became Tobias. While it happened I saw the bubble of *dominion* shield him, visible the way spider webs catch the light. Not there but there. And after that he was formed.

I got levered out of the *Gray* by *dominion.* I left as fast as I could, to escape the loneliness, the dislocation. When ghosts were around, the *Gray* sucked. It was the feeling of not being able to get back what you'd lost.

The waves turned green, and farther off, plumberry-blue. Tobias had the ghost expression. His right hand extended, and he offered a ring. A gold ring matching the ghost ring circled his dead pinky finger. So I stripped the dead man's ring off his salty wet finger. I sighed. What could you do? You had to keep breathing. I slipped the ring on my own pinky. Because I lose that kind of thing. And I had no pockets.

Behind me on the hillside I heard voices. The EMTs arrived, rushing to discover that they were too late, and that it wouldn't have mattered if they'd been here thirty minutes earlier. At my feet was my phone, wave-washed, and I bent to pick it up. Housekeeping things. I thought about being naked, and decided it was far too late to think about that. When I looked up, there was Hennessy, rubbing his face with his eyebrows. He had his hand at his belt on his gun, looking at me, looking at Tobias, concluding.

"I know how this might look," I told him.

"And yet. Here you are. Doing it anyway."

"*I* called the police. I'm the one who got you here."

"You were just down here. Doing some naked blood bathing with the dead body."

"The Brazilians did it."

"The gum chewers. And they are where?"

"They attacked me. I passed out. I don't know."

"Put the phone down. You get to visit the precinct."

"I have to make one call."

"Put down the phone. *Now*."

His hand tightened on the stock of his gun. His eyebrows ceased dancing.

"Hennessy, I swear to god," I gestured to my nudity and my phone, "what am I going to do, call in a drone strike? I'm a law-abiding citizen with the highest respect for the police. I'm practically a victim myself. Let me make one call, I have to call ahead, I can't just show up."

We watched me breathing and pleading. Some of the curl left the hand on his gun. He glanced down the beach, at the EMTs keeping Tobias dead, and sucked his teeth. He liked dispensing meaningless largess. You could see it.

"One call," he said. "Fast."

I made the call.

"Hello," Caroline said.

"Hey, it's Asher," I told her. "I'm calling because I need an appointment."

"Well I have some openings." Another wave came, behind me, and some silence, and Caroline said softly, "It's real nice to have you call."

The wave curled back out into the water. I wanted to tell Caroline about Tobias's ghost, but Hennessy was interested in everything I said, and Caroline would just deny it was a ghost. A crab crawled onto Tobias' cold white hand when the EMTs weren't looking. It seemed like a very bold crab. To the bold go the fingers, I thought. That's the law of the sea.

"You sound far away, Asher."

"It's the ocean."

She gave me an appointment the following day, which is what I asked for, then I gave the phone to Hennessy. The crab was gone. The waves kept rolling. I left Tobias screaming expressionless Higher light on the beach, and let the wheels of justice roll me forward.

CHAPTER TWENTY-SEVEN

Apparently some homeless people had disappeared on the beach recently, and the police were excited to connect me to that. But I kept returning them to the Brazilians. I told the police everything I was sure about. I pointed to the murder knife with Brazilian DNA and Tobias blood. I told them my cryptocurrency theory, and added some observations about crime syndicates and money laundering that I'd picked up from my Google search, and I described the one with the scar and the one with the scar tattoo. I gathered they were not unfamiliar with Brazilian money laundering, but they were convinced my personal Brazilians had long since returned south. That part was a relief.

Eventually, late that evening, I'd been placed in a pool of *provisional criminals,* with restrictions on my unalienable rights but permission to go home. The next morning I rolled my car downcoast toward Psychic Touch, thinking about being a ghost.

My concern was that— ghost canon as I understood it—you only become a ghost after you die. And I tried to decide if that's what had happened, if I'd been dead. I had a hard time letting it go. I seldom stumble on a thought so troubling I can't toss it on the slush pile of

I'm Not Interested. That skill helps me sleep, it's responsible for most of my boyish effervescence. But through police interrogations, then sleeping, then coffee, then driving, the thought persisted: Had I been dead? Had I been dead?

What happened now?

I got to Caroline's corner. On the sidewalk was a fantasy diorama of floating spirits.

Samantha and Tobias outgassed spectral light like fog off dry ice. I parked. I watched an older couple leave Empty Nest furniture and turn right and walk straight through Tobias. I squeezed out of the car, and the ghosts rotated toward me. I stopped in front of them to listen. To give them a chance to unburden themselves. We'd all been ghosts here—if they couldn't talk to me, who could they talk to?

Caroline's door swung and she stepped outside. She wore wood-shop jeans, boots scuffed on the tips, a sweater the color of autumn, loose woven, and I wondered what the sweater would feel like. It seemed like a *Gray* thought. But I wasn't *Gray,* there was Higher color everywhere.

She walked up a few steps and pointed where I'd faced the specters.

"So it's a new ghost," she said.

"Yeah. I'm having an issue, I'm finding more dead bodies than I'm used to."

"You know, you don't need a corpse to call here. That's not a prerequisite, in case you wondered."

"I'm hoping it's just a phase."

"I had a cat once, lord I loved that cat." From her expression I could tell it was going to be a hard memory with a mixed message. "Every morning he came in my bedroom and dropped off something dead. Are you like that?"

"With a cat it means he loves you."

"Well, I know Asher. That's why I let him in my bedroom."

"I feel like, yes, I'm a little bit like your cat."

"Uh huh. That was a cautionary story, by the way. That cat got killed by a TV repair truck."

"That's oddly specific. Did you ever get another one?"

"No, Asher, I did not. It's real hard to find the perfect cat."

After that it was time to go inside. Caroline led. She stepped back and held the door. I'd taken off the ring, but I knew not to hand it to her.

"I hope this isn't too much of an inconvenience," I said as we went into her den.

"No, you made an appointment—this is how appointments work. You're pretty weak on that concept, aren't you? Well, somehow you got here. You remind me more and more of that cat."

She set two glasses on her little table. She assumed her councilors chair across from me. I sat on my side and drank and held Tobias' ring between my thumb and finger. Morning sun mixed with ghost light came in the front window and fell on her heavy furniture and metal filing cabinets.

Caroline put one heel up on her chair, under her other leg, and leaned on her elbow. The sun hit her eyes but they didn't give any of it back. They were steady as fixed stars. I put the ring on the table.

"The new ghost, he's holding this ring," I said.

She nodded.

"How'd he die?"

"Knife wounds."

"Suicide?"

"No. He stole some cryptocurrency. Some people came to get it back, with knives."

I wondered if they ever *had* gotten it back, but thought of the Brazilian half loafers, and it occurred to me that anyone who could likely answer my question was dead.

"Can you describe this... I'll call it *ghost* for convenience, even though you know my reservations."

I did know, and I described Tobias, leaving out the Higher color and swapping in shiny white light instead. For some reason it felt impossible, in ways it usually is not for me, to speak about Higher color. Not to Caroline, not to anyone. I wanted to tell her. I felt like I needed to confess all my irregularities. But when I tried, I stuttered and grew confused, and had to use the water. Caroline was focused on the ring.

"And if I read the ring, you think Tobias'll go?" she asked.

"It happened to Waylon with the picture. It might have been a coincidence, but I don't think so."

"Get it off the table a minute," she said, and I lifted the ring and she spread the cloth, then I put the ring down. Caroline closed her eyes, held her hands and brought them down, and touched the ring. After a few breaths she spoke.

"Are you ready to hear the story in here?" she asked, her eyes closed.

"Ok," I told her.

"I can only tell it once. So pay attention. It's a real old ring. It's from Russia. A lot of people are in this story. It starts a hundred years ago, more. The ring was a wedding present, a bride in St. Petersburg. The newlyweds were aristocrats. Relatives of the Tsar. They had a baby boy. But then a... not a war... a revolution, Stalin took power... the newlyweds were enemies of the Soviet State. They lost everything. Almost. They were relocated and they found this ring in their chest of clothes. Before long, the wife died. Consumption. The father and son got relocated even further away, to live in the snow. The father died. Now the boy wore the ring.

"World War Two came, that boy fought with the Soviet Army. Though he came home changed, he still wore the ring. He married, had a daughter—a little girl, she was lame—but the war consumed him. Secretly he fought the communist government - he was arrested, a dissident like his own father, and he died in prison. His wife and lame daughter got relocated even farther, Siberia, with nothing but some books and clothes and cooking utensils. But they still had the ring. The wife was wearing it when she died, poor and hungry, and it was the only thing she had that the daughter took.

"The lame daughter grew up wanting change in her country. Spied for the west, like her father. She had a son, out of wedlock, with an artist, and when her son was old enough she used her contacts to have him smuggled to America. She made sure he had the ring, her single piece of history, so he wouldn't forget the communists, the repression, so he knew why she stayed to fight.

"Her son never fit in, in America. He was lonely. Went to school, worked as a carpenter, met a woman, together they had a son. The carpenter was old when he passed away, but his son was young. He had nothing to give the boy. Except the ring.

"That boy, the carpenter's son, is your ghost.

"He was an artist like his grandfather in Russia. He knew the whole history, the carpenter had taught him. But he wanted a different life. He wanted less suffering, more success. He wanted to be great. He got a scholarship to a prestigious art school, he thought he was on his way, and came to live in Skysill Beach. But as time went on he discovered he wasn't good enough. History seemed to weigh him down, all the suffering and persecution in his family. He felt it. If he had his own gallery, he felt people would love him, his history would be worth something. He stole the cryptocurrency wallet, then. So he was a thief. But he painted what was in his heart, authentic. He was proud of that. He felt connected to the place he had come from." She opened her eyes. "Asher?"

I was standing by that time, looking out the front window as light began pounding in. Tobias the ghost started to spin, twirling between *dominion* pinchers, while the Higher spectrum began exploding. Everywhere. I went outside.

Tobias's right hand was empty by that time, and hung at his side. I saw his face, where I thought there was an expression. Not gratitude. Or maybe it was, what do I know about gratitude? I watched as he whirled faster. The tendrils holding him down pulled away, he got thinner, faster, and then, a spasm of Higher gleam, he was gone. In a blink.

The sun eclipsed *dominion* as it retreated into the sky. I watched it.

Caroline stood by my arm and looked at my face.

I asked her, "What do your stories mean?" I don't know why.

"Meaning's not what I provide, Asher. All I know is, the stories are true." She watched me more. I felt transparent. It wasn't a bad feeling. "Asher, I swear to god sometimes you look like an angel. Can you give me a break?"

"What'd I do?"

"Boys who cry when they're moved is my terrible weakness. Are you okay?"

My face was wet. I couldn't remember when it started, or the last time I'd done it without being in a *chroma storm*. I wiped until I could see her clearly.

"I was just thinking," I said, "of being such an arrogant asshole, the things I said to Tobias while he was dying. Soviet constructivism. That's *his thing*. Totally his. I called him a thief."

"Wasn't he? Didn't he take that cryptocurrency?"

"I guess. Who cares about that?"

She studied me.

"Asher, do you believe in fate?"

"No. Why?"

"I'm just trying to figure out how crazy you are."

"What difference does that make?"

"None, probably. It's too late now, isn't it?"

She stepped closer and kept leaning until there were freckles again and her sweater under my hands, on her hips. The freckles broke in waves. They blurred as her lips came up to mine.

There are two kinds of *first kiss*. The first one is the classic, which starts pretty warm, expands balanced in a rush and ends like you glided with someone a hundred yards on a skating rink, symmetrical and a little drunk.

The other kind of first kiss is unbelievably rare, not balanced at all or symmetrical, not gliding—it's tumbling down a mineshaft. It starts during the first kind of kiss, the moment two people stop kissing *each othe*r, and one of them, for a second, starts to kiss the other one. The balance is interrupted. There's a lean, a hand, one of them means something the other hadn't thought of but instantly wants more of. With *this* kiss you trade that thing, the meaning, trade it back and forth. Maybe once, maybe a thousand times.

We got that second kind. Usually those send me *chromatic,* or push me *Gray.* The kiss felt unnatural, like it might not stop, but we stopped eventually, a little shocked. I felt damp on my lips and parts of my mind. Caroline recovered faster.

"I need to warn you," she murmured, "the people I kiss always end up sort of staying kissed. I usually issue the warning first, but I got swept away."

"The warnings for my own safety, I suppose?"

"I just like everything laid out before the snowball starts rolling."

"Like a disclaimer."

"A disclaimer! Because, you realize *something's* funny, right? Everything's moving faster than normal. Anyway, I said it, now both parties can go forward, fully consenting."

"I appreciate that. It's very romantic, like kissing the world's most beautiful, romantic Supreme Court justice."

"Well, I guess we'll just keep our fingers crossed."

A second kiss is completely different from a first. I felt Caroline taking over, spreading her shoulders, pressing her belly, pulling me down. I leaned and her waist slid in my hands. I saw why she'd brought up the disclaimer. I know a dozen kinds of second kiss. They branch off in different directions. I've had them all. I'd never had what we had then. I had to agree something unusual was happening. I'm usually harder to amaze.

"Can I take you someplace?" I asked when we stopped again. A breeze blew hair across her face. I moved it so we could see each other.

"Why do you want to?" she asked.

"You asked me how crazy I am, so there's some crazy-adjacent stuff I should warn you about. I just want to do it someplace other than this particular sidewalk."

"Oh? I'm starting to like it out here."

I didn't trust her peaceful expression. "You don't seem worried what craziness I'm going to tell you."

"I doubt it could be worse than what you showed already."

"Fair point. Now, I know you don't drink, but I'd like to take you to a bar I know."

"Don't drink. Me?"

"You don't drink... you mean you drink? I thought, all the water - "

"Oh, my god, I don't drink when I'm *working*, Asher. You don't do shots while you're performing art authentication, do you?"

"No," I told her, "not every time. It really depends on the art. Listen, the thing about this bar, it has its own disclaimer; it can get humid, the seats are worn, sometimes they don't have peanuts, and the bartender is very unreliable. What do you say?"

"You had me at disclaimer. When do we go?"

"Well, do you have a lot of appointments today?"

"Look at you, making an effort! That's real sweet. No, I canceled today's appointments yesterday after you called. I told everybody I was about to be busy."

I paused a moment, caught in the freckles spanning her nose but wondering, was this going to be one of those things where every time I turned around she revealed some new, unsettling extrasensory ability?

"So," I complained, "you get what, impressions of the future?"

"God no," she said, "I'm terrible at the future. I'm just decent with boys."

She boot stepped away to close her shop, and I was left to face Samantha. It was hard to see where her hair stopped being hair and became her *dominion* nimbus. She faced me and *stormed*. When I'd been like this, a ghost like her, I'd been able to think. I thought I had. So, was she thinking, right now?

"Listen," I told her, doubling down on talking to nobody in public, which really is liberating. I found I couldn't stop looking at her goblet.

"I doubt you can hear me," I told her. "Can you hear me? It's time for us to say... well before that I wanted to say I'm sorry. About the exorcism. That was kind of shitty. You probably don't care. Also, I loved your collection. It was brutal. I wonder what you would have thought about mine, it's down in Asher Gale's office. *Your* fakes were real though. The real thing. Mine are just forgeries. It's too bad we never met, we had a lot of... your father was an asshole, you know, but in the end... he loved you, at least you had that... he loved you, maybe he didn't know how to show it, but if you'd had *my* parents you'd see the difference..."

Somehow I always manage to bring it back to me. Even with ghosts. I'm very consistent. I think it's why I have my rich social life.

"Well," I said, hurrying now because Caroline was coming back, "I don't know, is this goodbye? If your plan is to haunt sidewalks in town then we'll see each other. I find myself out on the sidewalk pretty frequently ... so is it my imagination or — I have this feeling you're in trouble. Is that true? I can't tell. My area of expertise, I've told other people this, it's vodka not ghosts, but you seemed like you picked me, so I don't know ... anyway good luck with all your ghost shit. See you—"

Without warning I felt my hands spasm closed into *chroma* balls, shocking and sudden, and then, for the longest split second ever experienced, I went *chromatic.* But instead of finding madness, I found myself in two different places at the same time: Asher Gale the person had legs holding up a body, motionless, on a sidewalk. And a few feet from him was Asher Gale the ghost, who zested Higher light and floated in the air. My vision and my mind seemed bound inside Asher Gale the ghost, hovering in front of Samantha. I used my ghost eyes to see her. With my ghost peripheral vision I saw my physical body, doing nothing, not seeming to miss me, standing in place.

Samantha and I stared and hung silent in our Higher light, I don't know how long.

Until the split-second ended I guess.

My hands unsnarled, I found myself back. In flesh.

It was all too sudden, the split-second too fleeting, for me to form an opinion about the episode. But I didn't think I was going to like it when I had the time.

Caroline skipped back and as Asher Gale the real person I was able to put my thoughts of ghosts, being them, seeing them, them existing at all, onto the *I'm Not Interested* slush pile, and show Caroline the inside of my car, where she put her boots on the dash because it was that kind of car and she was that kind of girl. And I got in and pulled onto the highway.

Behind me, alone on her corner, Samantha stood, breaking Higher like a glass factory meltdown, compassing me north up the early morning coastline between the psychic girl and the deep, prismatic sea.

The End of Book One

And here's a sneak peak at Book Two:
The Queation in the Dancer's Kiss

CHAPTER ONE

I MADE my plan to warn Caroline of all my dangerous character flaws just as we were jumping in my car to go get drunk. It was a plan made on the fly, so it wasn't very thorough. And I was still confused by her mind-blowing kiss and Samantha's ghost on the sidewalk.

But all that—lack of time, confusion from kissing and ghosts—those are just excuses. The truth is none of my plans are more than placeholders for whatever was already going to happen.

A thorough plan would've taken Caroline's appointments into consideration, and all the murdered bodies I'd seen, and her psychic skills and the various crimes I might or might not be wanted for. But I was in no condition to juggle a plan that complex. So I settled on a simple warning—be aware I have bad judgment and unpredictable seizures and I melted a car with my bare hands a few days ago—which I'd deliver then let the suspended chips fall. I still hoped we'd end up getting drunk.

But a hundred yards into our drive to the bar we stopped for breakfast burritos, which I hadn't anticipated. Ordering burritos somehow led to a round of irrational kissing beside the take-out window. Her lips were warm and sweet like she'd dipped them in churro sugar, which seemed unlikely, and though I tried giving my warning there, her taste confused me. Then we drove away and forgot our burritos. For a few hours, I forgot I had any dangerous flaws to warn her about. She kept frowning and coming back to my mouth like she was surprised she hadn't gotten tired of it yet. The whole day passed that way.

At four in the afternoon we were still making out, like high school truants, just intoxicating, rabid, endless sweet kissing. It was impossible to stop but it seemed a little out of control. I'd skidded my car into a safety pullout along the Pacific Coast Highway and I still hadn't warned Caroline about my bad judgment—though some of it had to be obvious by then I felt—when a police cruiser pulled off the highway and stopped behind us.

I was wanted at the precinct for questioning, it turned out. The officers had been searching for me all day and it hadn't made them generous. I had to follow them to the station in my car, and I brought Caroline with me because they hadn't told me what else to do with her. She took roadside questioning by law enforcement as a matter of very little concern. She seemed to enjoy it. I started wondering if her judgment might not be even worse than mine.

Getting out of the car at the station yard I offered my keys to her but she said she'd walk. So together we strolled toward the gate and the impatient cop there. It'd grown cool. The sky was a slanting canvas of clouds on fire. With the day almost over I felt leaving her this final image of me as a person of interest in ongoing murder investigations made me look more murdery than I really was. And still she hadn't been warned.

"Here's a question," I said, watching as she walked, her tongue on her lips like it remembered being elsewhere, "I guess I'll just say it—I feel like I have things some people would call issues, well, everyone calls them that, which for full disclosure you should hear, also for your personal safety, but now I have a problem. I don't know if this is the perfect time to bring it up, in a police impound lot. What do you think?" I said it really casual and charming, in my way.

"You're wondering does revealing these safety issues of yours at the police station put them in the worst possible light?" she asked. I nodded. She really understood me.

"No," she shook her head, "because early on I factored police visits into my idea of you, since you kept showing up trailing crimes I could see you hadn't committed. I don't understand half of what's happening to me. I don't know why I feel like this. I swear you taste like a coke float and usually I don't like a coke float, so how come I like it when we kiss?"

An idea came to me in a flash—the worst ones always come that way, you'd think I'd learn—to ask her to meet me tomorrow morning at the office of *Asher Gale: Authentication and Investigation*. If she saw they'd officially put my name on a door I thought I might appear more law-abiding. It's not something I'm used to worrying about so I didn't know if it was a good idea.

She considered it though, as we ignored the cop who wanted us out of his impound *faster*. We'd stopped kissing for the moment. We just strolled through the end-of-days tangerine sunset shimmer, among confiscated getaway cars and drug cartel panel trucks, making memories.

"I'm sorry," she said after a minute, "I forgot your question. I got lost picturing you in an office. What's *that* like?"

"I admit I don't remember," I said. "There's a reception desk and... oh, my forgeries are in there. I mean the forgeries aren't mine. Or... I don't know. It might be a grey area."

"There's forgeries! There's a little of everything. This isn't forgeries they want you for tonight, though, right?"

"No. Tonight it's the other thing. The murders of Waylon and Tobias."

She took my hand. We let our fingers bridge the pieces of us. It felt structural and undeniable and almost totally insane.

"It's been a long time since a boy brought me on one of his police interrogations," she smiled.

"For a lot of people those are too personal. But nothing's too personal for me. And honestly this might *not* be the murders, it might be that cryptocurrency or those Brazilian hitmen that disappeared from that beach where those officers found me covered in blood. It might be that."

"Or money laundering," she said, remembering. "Don't forget money laundering."

"Right, the laundering. It could be anything. It could be Samantha committing suicide."

"Oh," she said and took a sad breath. "That poor girl."

We were walking slower. I wondered if I'd spoiled my lawn-abiding image by bringing up all my police interactions. Then she stopped. She turned to me and her brown eyes were overfull of all her worst judgment and it was beautiful. I was sorry I'd doubted her.

"I'd like seeing your office of forgeries," she said. "They keep coming up so I should probably get familiar. You have my number. Let me know to come find you."

Then we started making out in the impound lot. Neither of us planned it, it was just what we did whenever there was some spare time. The cop got sick of waiting and chased Caroline away. I tried to watch her go but they wouldn't let me.

In the station they sat me in a hard chair and pitched questions, the same ones from the day before but at different velocities. At the beginning we were friends. They were sure I'd done something murder related, I couldn't fault their suspicions, and they encouraged me in different ways to confess. But I kept reminding them of the Brazilians who'd donated the blood evidence on the beach, and the actual murder weapon used on Tobias where I said there had to be Brazilian DNA but none of mine, plus at Waylon's scene *his* blood everywhere but not on me and all the other exonerating evidence. I pointed out it had actually been me who *called* the police at all my murders, and it was me who reported the Brazilians breaking in at the Klimt. I joked it seemed like me doing their job for them, which we all thought was funny. I pointed their whole case out because I told them it seemed like they hadn't been paying attention, and we laughed.

Yes, they agreed, they had all that evidence, but what they really wanted was a story they liked that accounted for a man, naked on a beach with a murder victim, covered in blood but it's *his own blood* but he doesn't have any wounds. I told them I sympathized and shared some of the same questions. I didn't tell them they were asking the wrong questions. The question they should have asked was, *did it seem like you died getting stabbed by two Brazilians who then vanished except for a piece of one shoe while you became a ghost before returning to your body with no stab wounds and found Veronica Night offering you an internship—on the beach where she also might have healed your wounds with magic light—or maybe you healed yourself—or maybe it was a ghost?* If they'd asked that, I would've admitted everything. That's why it's important to know the right questions.

They had their own theories anyway. Since they'd recently had a few extraneous beach dwellers go missing, they started putting pressure on all the wild coincidences they were finding in my story: all the crimes on beaches, all the murders and missing people and break-ins, not to mention the suicide, and me in the middle of everything, just innocent.

Hours later they released me on the sidewalk.

That night in my living room, in moonlight through my bay windows, I ate cold pad Thai and observed my final, unfinished painting. After I ate I sat in front of the easel and touched a brush to the canvas, a moth weight, tracing abandoned strokes of Higher color. I stroked the tip up-down, back-forth, but without paint. I don't own paint.

My mind surprised me picturing the soft bristles sliding inside Caroline's open shirt, between her breasts and down the middle of her. Her lips pulled open, she whispered. Then because my mind darts around a lot I wondered if I shouldn't go to Asher Gale's office early the next morning before Caroline got there to make sure her visit wasn't an incredibly bad idea, since being associated with an office wouldn't be playing to any of my known strengths, and probably, yes, was an incredibly bad idea.

And that is why, jogging across PCH in the damp of that Skysill Beach dawn, mounting the Bradley Building steps and hurrying across lobby marble to the elevator, then keying open Asher Gale's door and charging into his office, I didn't see the ghost until it was too late...

BUY BOOK TWO NOW!

The Question in the Dancer's Kiss: The Book of Sound

THE QUESTION IN THE DANCER'S KISS

THE BOOK OF SOUND

From here the series gets ever wilder.

The Question in the Dancer's Kiss: The Book of Sound, begins as Book One is ending, as Asher and Caroline drive away from her psychic shop right after Asher became a ghost, going to maybe get drunk. But they find Skysill's suddenly too confusing and dangerous for that kind of casual day drinking. And as Asher's family secrets are revealed and his own powers grow, there's one question - hidden in a painting - he's desperate to answer: *The Question in the Dancer's Kiss.*

The Question in the Dancer's Kiss: The Book of Sound

THE HISTORY OF LIGHT

BOOKS 1 THROUGH 5

— THE GHOST WITH A KNIFE AT HER THROAT: The Book of Sight

— THE QUESTION IN THE DANCER'S KISS: The Book of Sound

— THE SHADOW WAITING ON ITS THRONE: The Book of Scent

— THE SACRIFICE THE DEAD WILL MAKE: The Book of Taste

— THE CURSE AT THE END OF THE WORLD: The Book of Touch

ALSO BY KEVIN HINCKER

The Little Queen

The Einstein Object

A Debt to the Stars

ABOUT THE AUTHOR

Kevin Hincker writes speculative fiction for curious readers. If you'd like to join his mailing list, or find extra information about his books, you can signup, or just explore, at https://kevinhincker.com/

If you want Amazon to send you updates on his future releases—such as Book Five of this series—go to his author page, https://www.amazon.com/author/kevinhincker and click the "Follow" button in the upper left next to his picture.

Made in the USA
Las Vegas, NV
09 May 2024